# Her eyes widened with delight

*It's Edouard Fergusson!* He must have rung home, been told where she was, and come in search of her. Monique's lips parted in anticipation.

A wave of happiness swept over her. This was magic to have him here. She took a few eager steps toward him, then stopped in her tracks.

He had looked up, an amazed look on his face as he took in the busy scene at Beauchamp House. Then as he saw her, he looked even more astounded. And angry. But why? Why should he come here if he hadn't expected to find her?

"What the hell are you doing here?" he demanded.

They'd only met once in Christchurch. But he'd been debonair, daring and altogether charming—nothing like the dour stranger confronting her now.

New Zealand born **Essie Summers** comes from a
long line of storytellers, and she herself began writing
verses when she was eight. At eighteen she submitted
her writing for publication and soon saw her poems,
articles and short stories in print. Essie Summers
debuted as a Harlequin author in 1961, has more than
forty books to her credit and, as readers around the
world will confirm, is one of the best-loved writers. Her
husband, Bill, a retired clergyman, is a kindred spirit
who shares her delight in words and poetry. They now
live in New Zealand's North Island, the parents of two,
and the proud grandparents of seven.

## Books by Essie Summers

HARLEQUIN ROMANCE

2068—GOBLIN HILL
2133—ADAIR OF STARLIGHT PEAKS
2148—SPRING IN SEPTEMBER
2281—MY LADY OF THE FUCHSIAS
2322—ONE MORE RIVER TO CROSS
2453—THE TENDER LEAVES
2525—DAUGHTER OF THE MISTY GORGES
2590—A MOUNTAIN FOR LUENDA
2622—A LAMP FOR JONATHAN
2645—SEASON OF FORGETFULNESS
2688—WINTER IN JULY
2766—TO BRING YOU JOY

These books may be available at your local bookseller.

Don't miss any of our special offers. Write to us at the
following address for information on our newest releases.

Harlequin Reader Service
901 Fuhrmann Blvd., P.O. Box 1397, Buffalo, NY 14240
Canadian address: P.O. Box 2800, Postal Station A,
5170 Yonge St., Willowdale, Ont. M2N 6J3

# To Bring You Joy

## Essie Summers

# Harlequin Books

TORONTO • NEW YORK • LONDON
AMSTERDAM • PARIS • SYDNEY • HAMBURG
STOCKHOLM • ATHENS • TOKYO • MILAN

Original hardcover edition published in 1985
by Mills & Boon Limited

ISBN 0-373-02766-4

Harlequin Romance first edition May 1986

For Ursel Boudry
of
Fond du Lac
Who knows and loves France.
Here is our tiny corner of
France within New Zealand

The author wishes to record her thanks to Professor Langer and
D.B. Sweeney, Director, Rural Development and Extension
Centre, Lincoln College, Canterbury, New Zealand, for much
advice and help concerning experimental field work on Banks
Peninsula, setting of my story.

# CHAPTER ONE

Monique made a wild clutch and steadied the Spode plate on its stand. That would have been the last straw. She mustn't lose her concentration. Not in work hours, surrounded by costly treasures. If only she could keep her thoughts from straying to her personal problems! Oh, what turmoil of mind you thrust me into, Aunt Amabel, when you deeded me that money, with that condition!

It had been so sweet of her, so understanding, so disturbing. And disturbing it was meant to be. Aunt Amabel had never been patient with the way Monique had shouldered the family burdens. This was her way of throwing a spanner into the works.

The note she'd left for her had been so typical. No beating about the bush.

Don't flap about this, darling. It's meant to bring you joy. Get out from under. Let the others stand on their own feet. It will be good for them. They won't be able to blame you, as they would, had you done it off your own bat. They are too shrewd themselves to expect you to renounce this. When the first shock has worn off they'll mutter: 'It's that eccentric aunt of Monique's ... absolutely unpredictable ... like marrying at her age and going off to Canada with her new husband!' I'd love to be a fly on the wall and hear it all. Anyway, dearest of girls, this gift is yours, to give you one year in which to do as you jolly well like, provided you take off for parts unknown and live your own life.

Mischievously yours,
Amabel Hurst

'P.S. Isn't it absurd to sign my new surname to

you? But oh, how I love my new name, the one I thought I might never wear. It means a grove of trees, you know. I can't think of anything more delightful, and Gregory's retirement home is surrounded by trees. It sounds like heaven. He is so thrilled I'm doing this. He loved you on sight, you know and remembering *my* sense of duty kept us apart for all of our young, green years, made him want me to do this before you succumb too. So take this chance with both hands, love, and spread your wings.'

*It's meant to bring you joy.*

So far it hadn't. Only a week of nights of indecision, tossing from side to side. Of course she knew exactly what Aunt Amabel meant her to do . . . take a cruise, go to the other side of the world, sail away from these shores to find adventure, freedom, possibly romance . . . but Monique knew full well what *she* wanted to do. Amabel might think it crazy, think she was dooming herself into another kind of bondage, but it was of all things dearest to her heart.

The fact that it was only sixty-odd miles from Christchurch would condemn it in her aunt's eyes. Nevertheless, it wouldn't be some strange place, frighteningly new. It would be the spot where her roots had been nourished, all unknown to her; the place that had been responsible for that note of nostalgia in her grandfather's voice, though he had never told her where it was.

Was it just a coincidence she had found it, or was it Providence, that glorious day of sunshine and sea-winds, on that far headland of Banks Peninsula? She would never forget her first sight of it, the narrow turquoise inlet gashed into the tawny hills, fringed with dark pines, and that white dusty ribbon of a road running out to the old gabled farmhouse, so French in its style.

How strange that she'd so often gone antique buying in Akaroa and the other bays of the fretted coastline of the Peninsula, but never to Port Beauchamp. It was so small, so remote, so exquisite.

The magic of it was with her still ... sorting through those dusty volumes stored in the old loft and suddenly seeing her grandfather's name, in childish but still recognisable handwriting staring up at her. Hilaire Beauchamp. Oh, that added up ... Beauchamp, the field beautiful. So when he had put the painful past behind him he had changed his name to Belfield.

But now wasn't the time to be going over that and the tantalising suggestion that had eventuated in that house, the chance she was still milling over. Here was a customer ... or possibly just a 'having a browse, thank you,' one. This one had a rugged look, tallish, broad, fair, with the high cheekbones of the Scot, but otherwise a square Saxon-type face. Oh, stop it, Monique Belfield ... you're so accustomed to placing goods in the country of their origin, to assessing and valuing, you carry it over into the personal field.

She went towards him, moving with the easy grace that came from years in this trade, one that demanded a careful threading-through of tables displaying valuable merchandise. He was examining closely a French clock.

She said pleasantly, 'You're very interested in that piece, aren't you? A very good example of its time and style and though these combined vase and clock items are rarely in working order, this one is. It's French, as you probably know.'

He straightened up, looked squarely at her, and she was aware that his eyes had a searching look, grey eyes, steely. 'That was what surprised me. I thought I knew this piece, knew it so well I was surprised to see it going. To the best of my knowledge it hasn't gone for the last fifty years. So          '

The eyes were questioning now, even slightly suspicious. She laughed lightly. 'So it isn't the same clock you knew.'

His lips tightened a little. 'I thought it could be that perhaps you bought it in run-down condition, and some watchmaker here, with the alchemist's touch, restored it to be useful as well as ornamental.'

She shook her head. 'No, I can guarantee that. I

bought it myself. A stroke of real luck. From the mantelpiece where it had ticked away for many years.'

He said, 'Are you sure the removal didn't just trigger the mechanism off again? It can happen. At a guess I'd say you bought it from one of the French settlements near Akaroa.'

A gleam of amusement lit her eyes. 'Fair enough, to expect it comes from our nearest French area, though right through New Zealand there are French antiques. But you aren't far out. A friend of mine, who lives at Ngahuru-Marama found it for me. Do you know it?'

'Yes, I know it. A romantic translation, that name . . . The Bay of the Harvest Moon.'

'My friend is Elizabeth Stirling, the author, who's married to Jeremy Ffoulkes, editor of the *Canterbury Argus*. Elizabeth does a lot of visiting around the village. She is fond of one old lady living in a rather dilapidated cottage to which she is much attached. Lives entirely on the age benefit, needed money for urgent repairs to her roof. Elizabeth had always recognised the clock as valuable and called me in.'

'The old lady didn't mind parting with an heirloom?'

(Did she just imagine his look was censorious?)

Her tone became cool. 'Not all possessions are heirlooms. Her late husband was an inveterate buyer at auctions. The poor woman's sheds on the property bear testimony to that. But, as with all such obsessions, some pay off. He'd bought this many years ago, kept it in good order, fortunately, and didn't recognise the value.'

He looked at the price tag, said, 'So you managed to buy it and make a handsome profit—or so I should guess, at this price.'

There could be no mistaking the flush of anger that stained her cheeks. 'You are implying we bought it for a song, taking advantage of her lack of knowledge. I assure you we didn't. Normally we don't do business this way, but we are selling the clock solely on a commission basis, so what her junk-collecting husband bought cheaply long ago, is going to be mainly profit to this dear little lady. When I used the word fortunately, I didn't mean fortunately for us, but for her. Her roof won't leak this winter and she will have a tidy sum over.'

For a moment he looked incredulous, but as a spark of anger shot into the brown eyes looking into his, he said quickly, 'I do beg your pardon. I jumped to a hasty conclusion.'

She nodded, her tone only a degree less hostile, said, 'We are used to it of course ... the preconceived idea that all antique dealers buy for a song and sell for a price that is beyond the dreams of avarice. The same people I'm told, dub all land agents as sharks, and they aren't. That I know.'

His lips twitched and his tone was one of pure interest, surprisingly. 'Ah ... perhaps you have an interest in a land agent. Lucky man to have so fair a champion fly to his defence.'

She stared. 'You sound like something out of a book.'

He chuckled. 'Blame yourself. That's how *you* sounded. I don't think I've ever heard anyone your age use that phrase, "beyond the dreams of avarice." Must be the atmosphere of this place, genuinely antique. Oh, sorry ... I'm not suggesting you're antique. But a phrase like that goes with bustles and bows and all this Victoriana, don't you think?'

Monique put a hand to her head, said, 'Perhaps it *is* the atmosphere ... I deal in period stuff and read a lot of period and historical novels. Perhaps I'm even thinking that way. But I don't remember ever having a conversation like this, with any other customer in all the years I've been in the trade.'

She couldn't think why, but an odd glint appeared in his eye. He said, 'In all the years? Surely they can't be as many as that sounds. You don't look more than twenty-three or four.'

She was surprised to hear herself say very promptly, 'Twenty-seven in actual fact, and I began in this line at eighteen.'

'Then you're the buyer of this establishment. The famed Monique of Montmorency's?'

For a moment she wondered why he thought she had

to be Monique, then thought he might have been in looking round earlier and heard Clint calling her by her name. She tried to sound snubbing. 'Yes, I am. Though I don't know about famed.'

'It's got a fine ring to it, that. Monique of Montmorency's.' She could have sworn he said it mockingly. 'Like Elizabeth of England, or Joan of Arc ... who else? A good name for an antique shop. Some ordinary New Zealand name wouldn't have had half the fine ring to it. Like Emma Smith, or Nellie Jones.'

A line appeared between the brown brows. 'I rather fancy you imagine I adopted that name for commercial purposes. Let me assure you I didn't. I was baptised Monique Belfield in Australia. And in case you think Montmorency is also a made-up name, you had better know the owner's name is really that. Claude Montmorency. I think his family was called that before the first Claude went over to England with the Conqueror! There's nothing sham about my employer!'

'And he has a very loyal employee. I hope to meet him some day and I'll tell him then what a lucky man he is. I take it he does meet some of his customers?'

'He does, but not in Christchurch. Our head shop is in Auckland. I was with him there till five years ago.'

This man was disconcerting the way he kept switching the conversation. He suddenly stared at her, said, with that annoying twitch to his lips as if he wanted to laugh, 'Would you mind keeping that angry look for a few moments longer? It makes me think we've met before.'

Words failed her temporarily. Then she rallied, said, 'I've never seen you before in my life ... and what's anger got to do with it?'

He grinned and for some reason it made her hackles rise again. His eyes narrowed consideringly. 'That's it,' he said maddeningly.

She said icily, subduing her rising temper, 'This is a ridiculous conversation. If I'd ever been angry with you before, I'd have remembered you.'

His laugh rang out. He seemed to dismiss that, said, 'I take it then you are the manageress here?'

'No, just the buyer. Mr Clinton Wood is the manager.'

'Then he must be the same calibre as you, if he allowed you to let your sympathies run away with you and sell this merely on commission.'

Monique didn't reply. She and Clint didn't see eye to eye on this. But she mustn't judge him harshly on that. Nevertheless she'd be glad when it was sold and out of his sight. After all, Clint had to prove himself as manager, had to make this branch pay and he hadn't been very long with the firm.

He was a good businessman, if a little over-ambitious. It had been very pleasant having him as an escort but she'd now come to the conclusion he wasn't a kindred spirit. At the back of her mind, from the very start of their association, had been the niggling suspicion that because Claude Montmorency thought so much of her, Clint had set himself out to win her approval. That was another reason why she would be glad to end her time here.

She came back to herself to find this odd customer staring at her. She coloured up, said, 'Sorry, it may seem rude not replying to that, but it was awkward to answer. I'll have to take refuge in the traditional TV retort and say: "No comment."'

Suddenly the slight animosity between them disappeared. He smiled, said, 'It shouldn't have been said at all. And I've been sounding censorious about business methods. I don't know what's come over me. I've never gone on like this before.'

She looked at him and grinned, the cool businesswoman submerging for a moment under a rueful grin. 'Neither have I! Well, it makes a change. Trading is so apt to get stereotyped. But back to normal: Now you know the clock isn't the one belonging to someone you know I suppose you're satisfied. I mean you aren't interested in buying it, are you? Oh dear, that's not my usual sales manner either.'

He laughed, nodded, said, 'But I'll take that blue ironstone plate. My mother collects those.'

He paid her, said, 'All right if I leave it to call for it

later? I've got to go for lunch now and it could be a nuisance.'

She carefully wrapped it, attached a small label, asked his name.

'Fergusson. With a double S. Edward Fergusson.'

She hid a smile. She'd been right about the Scots strain. She gazed at his back reflectively as he went out. An interesting contact. Rather anti at first, but quick to mellow. Well, now she must have lunch herself. She thought she'd sit on a seat by the Avon and eat. Christchurch was still a market town on Wednesdays, despite its phenomenal development and urban sprawl. The restaurants would be crowded. The tranquility of the Avon's emerald banks might be conducive to thought. By the end of this day she must be committed to a definite sequence of action.

One, she must ring Mr Montmorency tonight and give in her notice. Two, she would tell them at home she would no longer be in charge of the household. Kerry was near the age she had been when she took over the reins. Sylvie was now settled in a job she liked and it wouldn't hurt her to take on a few more chores. Noel was into his second year at Varsity. Her stepfather mightn't find it as comfortable as of yore, but he'd always been very understanding even if he'd leaned on her too much after her mother had died.

Three . . . ah, there was the rub . . . she would have to tell Clint what she was taking on, and in fairness to him she must make it clear she wanted their attachment to go no further. That this was finish. It had been pleasant, but never deeply satisfying.

Four . . . oh, she had no qualms about that, she would ring those two women at Beauchamp House to let them know she herself would come to them, value and classify all their treasures and take the necessary steps to turn it into a tourist attraction. That much she would be able to do for the two who were, though they didn't know it, her own great-aunts. *They* had believed in her grandfather even when his harsh father hadn't. Now they were the sole survivors of that pioneer French family; how ironic that old François

Beauchamp, who had had so fierce a pride in his possessions, in his property, had been the cause of it having to pass out of the family. How strange that both the sisters should have been childless. Ironic the first, strange the second, but wonderful, gloriously wonderful the third thing, that Aunt Amabel should have made it possible for Monique to offer her services to those two gallant souls, struggling along in that great house, against the ravages of the weather, the encroachment of their old age, and the knowledge that some day the magnificent estate the first Beauchamp had created in a raw, new land, would cease to exist, or at best be turned into a guest-house.

It would be unthinkable for her, Monique, to be so afraid of striking out on her own that she stayed in her comfortable family and well-paid business rut. Maybe she didn't need to think it out on the banks of the Avon. Maybe she had already made up her mind to those four steps. But she'd go to the river just the same.

She went along to Clint's office. He looked up. 'Oh, you're off? Thought you were leaving it a bit late. Look, don't hurry back. I'll cope. Pity Miss Sebright is away today but she rang to say she'll be back tomorrow. I don't want you skimping your lunch-hour though. You haven't seemed yourself lately.'

Monique immediately felt guilty. She'd sometimes thought Clint rather unperceptive where feminine moods were concerned. She'd done him an injustice. She managed a smile, said, 'I'm not off-colour. I've had a few family matters on my mind, that's all.'

He looked at her sharply. 'I'm not surprised. There could come a time when you'd have to make up your mind to shed some of your responsibilities in that direction. It would be fairer to yourself and possibly to them. Not good for their character development to lean on you so much.'

Monique felt like running. She thought she knew what he had in mind, but he was too late. She'd known for weeks she mustn't let their companionship deepen into something more intimate. He wasn't what she'd want in a husband. Whether that man of her dreams would ever materialise she knew not, but she wouldn't settle for Clinton Wood. She said quickly, 'Well, I'm off. But I'll try to get back at my usual time.'

He said smilingly, 'No, I insist you don't hurry back. I've had you on my conscience the last week or two. I take you too much for granted, in business as well. You're too good to me and to everyone else. We'll talk it over tonight or tomorrow night.'

She went out swiftly. Talk it over tonight? No, tonight was the night she would tell him she was leaving here. Or tomorrow night if what she had to tell the family provoked a full-scale discussion.

She walked two blocks along Colombo Street, turned towards the Worcester Street Bridge with its dainty ironwork, bought some sandwiches on the way. She turned into Oxford Terrace and bumped clean into her last customer. Recognition was mutual. She flashed him a smile and would have gone past him but he put out a hand, said, 'Oh, hullo, well met. I was just coming back to say I'm going to buy that French clock after all. I've a yen for it, now I know it's not the one I thought it was, and maybe the old dear at Harvest Moon Bay needs the money soon. I liked that. What time will you be returning to the shop? I can't sabotage your dinner-hour.'

Suddenly she was inexplicably glad this man would take Mrs Simpson's clock, despite the way he'd raised her ire earlier. She *would* be glad to see the old lady got the money before she left the firm. She was surprised to hear herself say, 'I could go back with you now. It would be a pity if someone else bought it in the interval. Can happen.'

'Good show. You're a sport. I ought to mutter I can't possibly impose on you, but if you aren't rushing to meet someone for lunch, I'll take you up on that.'

She shrugged, waved a paperbag at him. 'I was just going to eat this beside Captain Scott's statue and think something out.'

The grey eyes looked curious. 'Think something out? Then can you do it without solitude and the ducks by the river?'

She laughed lightly. 'I don't need to really. My mind *is* made up. I'm just being silly. I'll come back with you. The manager and myself didn't see eye to eye on the terms of that sale, and as our assistant is on the sick list today, he'd have to serve you. I'd rather attend to it myself.'

The customer said shrewdly, 'He'd rather have had a profit from it showing in his monthly sales analysis. Fair enough, and very natural, but I'm glad to think there's still room in business for some sentiment.' He hesitated. 'He'll recognise you've sacrificed some of your lunch-hour to return to serve me. Would he make it up to you ... extend your time and let me give you your lunch?'

She knew she wanted to. 'That's a handsome offer ... as long as it's not an elaborate meal. I couldn't expect time for several courses, but I'm sure a snack at a grill-bar wouldn't upset the timetable too much. He told me in any case not to hurry back.'

'Not a tyrant then?'

'No, mustn't give you that idea. We are—we're quite close friends.'

They came to a side-alley first. Monique said, 'No need to take you right through the showroom again. I've got a key to this.'

She unlocked the door and they were in a tiny passage. She re-locked the door. Clint would be in the showroom. But Clint wasn't. He was in the office. They could see him through the frosted glass wall and his arms were round a red-haired girl whose bright head was against his shoulder. As they stopped, shocked on Monique's part, embarrassed on her customer's, the girl cried passionately, with a hint of desperation in her voice. 'You'll just *have* to tell Monique. I can't stand it any longer. I can't understand you. It happens all the time ... a man or a girl meets someone else ... finds out this time it's true love ... and the old attachment has to be broken up. You promised you'd put an end to it. It's not even fair to her. You promised.'

His voice was reluctant, cornered. 'Glenys, I know I did. But it isn't as simple as that. Montmorency's due down here next month. You know how highly he thinks of her. He's not going to be very pleased with me for ditching her. I'd rather wait till after that visit. He only comes once a year. I've got to have time. Got to think it out. Please . . .'

Monique had stopped as if turned to stone. She was aware this stranger had caught her arm, that he too had frozen, apart from that, into an appalled stillness. Now he was turning her round, propelling her back to the door and doing it with such stealthiness he must've realised a sudden movement could catch the eye of the man with the girl in his arms through the patterned glass.

Mercifully it was just a few steps. Wordlessly he held out his hand. She gave him the key, he turned it with utmost care, put his hand beneath her elbow to help her over the shallow step down, closed and locked the door, returned her the key.

They stood in the deserted alleyway, facing each other, both breathing heavily, eyes locked. Then the man found words. 'How damnable! What can I say?'

Monique drew in a deep, necessary breath, though her colour didn't return. Then she produced a grin, said, 'You could congratulate me on a lucky escape, perhaps!'

'Good for you!' he exclaimed. 'You beaut! But I could knock his block off! The calculating devil!'

The next moment he was staring at her because she laughed and he was staggered at the natural sound of it. She sensed his surprise and said in a very objective tone, 'You see, this lets me out. I had already decided to give in my notice. Oh, not to Clint, to Mr Montmorency in Auckland, then to Clint. Oh, don't look like that, Mr Fergusson, I'm not trying to save face. That was what I was going to think about beside the river. Not whether I would, but who to tell first tonight . . . my family or Mr Montmorency. I was feeling guilty as far as Clint was concerned, now I needn't. I won't be breaking my heart over him. I'm not that way inclined.

'I think—would you mind if I didn't go back in now, even through the front entrance? I'd rather go back when she's gone, and when he'll expect me. At the end of my lunch-hour. You could come in and get your clock then. I think I'll change my plans. I'll tell Clint today, when we close. That'll let him off the hook and he need never know I heard. Say you come in at two-thirty?'

She swayed slightly. The big man in front of her put out both hands, caught her by the elbows. 'Steady. Even though you sound as cool as a cucumber, it's still been a shock. Sure the clock can wait. I'm taking you for some lunch and to hell with Mr Clinton Wood's own dinner. Let him starve. He must be mad to let a girl like you go for an empty-headed tough female like that! Let's get out of here. He might let her out this way. Did you hear what she said as I was unlocking the door?'

'Yes. She said: "If you don't tell her soon I'll tell her myself." That's why I'd rather get my notice into Clint before it gets too much for her. It'll save a lot of embarrassment. Then he can ring her and everything in the garden will be lovely for them. Clint won't fear any displeasure from Mr Montmorency then.'

Suddenly the man Fergusson squared his shoulders as if he'd come to a decision. He had. 'I've a better idea, but let's get back into the street.' He hurried her along, turned her into the crowd, glanced about, saw the entrance to a shopping mall, with cobbled paving, palms and pot-plants and, mercifully, a seat.

He steered her to it, sat her down. It was screened into a semblance of privacy by the drooping foliage of the tree it surrounded.

He spoke rapidly but enunciated clearly as if beating his instructions into her brain. 'You've been a brick. I think you need some support. I've got a splendid idea. I can't knock his block off but I'd like to do it another way. Let's go back in through the front door. A warning bell rings there, doesn't it? That'll bring him out. We'll pretend we've met before, fallen for each other. I'll ask your boss if you can have an extended lunch-hour because I've got to take a sudden trip to Australia and won't be able to see you for three weeks or so. That'll give him something to think about! You aren't engaged, are you? I can't see a ring.'

It almost took her breath away. 'No, not engaged. Most folk think we're on the brink. Except me. And I've got another job lined up already. Oh, there's no time to explain, but I can't let you involve yourself like this. I——'

'You can't stop me. And we haven't time to discuss it. Leave it to me. Follow my lead. Besides, it won't really involve me. I *am* off to Australia this afternoon.'

She felt dazed, mesmerised. She yielded to the insistence of his hand, stood up.

Half a dozen steps brought them to the door of a florist's shop. He let go of her arm, dived in, came out with a huge bunch of violets, dewy-wet from sprinkling, fringed with a circle of pale blue paper. His eyes, those grey eyes she'd deemed sober at first, were sparkling with mirth. 'A token of love from a reluctant traveller, who, a week after meeting a girl who bowled him over at first sight, has to quit these shores for what seems like an eternity to him. How's that?'

Monique couldn't help a laugh breaking through, heard his approving, 'Good ... you've more colour now. Come on,' and willy-nilly, clasped by his hand, she was hustled along, her bag and her violets in her other hand.

Within seconds the bell was ringing as they stepped over the threshold and threaded through the first showcases. They heard hasty footsteps coming from the direction of the office, and there was the flicker of a skirt disappearing into a corner devoted to terracotta ornaments, partially screened by a dividing stand.

Clint came towards them, dark, debonair, tall, in his grey chalk-striped suit, pale-green tie, ready to meet a customer. Monique said clearly, unhurriedly, 'Oh, there you are, Clint. I'm glad you aren't tied up with a customer because we haven't much time. Did you mean it when you said I could take extra time for my lunch-hour? Because I'd very much like to take you up on that. You see I'd no idea Edward would be in town or that he'd have to go to Australia so suddenly. He'd like me to have lunch with him before he leaves.' She brought the bunch of violets up against her rose-pink frock in a happy gesture and added, 'This is Mr Edward Fergusson . . . my boss, Mr Clinton Woods, Edward.'

They were rewarded by seeing Clint look astounded for one satisfying moment, then recover. He shook hands, said, 'I don't remember hearing you mention him before.'

It was fortunate Monique didn't have to reply because she was feeling dazed. Her companion did it for her, said, suavely, 'Well, our—er—friendship is quite recent, really, but as the saying goes, is counted in heartbeats, not hours and days.' He made a most effective pause, twinkled, as if expecting the other man to read between the lines, went on, 'Well, you know how it is. We feel we've known each other for ages. We met in Akaroa. I knew this trip would be coming off soon, but not as soon as this. Ministry of Agriculture's office rang me from Wellington yesterday afternoon and said there was a preliminary meeting in Canberra ahead of the other. I'm to visit areas in Victoria and South Australia too during the next three weeks. It's going to seem a long time. But the big meeting after the visiting won't take more than three days. And I can make my reports to Lincoln College and the Ministry back here.'

Monique felt as if her eyes were turning inwards with the effort to assimilate it all and daren't speak.

This man Fergusson said with a sort of confident effrontery, 'So I was sure Monique would be allowed extra time, Mr Wood. In fact . . .'

Clint found himself echoing: 'In fact . . .?'

'In fact, I wondered if you'd give her enough time to come out to the airport and see me off? We could've taken a taxi and had lunch there but she vetoed that. You'll know, of course, that she has an over-developed sense of duty.'

As if mesmerised, Clint found himself saying, 'Yes, yes. Of course. I'll stay on here. I'll ring up the restaurant in the mall and have a tray sent in. Take all the time you want, Monique.'

'Oh, good show. Thank you. Monique, give me that plate you wrapped for me. I'll take that with me, but perhaps Mr Wood would put the French clock aside for me. That one over there. The one that goes! Monique can give it to my mother. She lives in Christchurch.'

At that moment they both became aware that a girl with red hair was peering at them between tall terracotta urns on the divider stand.

Monique said hurriedly, 'I see you have a customer, Mr Wood. We must fly, anyway.'

Clinton muttered feebly, 'Oh, she's just browsing. But yes, hurry. There's a taxi-stand past the Phoenix. I'll get your parcel.'

But Monique's amazing customer moved too fast for him. He was at the counter in a jiffy, scooped it up, hurried her out of the shop.

It wasn't till they'd subsided into the cab that Monique found her voice. 'But if your mother lives in Christchurch and you're off to Australia, couldn't the plate be delivered with the clock?'

'Yes, but I dare not let him see you'd spelt my name wrong. In case later he finds out mine is spelt the French way: E-d-o-u-a-r-d. He could expect you to know. I feel proud of myself. I reckon a good detective was lost in me. I'd always be one jump ahead of the criminal mind.'

It was no use. Monique giggled feebly. It somehow relieved her inward tensions. 'Oh, poor Clinton. A criminal!'

'One who deserves to be deceived.'

Monique said, 'Where is your luggage?'

'At Mother's. With my car. She was going to drive me to the airport, but not to worry. I had already said I wouldn't be in for lunch. I'll ring her from Harewood and she can bring my case to us. But not too soon. We have a lot to talk about.'

Monique gulped. 'But how will you explain *me*? Oh, I get it. I'll leave as soon as we have eaten.'

'You won't, you know. I shall tell her the truth, if not the whole truth. I had told her I wanted to go to Montmorency's. She asked why and I told her I wanted to meet this Monique I'd heard about from friends in Akaroa who are interested in antiques. Mother thinks

I'm heading for an existence as a confirmed bachelor so any mention of a female on my horizon and she asks no putting-off questions. So I shall tell her the truth up to a point. What did you say?'

'I said I didn't think you'd recognise truth if you met it face to face,' said Monique. 'Your imagination would get in the way. I've never met a man like you in my whole life.'

'But aren't you glad you've met one now?' asked Edouard Fergusson.

# CHAPTER TWO

FORTUITOUSLY the intercom system of the taxi had been blaring away, giving and receiving messages, but now it stopped and the taxi-driver was chatting away to them. Monique was glad, felt she could now draw breath. Things were moving too fast.

They sped through the Christchurch suburbs, sweet with flowering cherry and prunus, gay with daffodils and polyanthus, with the golden fountains of forsythia and the multi-coloured burgeoning of a Southern Hemisphere September.

The man beside her was very much at ease, exchanging small talk with the driver. Perhaps he was giving her time to recover from what he might still think was a mortal blow despite her instant reaction to the scene in the office. She needed time to marshal her thoughts. Who would've thought things would come to a head so swiftly? She was conscious of an overwhelming relief . . . she needn't feel remorseful over breaking her association with Clint. So he'd promised this girl he'd tell Monique someone else had entered his life, but hadn't because he doubted if it would be policy, when the proprietor of the firm thought so highly of her! What a motive! She curled her lip wryly. Also, he'd taken an exorbitant interest in the telephone message he had relayed to her from Aunt Amabel's lawyers. Naturally, she'd speculated, aloud, as to what it could mean.

Clint had said instantly, 'Must be to your advantage, darling. Amabel was so fond of you. I mean, with no one of her very own, till Gregory appeared out of her past, she's looked on you as the daughter she might've had. I'm sure it will be good news. She sold that house of hers for a fabulous sum, it had appreciated so much since her mother left it to her. It doesn't look as if Gregory Hurst lacks for much. Could be she wants you

24

to have a nest-egg in her lifetime in addition to leaving you her car. Good thing she's no real relation, otherwise your half-sisters and brothers might've cashed in on it. I reckon they've all got an eye to the main chance. And mind, if she has decided to make you a gift of money now, no sharing it with them. You're a soft touch, you know, and you've done enough for them already.'

Monique knew that was true, but Clint saying it jarred her. He was assuming too much. A fiancé might've been justified in saying so, but he wasn't that. She'd shrugged it away, said, 'I don't think it'll be any more than a few keepsakes she didn't want to take to Canada, if indeed it's any sort of a gift at all. It may be just a few odds and ends of business she wants me to tie up. She didn't want to stay here long once the house was sold. She wanted to be away with Gregory, bless her.'

Naturally Clint had asked outright when she came back from the interview. But she hadn't told him. Impossible to say to the man who was manager of this branch, 'It's quite a sum of money provided I up-and-off,' especially when for months now she had found doubt after doubt creeping in about their relationship.

Now she and this amazing stranger swung in to the International Airport; Edouard Fergusson asked the driver to order a taxi to take Monique back to the shop five minutes after his plane was due to leave, then they went in, he reported, said his baggage would be arriving later, and they went upstairs to the restaurant.

Suddenly it didn't seem strange any more. It was like he'd pretended it was, as if they'd known each other a long time. 'I do hope you're starving,' he said, studying the menu, 'I am. It's interesting to find that such an adventure can sharpen one's appetite.'

Monique felt a surge of something, she didn't know what, perhaps a sense of anticipation, that now possibly wonderful adventures were ahead of her, after being in a rut so long, hemmed in by duty and people for whom she'd felt responsible.

She looked saucy, one dimple appearing. 'It's a wonder you've not found out before, St George!'

He looked up, said, 'St George? What . . .?'

The dimple remained in evidence. 'I can only suppose you've been rescuing maidens from dragons all your life, the cool way you set about it. The aplomb! The colossal cheek! And how you could be bothered when you're setting off on a Government mission, I can't imagine!'

He chuckled. 'It's just sort of happened, didn't it? One moment I was as mad as hell with you because I had a feeling you'd done someone brown, someone I'm very fond of, over that clock. The next . . . well a few minutes later I was madder over that office scene than I've ever been in my life. I just had to do something about it. I even feel bewildered myself so what you feel I just don't know!'

The sparkle remained. 'Don't worry about me. I'm bewildered, yes, but not for the reason you think. I'm more shocked, shocked at myself. I must have a horrible nature because I enjoyed the whole thing. At least from the time we entered the showroom from the front entrance. I was feeling horribly guilty over having to tell Clint and Mr Montmorency I was finishing at the shop.'

The waiter arrived. They ordered mushroom-stuffed pancakes as an entrée, and roast lamb with redcurrant jelly as a dinner order. Edouard grinned. 'I must be mad, as a farmer, ordering lamb. Ought to be going for something exotic but mutton, in fact any sheepmeat, will do me most of the time.'

She blinked. 'You're a farmer? I thought you must be in the Civil Service when you spoke of delivering reports, and so on.'

He grinned. 'It did sound that way. I run an experimental farm—at least part of it's experimental—under the auspices of Lincoln College. Still mainly sheep, though. My own. I enjoy it. But tell me, what's your new job and where?'

She hesitated, then said, 'It's to be confidential as yet. Sorry to be less than frank but I feel it's best to keep it under wraps till certain formalities, permits and so on, are through.'

The grey eyes regarded her steadily. 'I like a girl who can keep her own counsel. I'm so often in that position. Experimenting often means keeping your mouth shut till a certain stage is reached, till a report is given to the department most concerned. But you'll give me your house telephone number, won't you, so I can ring you on return? I can well imagine Mr Clint Wood might not be disposed to give it to me if I applied to him, or think it odd I didn't know it.'

She laughed, 'Yes, even if he might be relieved in one direction, he might feel chagrin in another. The sort of chap who'd rather drop a girl than be dropped by her. How are we for time? I suppose we should be in the foyer when your mother arrives?' He nodded and fell to.

It was dreamlike to Monique. Things went on in the same old way for so long, then suddenly your world turned upside-down. The perfume of the violets she'd laid beside her plate came up to her, sweetly redolent of woodsy dells and cushiony mosses, birdsong and singing brooks. The world that was opening up before her would be like that, an old, old house where tranquillity and tradition held sway, where wide paddocks sloped to the clifftops that rimmed an aquamarine sea above the deep cleft of the inlet. She would tread the very stairs her ancestors had trodden, stand under the pines they had planted, reach out to bring yesterday's history alive for her.

They finished their dessert, decided to skip coffee, went downstairs. Edouard looked at his watch a little anxiously and at that moment a girl trundled one suitcase in on a trolley towards them, a boy of about four trotting beside her, a tiny girl on the top tray.

'Good grief, Francine, not Mother!' Edouard rushed towards her, took the case and said, 'What's happened? Is Mother all right?'

Obviously a sister. She laughed, 'Yes, but you know Mother's plans so often go astray ... an old school friend not seen for thirty years turned up. She'd married an American, is visiting here, and had called on that woman who lives over Mother's back fence. When that neighbour mentioned Mother by her unusual Christian name, the school friend decided it must be her old mate and rushed round. She was leaving at three-thirty for Queenstown, so Mother didn't want to waste a moment, threw your case at me, and here I am. And just look at the children. They were blissfully playing in the sandpit! When Mother 'phoned and said, "Francine, I need you here, with the car, immediately," I just plucked the filthy imps up as they were. I love you dearly, brother, but why on earth couldn't you travel with your luggage?'

He laughed. 'If I told you the whole tale you'd never believe it, but it would satisfy even your romantic heart if I had the time. Francine, this is Monique.'

Francine blinked, said, 'Hullo, Monique.' Then: 'Monique who?'

Her brother stared. 'Good heavens . . . I didn't even have the time to ask her that! I've been too busy rescuing her from unimaginable dangers to find out. I wonder if St George had the same trouble!'

This time his sister positively boggled. 'Edouard . . . have you got sunstroke or something?'

Monique decided she'd better lend a hand. 'I'm Monique Belfield and he did rescue me, from an extremely embarrassing situation with my boss. So he was kind enough to give me lunch here to restore my shattered nerves.'

The Fergusson man looked at her reproachfully. 'Reduced to those terms it completely wipes my feeling of having risen to great heights of knightly chivalry. But I guess that about sums it up.'

His sister sighed. 'I've a feeling that I'm not going to be told any more than that. I know you! When you talk like that you might as well be an oyster and say nothing. Oh dear, is that your call? How tantalising. Well, we'll walk to the barrier with you. And of course if you want me to run any more messages for you, I'll submit.'

'Well, you can tell Mother I'll let her have the whole

story in about three weeks' time. Might even let you on it. There could be more to reveal by then.'

They walked to the glass doors through which only boarding passengers were allowed to pass. Edouard produced fifty-cent pieces for his niece and nephew for ice-creams, bent and kissed his sister goodbye, then with a sudden swoop before she could draw back, kissed Monique full on the mouth. 'I'll ring you when I return,' he said, 'Best of luck in the new job. Take care and don't worry.'

Francine and Monique were left looking at each other, Monique slightly apprehensively. Suddenly Francine smiled, looking more like her brother than ever in feature and colouring, if not in build. 'He said not to worry. So don't be afraid I'm going to ask questions even if it does sound delightfully intriguing. He's quite mad and capable of anything. Mother will be thrilled. She said the other day he hadn't got involved in anything for ages and she was afraid he was getting stodgy.'

Monique's 'Stodgy!' was jerked out of her and was completely indicative of the fact that stodgy was the last word she would have applied to Edouard.

Francine took pity on her, said crisply, 'Now, tell me, can I drop you anywhere?'

Monique shook her shining browny-gold head, 'But thanks all the same. Edouard ordered me a taxi for five minutes after take-off. I've got to get back to work. My boss was having his lunch sent in so I could have this extra time, so I mustn't take advantage of him.'

Again Francine looked puzzled. 'Your boss ... the one Edouard rescued you from? I mean from the embarrassing position. Yet the same boss was in a mood to do you a favour ... you must be some girl!'

Monique said lightly, 'Let's just say by now that my boss is possibly very grateful to your brother. He was saved by his lightning actions too. By the way, would you give this parcel to your mother? Edouard bought it for her.'

Francine looked down at the lavender paper embossed all over with *Montmorency's Antiques* in

Gothic lettering. 'My word ... Edouard *has* been spreading himself. Were you with him when he bought this? What is it?'

'Yes, you could say I was with him. It's one of those dark blue ironstone plates. He said your mother collected them.'

'She'll love it. Oh, this could be your taxi now. Well, Monique Belfield, I'll hope to see you again ... when my impetuous big brother returns from the seats of Government across the pond. 'Bye for now.'

''Bye, Francine. By the way, Edouard also bought a marble clock for himself. They are sending it to your mother's to keep for him. He scribbled the address on it.' She stepped into the taxi and was gone.

Monique found the showroom busy and plunged immediately into selling. Clint had called in a woman who worked for them part-time and it was just as well as the pressure kept up till almost closing-time. She and Clint occasionally eyed each other but nothing could be said till their assistant had departed, the shutters were up and they were alone.

Clint said, 'At last. Will you come into the office. I think I deserve an explanation.'

She dared not say he had forfeited the right to that, because that would have meant revealing his scene with Glenys had been witnessed.

She achieved an easy, 'Yes, I suppose so.'

'You *suppose* so! Isn't that a bit ridiculous?'

She said coolly, 'Oh, I don't think you need to take that tone, Clint. I think you know as well as I do that we aren't really committed to each other. So we're perfectly free to go out with whom we please.'

She'd rarely seen the self-possessed Clint so flummoxed. He was bereft of words for moments, then rallied, said, 'What an extraordinary idea. I mean you can't expect me to be pleased about this, or to take it as natural. I mean, how would *you* feel if *I* whisked off with another girl?'

She repressed a desire to hurl at him: 'You hypocrite! What about Glenys?' Instead she looked wide-eyed and naïve. 'I wouldn't mind a bit, Clint. I——'

He cut in indignantly, 'Then you jolly well should!'

She maintained the surprised look. 'But Clint, I never really took you seriously. I mean I wasn't looking on you in the light of a possible husband, you know. I enjoyed going out with you. Our tastes in concerts and plays were similar and I enjoyed the occasional dance, but I wasn't in the throes of an undying passion.' She permitted herself a twinkle. 'I think you'd have been a little uncomfortable if I had been.'

He fell silent, looking at her with an assessing expression, puzzled, still slightly aggrieved.

A hint of mischief lit the sherry-brown eyes looking into his. 'Watch it, Clint. Don't let the shock of this happening jolt you into a declaration. You know perfectly well you aren't head over heels in love with me. Don't let a sort of natural masculine chagrin land you in deep water.'

He said slowly, 'Monique, I don't understand you. I—feel I haven't known you at all. You've been so placid till now, content with our companionship. All of a sudden you're a different person.'

Now the eyes looking into his were serious, sincere. 'Clint, I'm not really placid, not particularly content, only fairly well disciplined because I've had to be. When Mother died I had to take on the responsibility of the family to a great extent, so all the things I wanted to do in life were shelved. I don't need to do that any longer. You were curious about what Aunt Amabel's lawyer wanted me for. Well, she's made me a gift during her lifetime instead of a legacy, a much nicer idea. But there are conditions. I have to clear out and do my own thing. I'm ringing Mr Montmorency tonight from home, giving him a fortnight's notice. I've got a whole wonderful year ahead of me free from financial worry, to do exactly as I please!'

Clinton said, 'So you'll be splashing out on travel? I suppose that'll take you to London, lucky you! You'll find yourself drawn to the famous antique shops there ... and in Paris and New York. You'll get your restlessness out of your system and come back to little old New Zealand more knowledgeable than ever.'

An impish smile touched her lips. 'You couldn't be more wrong. I'm staying in New Zealand. In fact less than a hundred miles from here. I've found my ideal spot. I'll be doing something I've always yearned to do, something very dear to my heart.'

Baffled, he gazed at her. 'A hundred miles? Sounds like Timaru.'

She said quite nicely, 'Clint, I have to keep this confidential for the moment. The details are still in the melting-pot. It concerns other people. But I don't have to keep the locale secret. It's Akaroa way.'

'Akaroa? But there's nothing in our line big enough there to tempt you. I——'

'Not an antique shop. And only in the vicinity of Akaroa. But I can't say more yet. It won't be anything in the way of rivalry to this place, so neither you nor Mr Montmorency need be upset.'

'He could be disappointed though. I thought he was rather pleased we were evidently more than friends.'

She shrugged. 'A very minor disappointment. Clint, no more discussion. When you think it over, you'll realise it's for the best. Now I'm off, I've a lot to do tonight.'

She was nearly out of the door when his voice recalled her. She turned, raised a brow. He was frowning. 'This chap was from Akaroa, wasn't he? So this decision is to do with him.'

She said swiftly, 'Well, he said we met there, didn't he? But I can assure you, Clint, this position was in the air before I met him.'

Phew! That had been a bit sticky, because she hadn't the faintest idea where Edouard Fergusson was farming. He'd made that mysterious remark about friends in Akaroa telling him he should meet Monique of Montmorency's. There'd been no time to question him further. It probably meant very little, anyway. He seemed to have an interest in antiques and no doubt had been prowling in one of the shops in Akaroa and it could've been someone there had mentioned to him that

he might find what he was after in Montmorency's and
had added, 'Ask for Monique, she was here the other
day and knows about such things.'

That would be it. He could have an interest in French
possessions. His surname might be as Scots as they
come, but his given name was French, so was his sister's
and possibly his mother's, since it had been said hers
was unusual. Oh, bother, she must get her mind off that
man. She must think about how and when she would
tell the family she was leaving home. Perhaps after
dinner, when they were replete and refreshed. She'd left
the vegetables prepared. Noel was going to switch the
casserole on when he got in from lectures and it was a
cold dessert made the night before. All she needed to
think about was how to start her announcement.
Dramatically or casually?

She needn't have worried, it was solved for her.
Jerked out of her in fact as she came round by the back
door. There she noticed that under the plumbago bush
where Muffles, their old cat, loved to lie, were long
tendrils of clingweed. So that was where he was getting
all those sticky seeds in his fur! Well, that weed came
out easily enough and no time like the present. She bent
down and seized some, right by the open window of the
porch.

Kerry's voice floated out. 'It's just not like Monique.
I can't understand it. She's anything but an oyster
usually. And there's been an air of suppressed excitement
about her. Usually if it's something nice, she wants to
share her news, but not this time. I'm sure it's to do
with old Amabel's lawyers. I've tried to worm it out of
her but the more I try, the more she clams up. Yet when
she doesn't know I'm watching her, she falls into a
daydream and gets positively starry-eyed. Then comes
back to herself. On the other hand, the day she came
back from Akaroa she had another air of suppressed
excitement about her. And that was three days before
she went to Amabel's wig-and-gown men.'

Noel gave a derisive hoot. 'I think you're just being
imaginative, Kerry. Can't the girl be in a happy mood
without it having to be money? Gosh, you've got a

materialistic outlook. Perhaps she's in love, and not, I hope, with that smoothy, Clinton.'

Sylvie chimed in, 'Well, the smoothy would do me. I like men that age. I'm sure he's not in love with Monique. Of course *she* might be in love with *him*. Perhaps he's been a laggard in love ... I say, that's a good phrase, isn't it? A laggard in love, but suddenly he's popped the question.'

'Good grief, I hope not. She runs this house like clockwork and I'm damned if I'd have a shot at it. But Dad would say if Monique could do it why not me? I wouldn't half make you lot sit up and do more chores if she got married ... but I'm not worried, for one thing Monique strikes me as a career girl and for another Clint doesn't exactly seem a man of passion. No, knowing Monique she's probably planning something.

'I reckon old Amabel was so carried away by her old calf-love returning to her, she's left Monique a tidy sum. I believe the price she got for her house was fantastic. I hope that's it because Monique's bound to share it out. She's a daftie, of course, but I'm sure we're deserving objects. Wouldn't it be marvellous if she decided to buy us a car? I mean she's got Amabel's and we can hardly ever get Dad's. A car between the three of us would be marvellous, we could have it in turns. Or she might give us all a fabulous holiday in Australia. I'm pretty sure that visit to the lawyers meant money.'

Sylvie's voice was excited. 'I'd settle for a trip to Australia myself. Lovely shopping. A girl at the office got——'

Noel cut in, 'You're both dafties, not Monique. If she's got a little legacy why the dickens should she spend it on you? On any of us? If I was her and that's what it is, I'd say to heck with everyone, I'm tired of being little Orphan Annie to the Lethbridges ... I'm off for pastures new.'

Monique, all this time, had been crouched below the window level, her hands still grasping the sticky clingweed, all sort of reactions chasing over her. But at Noel's words she rose up, looked through the window, said loudly and clearly, 'That's exactly what's happening. Good guess, Noel. Aunt Amabel's left me enough money to keep myself for a year. I gave in my notice today.'

Their reaction was as one. After their initial jump they were as still as statues. Monique said crisply, 'Open the french windows and let me in. I wasn't going to say a thing till we'd eaten but this has precipitated things and made me realise Amabel was right.'

The two girls rushed, opened them, Monique stepped inside. Kerry gulped. 'Sorry, Monique. Perhaps what I—what we said sounded worse than we meant. I— we——'

Monique held up a hand. Kerry stopped but Sylvie rushed in. 'You've given in your notice? But you *love* your job! You won't want to live on a lump sum, surely? I mean wouldn't you rather spend it . . . and keep on working? Or have——'

Noel said, 'Give Monique a chance, girls. I hope she's going to be sensible for once and do her own thing. Go on a cruise or something. Or fly off to Europe if there's enough; it's time she lived a life of her own. I've never thought Clint was the man for her, he'd lean on her too like we have and if he *was* slow to come to the point, who's to know it wasn't because of us? Probably thought her family'd be hung round her neck like the Old Man of the Sea, for the rest of their lives.'

His sisters gazed at him. 'You've done as much leaning as we have. You like your comfort, you——'

'Sure I have. It was Merle who opened my eyes. Ever since I brought her home she's made me see things in a different light. *She's* had to stand on her own feet. I realised finally, not all at once, how true it was. And the way you went on just now just made me sick.' He swung round. 'Monique . . . you *are* a daftie but a very nice one. But if Amabel left you some money it's jolly well going to be all yours if I have anything to do with it. And girls, none of this saying that Monique gets her greatest pleasure out of giving. I've heard you come out with that before. Keep your money to yourself, Monique!'

To their immense surprise she burst out laughing. 'I

can't do anything else,' she gasped. 'Aunt Amabel has deeded over some money on one condition . . . that I clear out and live my own life. I'm to have one year in which I do what I jolly well like!'

Noel fell back on the couch and laughed helplessly. 'The old pet! No flies on Mrs Gregory Hurst. That's priceless. No wonder her Gregory came to her from the ends of the earth. I never saw anything like it. I thought she was quite old, but he renewed her youth.'

Sylvie looked at him suspiciously. 'Going all romantic, aren't you? Who are you studying now? Byron or Tennyson or someone?'

If she expected her brother to be embarrassed she was disappointed. He said mildly, 'I am, as a matter of fact. Tennyson. And there's nothing wrong with romance. Or poetry. Do you know what our lecturer said yesterday, most unexpectedly? That romance sweetens life.'

Sylvie said nothing. It rang so true. What a day for bombshells. Suddenly Monique felt light-hearted and light-headed. It hadn't been as hard as she had anticipated. She'd been pitchforked into the announcement and what they'd been overheard saying had more or less shamed them into accepting this. It was true what Amabel had said, they were too shrewd to expect her to renounce it. How neat. All tied up and delivered to her. They were dismayed, yes, because they'd all have to buckle in, but it was accomplished. All of a sudden she felt swimmy.

She found herself swaying, said, 'I've had a very tough day. Well, more exciting than tough, I suppose, but I'll just have to flop before dinner. I'd like you to make me a cup of tea. In fact a whole pot of tea. In here.' She subsided into a chair.

Silently the girls went out together. Monique looked across at Noel with love in her eyes, said softly, 'Thank you, Noel. Today above all days, I needed a champion, and I found two!'

She hadn't meant to say it. Noel dropped down on the arm of her chair, hugged her. 'Two? Who was the other? And what did he champion you for? Monique,

you've not been in a spot of bother, have you? Come on
now, you've fought our battles all your life ... you tell
me.'

She shook her head, laughed to reassure him, 'For
Pete's sake, don't let on to the girls. It slipped out. It
was nothing. Just a—just a customer who came to my
rescue.' To her annoyance she felt her colour rise.

Noel chuckled, 'Dear Sis, I strongly suspect this Sir
Galahad is not in the sere and yellow. Do tell.'

'I can't, Noel, much as I'd like to. You'd have
enjoyed it, because we've got the same sense of humour
but it would mean giving a couple of people away, and
it wouldn't be fair. It was a kind of poetic justice.'

He looked rueful. 'How tantalising, but knowing you,
if you've decided it would be unethical, you'll be as
mysterious as the Sphinx. I just wish it hadn't been at
the shop, though. Must've curbed your style a bit.'

She couldn't resist it. 'Oh, it wasn't all at the shop.
He took me out to the airport for lunch. I suppose to
help me get over it.'

Noel whistled. 'Sounds a bit of all right to me but
why the airport?'

Her eyes danced, her spirits rising, 'Because he was
just leaving for Canberra.'

'For *Canberra*? You mean the seat of Federal
Government in Australia?'

'Of course. Is there any other Canberra?'

'No, of course not. I'm being daft. What is he? Some
sort of Government wallah here? Some political bod?'

'No, a farmer doing experimental work for Lincoln
College and giving reports.'

'Better and better. Where does he farm, Sis?'

'I haven't the faintest idea. We didn't have time. Oh,
that's not quite true. I suspect it might be Banks
Peninsula.'

Noel smacked two fists together. 'Beats me. You've
been having fun. Tell me, how has the dear Clint taken
all this ... I mean dashing off to the airport for lunch,
giving in notice? ... which means, I guess, more or less
brushing him off, giving him the go-by.'

'It does. I'm not sure how he took it. He made the

right sort of noises, even protested a little. But not too much. Poor Clint. It won't break his heart, Noel, that I know. He behaved very well under the circumstances, I'd say, and once the dear man gets over the shock to his vanity, he'll probably be as relieved as I am.'

Noel said in a vastly satisfied tone, 'That makes three of us. I couldn't have borne you to have married Clint. Someday I'd like to see you on Cloud Nine about someone. Perhaps about this Sir Galahad?'

She shook her head. 'I may never see him again, Noel. He could be a ship that passed in the night, and in passing, rescued me. The girls are coming back. No more now.'

They'd been long enough to have had a consultation and she guessed they'd decided to play it cool. There was a pretty cup and saucer on a silver tray, and two biscuits. Kerry poured. As soon as Monique felt revived she said, 'I'm not splashing it on a cruise or anything like that. That would be over in a flash. I'm realising a dream. I've always thought I'd love to restore some old historic house. That's exactly what I'm going to do. It's for two elderly ladies who couldn't afford today's wages for someone to assist them. I'm going to do it for my keep, and the legacy gives me enough for clothes and other expenses. I'm going to catalogue and value everything, and arrange the rooms so the general public can be charged admission.

'It's at Port Beauchamp, that delectable inlet past Little Akaroa, that I visited a month or so ago. It's haunted my dreams ever since. Henriette Olivier and Thérèse de Quincey live there. They look very frail, but they're whipcord tough really. They come from a long line of French pioneers. They are both childless widows and are the last of their line.' (They weren't really, but they didn't know that yet.)

Kerry nodded quite amiably, 'And if you give them this year, I daresay someone else could take over and you could come home at the end of it. You wouldn't find it hard to get a job in Christchurch again, with your experience.'

Noel drawled, 'Oh, I don't know. Banks Peninsula is

an enchanting sort of place ... she might never escape from it.' His dancing eyes met Monique's.

Sylvie looked across to where Monique had put her handbag, said, 'What fabulous violets. I'll put them in water. Where did you get them?'

Noel's voice was teasing, 'Did the chap who gave you lunch at the airport buy them for you?'

Monique was again conscious of warmth in her cheeks. 'Yes ... they certainly are beautiful, aren't they? And so fragrant.'

Kerry and Sylvie exchanged glances. 'Lunch at the airport?' Kerry's voice squeaked with surprise. 'Wasn't that a bit far for a lunch-hour? I mean to say!'

Monique managed to say casually, 'Oh, Clint had his lunch in the office and gave me extra time.'

'Cor!' said Sylvie. 'Beats me! How magnanimous of Clint. The poor bloke ... his girl ditches him, gives in her notice, and he lets her have extra time for lunch, all in the one day. Who was this guy, anyway? Some influential customer Clint dare not offend?'

'Hardly,' said Noel, with the smug air of knowing all, 'But probably a VIP ... he was off to Canberra on Government business. There's more to our Monique than we ever suspected, you know.'

Monique was terrified he'd go too far. What a blessing he knew so little.

Kerry looked consumed with curiosity. 'Have you known him long?'

Noel answered, eyes slits of merriment, 'She hasn't. It's just that this bloke's a fast worker, unlike the laggard Clint.'

Kerry disregarded him. 'What's his name? she demanded. Monique thought it better not to make too much of a mystery of it. 'Edouard Fergusson,' she said. 'And that's all I'm going to tell you.'

For the very good reason that was all she knew ... and she might never see him again. Though deep down in her heart she was sure that Edouard Fergusson would reappear in her life.

# CHAPTER THREE

ONCE you had taken a decisive step, smaller issues seemed to have a habit of resolving themselves. Monique had insisted her stepfather wasn't told till he'd had his meal and that she was going to see him on his own. Athol Lethbridge had married her mother when Monique was just seven and she loved him dearly.

He had a small study off his bedroom, and led her there. She often consulted him privately since she'd taken her mother's place in the household. He flung himself down, smiled at her, said, 'Nobody playing up, I hope? I'm going out later with one of the board members, to see the play at the Town Hall. But fire away.'

He had the rare knack of hearing one out to the end. Monique described her visit to Port Beauchamp, her delight in its beauty, and antiquity, the two charming elderly ladies, their problem in wanting to stay on, in the huge old home, the instant rapport she had had with them, and Henriette's touching sureness that because she was an expert in the world of antiques, she would be able to find someone willing to live there and to organise it as a tourist attraction.

She said nothing of opening that book and finding there sure and certain proof that this was where her beloved grandfather had spent his childhood, that grandfather who'd been estranged from his family when just a youth. She didn't want to hurt this man who had loved her as his own, by revealing this sudden heart-hunger for the scenes of Grandad Belfield's ancestors.

She hurried on instead to Aunt Amabel's bequest and condition. Athol rose, came to her as she leaned forward, talking earnestly, a plea in her voice for understanding. He brought her to her feet, held her to him, 'Darling girl, don't be nervous with me. I can see what you're afraid of. You're so like your mother.

40

Monique, I won't think you're feeling put upon, used by us, though you've every right to feel that. I've been concerned lately about Kerry's selfishness. This could be the making of her. Although it would upset my own pleasant existence, love, I've hoped someone might come along to give you a home of your own. But not Clint. He's not for you. But I dared not say so lest you thought it was only myself I was thinking of. Get cracking. Ring Mr Montmorency now. Pity if you dilly-dallied and he was out for the evening. And listen, no offering to give him a month's notice ... a fortnight these days, with so many looking for jobs, ought to be all right.'

He kissed her forehead, rubbed a hand over his chin, said, 'I think I need another shave. Ring from here. Give you more privacy than with the bunch listening in.'

Monique stared after him. She was sure he didn't need to shave again. Board member? There had been one or two such outings of late. Not necessarily another lonely guy. It was a private hospital board he worked for, nearly half were women. Well, good luck to him!

Claude Montmorency was another instance of the minor problems smoothing out. 'I regret this decision, of course, though I've often thought you could want to spread your wings, perhaps gain experience in Europe ... had you rung yesterday I'd have been utterly dismayed, but it's amazing. Just this morning a woman approached me. I was sorry I could offer her nothing. She's an English widow with a great experience in antiques. Her son and his wife were given the opportunity of a good position with a New Zealand firm. He's been fully trained in the Auckland branch to take over in Christchurch. She came out here to see if she liked New Zealand. She certainly does, and knowing we had a Christchurch branch, came to see if I could offer anything. This could be the solution. How about that?'

Monique's heart leapt and all traces of guilt at leaving a fine employer began to dissipate. He started to say something, stopped. Monique prompted him, 'Yes, Mr Montmorency?'

Again hesitation, then, 'No, sometimes second thoughts are wisest. This was too personal. Leave it at that.'

Mischief sounded in his employee's voice. 'Were you by any chance going to ask if it was all off with Clinton?'

He burst out laughing. 'I was, but unless you want to tell me, you needn't.'

'The only reason I would have for not telling you, Mr Montmorency, was if it reflected on Clint in any way. It's nothing to do with that. I've just drifted into being a steady partner of his at various functions and outings. I don't want it to go any further. And he's a splendid manager for our trade.'

'Thanks, Monique. I appreciate and value your opinion. I'll ring him tomorrow and tell him what's in the offing. I'll be in touch with you again very soon. Meantime, go ahead. I'll be most interested in your project. Given time Beauchamp House could become as famous as Olveston House in Dunedin. Incidentally, keep an eye open for antiques round the Peninsula, with Montmorency's in mind. We'd be prepared to be generous in the matter of commission. Not to strip that area of its rightful heirlooms but if things must be sold, we'd like the chance to purchase.'

She rang Beauchamp House. Henriette answered. Her voice warmed when she realised who it was. 'Monique Belfield, how lovely. I know by the pricking of my thumbs you've found someone for us. I told Thérèse that I felt your visit was meant to be, that if anyone could bring this dream of ours true, it would be you. Ever since we visited Olveston House we've yearned after this. If only the public can be induced to come the extra miles from Akaroa.'

'I don't see why not, Mrs Olivier. If they can go to Okain's Bay to Murray Thatcher's museum, why not that comparatively short distance on to the Port? I've an idea about this. The odd carload or family group isn't going to be very profitable, even though welcome, once we get known, but it could snowball if we concentrate on groups. If we get out an attractive brochure and send it to Women's Institutes, the Women's Division, the Townswomen's Guild and so on, various church clubs, Rotarians, Lions, Kiwanis, the lot, we'd soon be known. They pass it on by word of mouth. What did you say?'

Henriette sounded excited like a little girl. 'But Monique ... you are saying "we"! Are you going to retain an interest in it? Oh, how we would love that. We felt so drawn to you, somehow. Is it possible you have found a close friend and that you intend to give us the benefit of your own advice, your expertise?'

Monique said: 'Dear Mrs Olivier ... I've given *myself* the job ... if that's all right by you. When I came to Beauchamp House I knew beyond doubting that this was what I wanted to do in life. At times I've hated taking family treasures away from their rightful settings. In a job like this I can enhance those things, match them up, refurbish others, write out their history ... will you have me?'

Henriette's voice that was surprisingly young-sounding for her age, went all wobbly. There were tears in it. 'My dear, oh, my dear, *will we have you*? When you left the other day Thérèse said oh so wistfully, "If only she can find us someone of the same calibre as herself." But we didn't entertain the idea seriously because how could we possibly afford the sort of salary you must get at Montmorency's?'

Simply, without dramatising it, Monique told them of Aunt Amabel's bequest. She could hear Thérèse, who must have caught most of the conversation, twittering in the background and now softly clapping her hands. Monique added, 'Aunt Amabel wanted me to take time off my job, to do my own thing. There's enough money for a year even if I went travelling, but when I saw Beauchamp House the other week, I realised how I'd love to restore it. And when I knew about the money, I thought my heart's desire lay much closer than the other side of the world. Together the three of us could create something beautiful that would give pleasure, in time, to thousands of people. And because it's my dream, too, you must allow me to work without wages.

I just want my keep. I won't come otherwise. I couldn't allow you to put your financial resources at risk otherwise.'

Then Monique held her breath. Would they be too proud? The voice, still with a quaver in it, took up again. 'My dear ... I'm sure if there were any men in the family to advise us, they'd say we couldn't possibly accept a sacrifice like that ... that it would put us under an obligation, you know how men are ... stiff with pride. But we aren't going to. If you are quite, quite sure, dear child, and if you think this Amabel would approve, we will welcome you with open arms.

'Thérèse and I were trying to be oh, so sensible, to make up our minds that the time would come when this house would have to be sold, the farm has already gone; we retained only five acres for ourselves. We thought we might have to retire to some small place in Akaroa where we would not see strangers altering it, perhaps cutting the trees down that the first Beauchamp, Philippe, planted. But instead I am convinced, as our father used to say, that *le bon Dieu* sent you to us that day.' The voice paused and Henriette gave a wicked giggle. 'You will think me very unfilial, Monique, but that was a strange phrase to hear upon my father's lips. He had more in common really with *le diable*. Certainly the very devil got into him at times. Yet he was convinced the world was created solely for his benefit. Have I shocked you?'

Henriette would never know that Monique's laugh was almost pure relief. She'd thought it might be difficult, if ever she revealed she was the granddaughter of the reputed black sheep of the family, to refrain from flying to her Grandad's defence, but if Henriette and Thérèse had known their father for what he was, there was hope!

She said, 'Dear Mrs Olivier, how refreshingly honest and free of humbug you are. Me, I have never subscribed to the theory that all dead dogs were good dogs.'

'Bless you, my child. Monique, tell me, we are intrigued by your French name, and just now when you put it that way . . . I mean saying: "Me . . . I have never . . ." etcetera, is it possible your mother was French? Your surname, of course, is English.'

What a good thing she'd put the question that way. She could answer it truthfully. 'No, Mother was an Australian, fifth generation, and of Scots stock, pioneers.'

'Where did you get your name from, then? I mean was it after someone?'

'My mother once said she'd broken with Scots tradition . . . you know the one that decrees the first sons are named for their grandfathers, and the first daughters for their grandmothers. She had dozens of cousins so every second generation bore the same name. Mother was Anna. The rest used to try for variations, Nancy, Nan, Anne, Annie . . . but it was still awkward at family reunions. So she picked a name she just liked for us all. I have two half-sisters and a brother, Kerry, Sylvie, and Noel. Mrs Olivier, I'll come across to see you at the weekend. Oh, could I? I'd gladly stay the night. I want to get on to preliminaries right away. We must work out the wording of a leaflet to introduce the idea that soon a new tourist attraction will be opening in Port Beauchamp. You'll have to okay the wording. We have late night at the shop Fridays, so I'll come Saturday, leaving early.'

Athol was very late home, nevertheless Monique's light was still on. He came in, sat on the side of the bed, and said, 'Too excited to sleep?'

She nodded, putting her book down. 'You could say that. Dad, you know once Mother said you and she decided to bring new names into the family, and made them Kerry, Sylvie, Noel? Was it the same with me? Did she ever say?'

'It wasn't the same. I asked her once, because Monique is usually Monica in English-speaking countries. She said your grandfather, whom she adored, had asked diffidently if you could be called that. Said as a schoolboy he'd fallen for a little girl called Monique. Rather sweet, don't you think? Good night, dear.'

Yes, it was sweet. Wouldn't it be lovely if sometime

she met that long-ago Monique? Had she gone to the village school down near the shore? Oh what a pity Grandad hadn't talked more of his early days, but he had shut them off, bitter because his father hadn't believed him when he'd been questioned and accused wrongly. There had been the hint of steel, the uncompromising core at the heart of the man.

'My own father thought the worst of me. It was nothing I could refute, prove. It would've been so different had my mother been alive. She would have dragged the truth out of that girl. But the one person who really mattered hadn't believed it. Just a young girl, but she had enough faith for a dozen. I didn't know that for twenty-five years when I met her in a Sydney street. One of the sweetest moments of my life.

'But at the time the fact that my own father wouldn't take my word ate into my soul. When he was so old that his years were few and my older brother had died, he found me out and came to see me. But it was evident that all he was interested in was that I had a son who could inherit the estate.

'Oh, perhaps I was stiff-necked with pride, Monique, perhaps I was no better than he was, hard and unforgiving, but I couldn't risk my son, your father, coming under the domination of his grandfather. I loved and trusted my son, and he had inherited my mother's gift with brush and pencil, as you know. He worked hard to earn his living as a commercial artist and had he lived, would, I think, have become famous as an illustrator. I couldn't have put him under the tyranny of my father for the sake of a parcel of land.'

Well, Grandad had had a happy life, a long one, and his son had had a short happy one, but now Monique felt with her Great-aunt Henriette that in very truth *le bon Dieu* had led her to the home of her forebears that idyllic day last month. That was what made life so worthwhile, that you never knew what was lurking around the next corner, till, suddenly, when at some time things seemed drab and grey, you were, as Wordsworth put it, 'surprised by joy'.

The moments of truth she'd once read, so often come

to us on the verge of sleep and one came to her then, the swift and certain knowledge that out of all the good gifts that had come her way this day, the sweetest had been when an unknown man had rescued her from humiliation; who had made her laugh when she had been trembling on the edge of tears, the man whose sheer audacity and sense of fun had lifted her out of herself . . . the man whose lips on hers had stirred in her something she hadn't known existed, an awareness that other worlds awaited her beyond the dull present. The perfume of the violets he'd given her drifted across the room. He'd asked her to write her telephone number down for him and he said that someone in Akaroa had recommended her to him. Didn't that make it almost certain that in a small community like the Peninsula, their paths would converge again? A smile on her lips, she slid over the edge of slumber into deep sleep.

The rest of the week fled. Within two days the prospective saleswoman Mr Montmorency had mentioned arrived, an ideal applicant. Angela Freeman couldn't believe her good fortune. 'I'm dying to start. I know I'm not engaged yet but I'd like to come in and assist so I can get the feel of the place.'

It was only natural Clint was a little stiff with Monique, who occasionally had to hide a smile. Poor darling, he couldn't very well appear relieved though he ought to be . . . a capable assistant was taking Monique's place and there was no awkwardness with Montmorency as there might've been had he ditched Monique for Glenys. It was a whole new start for them both.

In a quiet moment she said to him, 'Clint, it's better this way. If we're honest we'll admit we struck no sparks off each other. We drifted into a second-rate attachment that in the end satisfied neither of us. Let's be as natural as possible with each other till I finish here.'

He looked at her searchingly, with less reserve than usual, then smiled and said, 'I think you only realised that when you met this chap from Akaroa, didn't you?'

She didn't answer. She wanted no probing. Edouard might or might not live in Akaroa. Clint smiled again and patted her hand saying, 'All right. I won't dig deeper. A bit mean if I did. You had the courage to break away and maybe it'll be best for me, too.'

She resisted the temptation to say, 'And love to Glenys.' She rose as Miss Sebright said, poking her head round the office door, 'Your sister's here if you can see her for a moment, Monique.'

Kerry said, 'I'm a customer for once. I want a birthday gift for a girl at the office. We're clubbing together on it. She's mad on horse-brasses and I knew you had some.'

They were looking at a selection when in came a florist's messenger. He had a huge swathe of pale green paper concealing something. 'Flowers for Miss Belfield,' he announced.

As Monique took them from him he said, 'I was to tell you they were sent Interflora and apologise if they are late for a special day, but this chap particularly asked for red rosebuds and it's too early from here. We had them flown in from the north.'

Monique looked blank. 'Are you sure they're for me? I mean it's not my birthday or anything like that.'

The young man grinned. 'If it means anything to you, the order came from Canberra.' He gazed at her with open curiosity and the grin widened as he saw her colour rise. 'Ah ... I think that rings a bell. Look!' With a flourish that did him credit he swirled the green translucent paper aside to reveal an exquisitely shaped basket, narrow-waisted with a flared-out top, holding red roses, just unfolding, lilies-of-the-valley and maidenhair fern in an arrangement that was sheer perfection in artistry and dewy sweetness.

They all oohed and aahed, the young man disappeared, Kerry said in a strange, envious voice, 'Aren't you going to open the envelope?'

Monique slid her nail under the deckled gilt edge, drew it out. She gazed down on it. Kerry, with cool effrontery, craned her neck over Monique's shoulder. It said, simply: 'Till I return. I hope you know your Robbie. Edouard.'

Kerry boggled. 'Robbie? He means Robbie Burns, doesn't he? Good God, the man's a poet as well as a dark horse.'

Monique decided the only thing to do was to ignore Kerry. She said, 'They're really something, aren't they? I think we'll give the customers the benefit of these till I take them home. Now where?'

She swung round, her eyes roving over the display stands till they came to one draped in black that had a Victorian tea-set on it, of rose-sprinkled china. 'Would you hold this basket, Angela? I'll just move these along.'

She cleared the space, took the basket, set it on the top tier. It could have been designed for there. Angela and Miss Sebright were enchanted. Clinton approached, stopped in admiration.

Kerry knew him well enough, of course, she waved to the offering. 'From Canberra, no less. From the lordly Edouard. I'm dying to meet him. Sounds like a spare-no-expense sort of wallah. Are you sure he's an ordinary run-of-the-mill farmer, Monique? By the look of those I'd put him down as no lower than a Minister of Agriculture. That, and the Canberra touch. How old is this chap? Must've been earning a packet for a good many years by the look of that. Is he in the sere and yellow?'

Kerry had never been a favourite of Clint's, but his reply to her still surprised Monique. 'I can assure you he's not,' he said, drawlingly, 'My guess is thirty-two or three? Am I right, Monique?'

Again Kerry boggled. 'You mean *you've* met him?'

'Of course. He picked your sister up here one day. He's what I imagine Sylvie would call a dish. And now, if you don't mind, back to business.'

Kerry said hurriedly, 'Of course. I'm a customer, actually. I'll have those three brasses, Monique. Gift-wrapped please.'

The others disappeared. Kerry said in a low tone, 'Your new swain isn't the only one who's a dark horse.

You are, too. You go on in the same old way for years, then suddenly you up and leave us, get yourself a new boyfriend, and your old one refers to him as a dish. I don't know how you do it. Didn't think you had it in you. Robbie Burns! Well, even I could guess that one. "O my Luve's like a red, red rose . . ." This one sounds serious. You must've been keeping him a secret for some time. Definitely a dark horse!'

Monique said coolly, 'Wrong sex. I'm a filly. Here's your change. Nine fifty-five, sixty, eighty, ten dollars. And Kerry, on your way home tonight would you get a bottle of cream and some hokey-pokey ice-cream? Bye-bye for now.'

She managed to work out some preliminary wording on the first leaflets she was sending out about Beauchamp House. Henriette and Thérèse could okay them on Saturday. No doubt there would be things they'd want added. When there she must itemise some of the more valuable treasures. They'd have to take out extra insurance, get a man versed in security locks to examine doors and windows. Oh, for the early days in the colony when such things as burglary and vandalism would be unknown on the Peninsula.

Saturday dawned as she had hoped it might, gently, with the promise of a glorious day to come. She was up early, breakfasted alone, left the table set for the others, and was away, her weekend bag on the back seat, her heart singing. Oh, dear Aunt Amabel. How heavenly it was to have your very own transport.

This widely spread city of the plains was stirring now for its short morning of trading that hadn't long been the custom. A few years ago only dairies had been open and everyone had a long weekend. Monique was glad Montmorency's kept to the old way. Theirs wasn't an essential service and a brief three hours shopping-time not so suitable for antiques. The city was left behind and the guardian hills, those hills she was going to live among, came closer. Could anything be lovelier than the Peninsula hills and bays?

Aquamarine and turquoise and sapphire inlets fretted the circle of the tawny-tussocked hills sweeping out into the Pacific.

She herself would be living within sight and sound of a small harbour that had been settled by her own ancestors, a darling inlet gashed into towering cliffs, with a village clustered at the southern side, farms sweeping back from it, unspoiled by the march of progress, only slightly more populated than in Philippe Beauchamp's days. He had arrived to establish that little colony of France just a few years after the first French settlers on the *Comte de Paris* had come ashore, to their meagre parcels of land, isolated, homesick, promised more than was given them. That had been in eighteen-forty, at Akaroa. In time those industrious people had created a small town of great beauty, thirteen thousand miles distant from all they had hitherto held dear.

Monique had swotted up the history of the place long before she first ventured there in search of antiques at the bidding of her Auckland boss. Even then, all unknowing that she was treading in the very footsteps of her ancestors, it had caught at her imagination, stirred her heart.

Now she was driving through these winding country roads, with rich farms on either side, towards those narrow streets that were still called *rues*, and countless lanes sweet with Normandy poplars and Bourbon roses, quaint gabled houses that could have been tucked into any French village in the Old World, whose gardens grew the same walnuts, mulberry trees, and spicy scented gilly-flowers.

The miles went by as she skirted the hills, through Tai-tapu, past Motukarara, and Little River Township, then she was climbing up the road to the Hilltop Hotel where she would get her first exquisite glimpse of Akaroa five miles on ... there it was, lying below her, contoured like a relief map. The road took her down to the waters of the harbour at Barry's Bay, then in to Duvauchelles with the County Council offices in the seaward triangle of a valley that ran back into the volcanic hills, then on past the shore-line of tiny bays with oyster-catchers wading, stilts, gulls, picking among the rocks. On a headland some stunted olives had been pointed out to her once before, then Akaroa itself, the Long Harbour, Rue Lavaud, the Rue Jolie, Rue Balguerie ... she turned away from the busy fishing harbour and into and over the hills at the back of the enchanting sleepy-hollow look of the town towards the Eastern Bays; here and there the summits afforded her a glimpse of the limitless leagues of the Pacific Ocean in the direction of the South Pole, but who could think of Antarctic wastes on a day as warm as this?

She dipped down and negotiated a bend that scooped through a cutting deep in a patch of red earth so different from the yellow clay of most of New Zealand. Tall, dark pines shut out the sunlight briefly, then she was through that balsamy tunnel and there before her it lay ... the narrow mini-harbour cleft into the rock-hard cliffs by that eruption of aeons ago, turquoise blue today with glints of green. There was the tiny wharf that in those roadless days had been Philippe Beauchamp's life-line for his provisions, his produce, his only link with the doctor in Lyttleton, whenever illness had threatened his large family.

The next bend widened out to the open white gates of Beauchamp House, set far back from the road, gabled in true Colonial style. Not Beauchamp House ... *home*.

She was early but they heard the car coming and came running out on to the wide verandah, Henriette and Thérèse, tall, slim, elegant, with a youthful eagerness that belied their age. Monique's heart leapt ... her own kin though they didn't know it yet. She stepped out of the car and up the wide stone steps and had the feeling that she had crossed a river and burned her bridges. A sentimental thought, perhaps, but satisfyingly true!

Thérèse, starry-eyed, reached her first, and knew no reserve, kissing her as indeed she might've greeted a niece. Henriette followed suit. 'Oh, we've been counting the days. So glad you were early ... the weekend will pass all too quickly. So every moment is precious ... oh, dear, that sounds as if we're going to work you to

death, but not so. Just that we're like children on
Christmas morning, wanting to show you everything.
The other time you were here was much too short. But
you are going to have coffee first. Then we'll take you
to your room.'

The coffee was perfection, topped with whipped
cream and powdered chocolate. There were wafer-thin
sandwiches and tiny light scones, with bramble jelly.
The house, of course, was ridiculously large for two
childless widows, but magnificent for the use they were
now going to give it. The rooms that were to be open to
the public could be kept dusted and polished, doubtless
by someone from the Bay eager for part-time work, and
with judicious planning it would pay for itself in no
time.

Philippe, from the start, had built his house wisely
and well, getting the coastal schooners of the day to
bring him *kauri* from the North Island for his beautiful
staircases and ceilings. Generations of loving care had
enriched and polished the wood. On the upstairs
landings were pointed arches overhead, and smaller
passageways led off as the house had been added to
sideways and upwards. Fortunately, there were skylights
and tall narrow windows slotted into the walls
everywhere, bringing light and sun in to twinkle on the
panelling, the brass and the glass lamp-brackets.

Every step enchanted Monique more. Henriette
turned another corner into a tiny passage. There was a
door each side. 'Those are our bedrooms. At the end,
up that tiny flight of stairs, is yours, if you like it.' She
opened the door into the quaintest room Monique had
ever seen and she was experienced in visiting old
Colonial houses. It was set into twin French gables and
was two rooms in one, but with one set two steps higher
than the other, and furnished as a tiny sitting-room. It
was like a suite.

She gave a little skip of pure delight. 'Oh, this will
give me a little apartment of my own. I love it. You
absolute darlings!'

The bed was a three-quarter one, covered with a
French knitted cotton quilt, and the pillows actually

had shams on them, with drawn-thread work edgings. That bed was, as Monique instantly recognised, French Imperial style, probably made in Akaroa in the early days, by a French carpenter. The towel rail and mirror stand were similar, the dressing-table stool was covered in soft pastel-shaded chintz, and there were glass powder-bowls and silver-capped scent bottles.

She found the two steps to the little sitting-room drew her feet. The small-paned casements, set in the gable with a windowseat below framed a view of the inlet, sparkling like myriads of diamonds in the late morning sun, and a fascinating glimpse of the quayside, little boats rocking lazily on the tide. There were a couple of easy chairs with loose covers, a long carved chest that had surely come out with Philippe and his Louise, a round French Provincial table, some more modern bookcases, well-filled, had French ornaments on the top and above, rather an incongruous note, a couple of muskets, crossed. At a glance she put them down as types used at Waterloo. There were some exquisite miniatures, a corner cupboard that was English Regency, not French, and a *kauri* davenport that had probably been copied and bore much evidence of use. Shabby, but mellow. Not a museum piece, a household article.

Henriette saw her looking at it, crossed to it, pulled out a drawer, demonstrated how it opened up. 'You could find this handy for your correspondence, Monique. It was Hilaire's . . . our younger brother. He was very good to two little girls who were always tagging after him.' She touched the wood caressingly. 'I still sometimes think I see him at it, poring over his stamp collection, his sketches of birds, his homework.' Monique felt her heart constrict. Hilaire's! Grandad's. He who had been Hilary Belfield to her. Henriette's tone had been one of love and nostalgia. They had mentioned him that day a month ago, all unknowing what it meant to her, as sinned against, not sinning. A wave of love for these two women washed over Monique. And a great longing to turn back the clock. Oh, if only Grandad could know she was here.

But perhaps he did.

# CHAPTER FOUR

Monique managed to choke back her emotions, said calmly, 'Was this his room, then? Or has the davenport been moved here?'

'No, this was his. He was a bookish little boy, different from Emile, whose world was horses and the farm. Emile had the room at the far end on the first landing. It overlooked the stables and had an outside staircase leading down. He was nearly always up at dawn riding over the hills. He was Father's right-hand man. He never married and one morning when he was fifty and Father was seventy-five, he didn't come home. They thought he'd been thrown but he hadn't. He'd tethered his horse to a willow and gone to get a cast ewe to her feet and suffered a coronary. Father was never the same again. In some ways it was for the better. He wasn't so harsh.'

Monique couldn't help it. 'And Hilaire?'

Thérèse sighed 'Father never understood him to begin with. To end with, he drove him from home. A family came here to the Bay to work. There was a girl, rather notorious, I'm afraid. She had a certain wild charm. Hilaire was blamed for the baby she was going to have. She came here and saw Father. He almost met his match in her. We were young but not as ignorant as Father thought we were. Mother had seen to that before she died. *We* never believed it. Hilaire was cut to the heart that Father wouldn't believe him. He offered to swear on the family Bible that he was innocent. Father was terrified that she and Hilaire might have to live under his roof; she was cheap and coarse and used appalling language. In actual fact and in fairness to Father, he'd have been sorry, had she been a different type, for a girl in that plight, but he shrank from having anyone of that calibre living here. He offered Hilaire a large sum of money to take her away from the district and marry her. Hilaire refused. The girl took the money and went to Australia. Hilaire left home. We think he went to sea. Because for years we got presents, on our birthdays, Henriette and me. We share a birthday, two years apart. I'm the younger. We got kimonos from Japan, small carved canoes from North America, shell necklaces from Tahiti, boomerangs from Australia, but always they came by cargo shipping and too late for Father to have him traced.'

Monique asked, unnecessarily, 'Was there never a reconciliation?'

Henriette sighed. 'They met again. I doubt if you could say it was a reconciliation. I think poor Father blundered again. We never heard the full details, but we think Hilaire felt it was only because he was the one Beauchamp left. That it was for the sake of the estate, not his own sake. Someone from here met Hilaire in Sydney and arranged for the two of them to meet. Father didn't even get an address, just a place to *rendezvous*. If only we'd known at the time, we could have gone, too. It might have helped. But I was on a voyage with my husband, he was a sea-captain. And Thérèse was living in Auckland.

'You see when Emile died and the solicitor came out here with his will, there was also a letter addressed to Father. We didn't know till much later. Emile confessed in it that he was the father of Muriel's baby. He knew his father would never tolerate Muriel at Beauchamp House and Emile hadn't wanted to be disinherited. So together she and Emile concocted the vile lie. Emile had thought Father would settle a good sum on Muriel, which she would have had no hesitation in accepting. Instead, he tried to insist on Hilaire marrying her.

'Poor Hilaire. Everything was against him. He didn't want to farm, he was always interested in birds and trees. Wanted to go into forestry, preserving our native trees. He always dreamed of finding a laughing owl and proving they were not extinct. So he used to slip out at night, in search of any kind of owls. He had copious notes on the subject. But so did Emile sneak out. Down that outside staircase.'

'Did you know much about the reconciliation?'

'Yes, but not till a long time after, when Father told us. Most surprising that, because he would never have admitted himself in the wrong in earlier years. But he had mellowed. In fact, being in the wrong had humbled him. He said Hilaire had been surprisingly forgiving, but only up to a point. He also said he was glad his father knew he wasn't guilty, but that his old life was dead to him and he wouldn't want to return. That he had no desire to revive the past. That he had achieved great happiness. Actually, when Father told us, he said that he had *had* to accept what had come to him. That he'd reaped as he'd sowed. I'm glad that at least he was fair in that respect. I felt it was true what the men on the estate used to say of him, that he was sure an old devil, but a fair devil! Oh, child, you've got tears in your eyes. I shouldn't have made you cry.'

Monique blinked rapidly, 'Oh, take no notice of me. It's easy to make me cry. I mean often when watching TV, I weep. Even when I hear little children singing Christmas carols I get all dewy, yet you can't really get anything more joyful that that, can you?'

(She was jabbering to hide her own surprise . . . that for once she wasn't shedding tears for the young lad who'd been her grandfather, but for the forbidding François, his father, who'd come to a sonless old age and known that because of his own behaviour so long ago, the Beauchamp estate, wrung from a Pacific wilderness by his own forebear, would pass into the hands of strangers.)

Henriette didn't pick anything. She touched a finger to Monique's cheek. 'We like people with ready tear ducts. They are human. Warm creatures, not icebergs. Mother couldn't bear icebergs . . . she was easily moved to both tears and laughter herself. She was so light-hearted and joyous, in spite of an autocratic husband. She retained her sweetness to the last. Pity she died comparatively young. Despite her sweetness, she was steel under the velvet when it came to her children. We must show you the photos of her sometime. We are old enough, I know, but Mother belonged to the days when they played tennis on the Beauchamp courts in floorlength skirts and rows of braid round the hems to stop them getting frayed. Isn't fashion odd? When you came in today with your cream frock with that sailor collar in pale blue, you reminded me of a picture of Mother in what she called a middy blouse.'

Monique turned away hastily to put her weekend bag down. Was it just the frock that had reminded her? They left the room. Monique said, 'There will be other, happier stories of course?'

'Scores. Some will unfold as you catalogue our treasures. About Emile's room. We'd better just point out that outside staircase to it when we show people round the stables. That room's usually occupied by the man we sold the farmland to. He needed the houses on the estate for the men, and besides, he got a bit worried about the two of us here alone in this great house. Time was when it didn't matter, we had very little crime, this end of the Peninsula was so isolated, but then there were burglaries in Akaroa, and Mac gave up his rooms over the stables to sleep over here. He's a dear soul, a grandson of a dear friend, Juliette de Courcy. He's away just now, so one of his young men sleeps here instead. He takes his meals at his mother's place, though. Comes and goes by that stairway.'

'Oh, I'm so glad. I thought that before we advertised we'd have to have dead-locks put in and the security of the windows seen to. And of course there'll be extra insurances, too. I hope the takings will soon justify that.'

'Well, with you not taking a wage, it will certainly be no hardship. I'm glad you're so sensible. Mac's a bit of a stickler over these things. He thinks we are innocents abroad, and we aren't. We're very shrewd. That, at least came from Father. And the French are, in any case.'

'I take it that the French intermarried greatly with the English settlers?'

'Yes, it came to that very quickly. There were half a dozen Germans on the *Comte de Paris* too, all intermingled now, plus a few Irish and Scots and other Europeans. We're all just New Zealanders now, and only in our names and also the occasional French phrase that has slipped into our everyday conversation, does one realise how mixed our ancestry is. Philippe's son married a Morag Macdonald and one of his daughters married a Schmidt from Takamatua, which used to be called German Bay.'

Time flew. The two sisters approved the first draft of notices to be sent to the various clubs, offered ideas of their own, many exceedingly well thought out. Some Monique deferred. 'Till we see what assistance we can get. Souvenirs are out meantime, but when they come as far as this, we must serve morning and afternoon teas.

'Certain areas must be roped off, or people will handle priceless treasures. I've already found a furnishing place in Christchurch who actually have on hand enough synthetic furnishing cord, with tassels, to do the job, and can supply the plastic carpet strip to protect, but not hide, the carpets from too much wear. Are there people in the Port who'd be glad of part-time work?'

'Plenty. The Bay is surrounded by farms, many under management, plus farm workers and wives, quite a few married couples need a bit of extra coming in. We've got a few names already.'

'We won't fly too high, just serve sandwiches like you gave me earlier, chocolate eclairs if we can find someone who'd make them in her own home, and the tiny scones or pikelets with cream and jam. I'm glad the verandah is partly glassed in, some tables could go there. It would be ideal.'

Thérèse said eagerly, 'And in the summerhouse, it's so pretty. We'll take you over. A few years ago we had windows put in. It needed renovating and we rather went to town on it. We had it wired so we could make ourselves tea when we spent an afternoon there. It has views of most of the Port.'

Monique's eyes sparkled. 'The guests will love it. Tell me, does it have honeysuckle and cottage roses over it? It does? Good.'

The weekend wasn't long enough. By Sunday it

became apparent to Monique she hadn't accomplished enough to get things moving in Christchurch for their advertising campaign, especially the printing of the interim catalogues. These would be added to when she knew more of the history of Port Beauchamp and the beautiful house Philippe Beauchamp dreamed up and finally erected. Later she'd get some of the choice pieces sketched. Oh, wasn't time a tyrant, dragging interminably in some hours, racing madly in others?

On impulse she walked to the telephone, dialled Clint's number. A girl's voice answered, a voice that could well belong to a red-headed girl last seen lurking behind the terra-cotta ware!

Monique said crisply, 'I want to speak to Mr Wood, please?'

A hesitation, then a reluctant, 'Who is speaking, please?'

Monique didn't want to be told he wasn't in so she said, 'This is a business call. Is he there, or not?'

It had the desired effect, Clint came on. She said, again crisply, 'It's Monique here, Clint. Oh, it's nothing personal. I realise you have company. Just that I find I can't quite get through these preliminaries. Any chance I could have tomorrow off? I'd like to get an interim catalogue out ready for Xeroxing Tuesday.'

He didn't repeat her name, said formally, 'Yes, that could be arranged. I may have some information for you then, anyway, so would you like to ring me at the salon tomorrow morning? About ten. I should be able to finalise things for you then.'

'Thank you immensely. I will. And Clint, if you feel it would be worthwhile, I can have a footnote at the bottom of these catalogues to the effect that anyone interested in buying antiques, is recommended to call at the Montmorency Salon, Christchurch. How about that?'

'Thank you. That would be much appreciated. Advertising of any sort is valuable. Then I'll hear from you around ten. Goodbye.'

Poor Clint. He'd hope she only imagined he felt it

was policy not to give anything away in front of visitors. He'd been cagey enough for Glenys not to suspect it was Monique. She smothered an inward giggle. He didn't realise he was fading rapidly into a past that had been very mediocre, emotionally speaking.

Her thoughts flew to the man who'd turned her humiliation into something that was more like a stage comedy. Dear Edouard! Her hand went out to the telephone book. He'd heard of her in Akaroa. If he was farming near here it would be interesting to find out just where. She flipped quickly through. Fergussons, yes, plus some spelt with one 's', but none that could be Edouard Fergusson. Well, she'd know quite soon . . . a man who'd asked her to write her number down (even if they'd quite forgotten he didn't know her surname then!) who sent costly roses out of season, Interflora, who was impulsive, warm-hearted, and sentimental enough to quote Robbie Burns . . . again her pulses stirred . . . was bound to follow up his timely eruption into her life.

At ten next morning Clint came straight to the point. 'Monique, I can tell you're dying to get stuck right into this venture. The firm will miss you, of course, but it was a stroke of luck getting Angela Freeman, especially when she was recommended by Mr Montmorency. She's had luck, too. Her son's managed to buy one of those houses with a granny flat attached. Not that she's in the granny category by any means, but you know what I mean. She doesn't even need to go back to Auckland to pack. The son's flying back and the packers can include her stuff with theirs. She's at a loose end, finds hotel life boring and would like to start work as soon as possible. If you came in from, say, Tuesday afternoon when you finish with the printers, till about Thursday, just to tidy up the orders, I could let you go. How about that?'

She subdued a giggle. Poor, dear Clint. The sooner she was out of his hair the better in case Glenys got impatient to flaunt him as hers! She felt gloriously free. Henriette and Thérèse were delighted. They finished the

listing in a grand burst of energy and Monique departed
after breakfast Tuesday.

By Friday she was heading back to Port Beauchamp,
her own dear place. She'd said to Clint, 'If anyone rings
for me, give them this address and number, would you?
And forward any letters there, not to my old home.'
One 'phone call, however, would be made to her home.
She hadn't expected that day she met Edouard, to be
away before he returned. She had thought then a
month's notice might be necessary, but it would make
little difference. He had some connection with Akaroa
and would probably be delighted when told she was
now living there.

She said to the family, 'Edouard Fergusson will be
ringing me on his return from Australia. I wrote this
number down for him, but not my address so be sure to
make it plain where I am. And I certainly wouldn't want
him ringing the shop.' A reminiscent smile flickered. 'He
knew I was moving on but not where. It wasn't finalised.'

Naturally the two girls had looked curious. Kerry
had said, 'Didn't you even hint? I mean he was so
obviously smitten . . . red roses . . . Robbie Burns . . .
and all that, and if he was the dish Clint said, *I'd* have
encouraged him all I could!'

Monique's eyes had danced, and now, driving, she
laughed to herself remembering how she had said, 'Our
acquaintance, in actual time, was of the briefest, though
full of action. No, girls, I am not going to tell all. Just
give him my new address and number when he rings.'

Ten days to go before his return . . . just as well those
days were going to be crammed full. Never had she
experienced such a feeling of delighted anticipation as
at the prospect of hearing that voice again. The voice of
her Saint George!

The little community at Port Beauchamp was delighted.
There had been a feeling of dread abroad that when the
two old ladies were forced to leave the Port because of
their age, and Beauchamp House would go out of the
family, become just another white elephant, mouldering
away to a ruin, the Bay would lose its identity. If it had,

the young schoolmaster said to Monique, even its history would fade and die away. He and his wife arrived to encourage, full of enthusiasm.

He offered to paint and erect a huge sign near the gateposts . . . he was quite an artist, and when he saw the cards Monique was doing in Gothic lettering, to place beside as many exhibits as possible, he offered to have some of his more artistic pupils produce some for her with tiny paintings of the garden flowers in the corners, and native birds and tree-leaves. 'They've already had some experience at making place-cards for dinners and parties. They'd love to do these. Makes them identify with the project.'

Monique's eyes sparkled. 'That would be magnificent. I want to get going but don't want to spoil things by rushing too much. Yet I must identify enough objects to have knowledgeable people keen to visit here. I'm used to valuing and assessing dates and origins, but to make it different, I felt I needed to delve into the history of how and when they were brought here. Henriette and Thérèse are marvellous but quite a few of the things they've lived with so long, they have taken them for granted and are vague about dates. If only there were some of a younger generation here who knew.'

'M'm, see what you mean. Of course Mac's very knowledgeable about these things. Pity he's away just now. His relations are close friends of the old ladies and have a great interest in antiques. I'm sure he'd help. Monique, Jen would like to give you a hand when you open. She's too shy to ask you herself. Jen, don't make faces at me, she can say no if she doesn't need you.'

'You'd be a godsend, Jen. I need someone interested enough to swot up the history, and as Errol gives it to his pupils, he'll have what you need. You would be able to relieve me at times, with the commentary, and if it's a success and some big busloads come, we might have to divide them into smaller lots, map out different routes through the house. It's constructed beautifully for that. And they'll want to see the garden. I'm told some of those camellias are practically unknown now. How about it, Jen?'

Jen looked delighted. 'I'd have settled for a French maid's outfit to serve tea in, but this I'd love. I know most of the treasures by look already but I'll need to be versed in more accurate detail. Would you let me help you clean that stuff you brought from the outhouses? I can't go wrong with that and you could put your expertise into cataloguing them. Wouldn't it be thrilling if we discovered some real masterpiece among the junk? Something to make this place famous, or, if it wasn't closely connected with the family, could be sold to defray the expense of all this. I believe old François was always buying things up at sales.'

'It's always possible,' said Monique. 'That's what makes the antique trade exciting, but we can't bank on it.' It wasn't to be among the junk she discovered what could be a treasure. But that was still to come.

Errol looked up at the sky. 'Jen . . . that sky means rain. In fact a thunderstorm, and we came on the motorbike. We'd better head for home. See you tomorrow, Monique. You won't be able to keep Jen away, now. She was beginning to get bored for the first time in her energetic life.'

It was just as well they had scooted. Monique had never seen such a spectacular storm. It came up from the south, whipping over Mount Bossu, the mountain of the friendly hunchback that kept guard over Akaroa Harbour, and whose peak could be seen from here, its shoulders hunched against the weather. There were clouds scudding before the wind in grotesque and frightening shapes, then an ominous stillness that somehow seemed more terrifying than the tumult, till great stabs of lightning zigzagged across the gunmetal sky and ripped it apart in spectacular display. Henriette, Thérèse and Monique stood spellbound, then the thunder rolled and reverberated among the hills, tossing its echoes from peak to peak across the valleys and gullies.

Thérèse's fine dark eyes were full of a youthful enjoyment, her crêpey old hands coming together in their soundless clapping movement that was so endearing. 'I shouldn't, I know, but I've always revelled in these electrical storms and I'm sure that nowhere do they come more royally than over Banks Peninsula.'

Henriette burst of laughing. 'Thérèse, you goose. Better not say that to the Beaudonais up at Dragonshill in the Alps. Or to someone from the Himalayas, but I know what you mean. Monique, there's a pattern about our storms ... see ... those clouds are travelling eastward, slightly to the north. They'll vanish over the open sea and all of a sudden the sun will pop out and this torrential rain will be seen as a curtain far out on the Pacific. Nevertheless, despite the magnificent show, I'm glad we had time to shut the windows. At this stage we don't want any wallpapers stained. Good job Mac cleared out the gutterings before he went away. It's a drawback having so many trees so close, though when I used to say that to my grandfather, he used to shake his head and say that *his* father, Philippe, wouldn't have agreed. This was one of the places where the thick native bush didn't come down to the water's edge. Philippe built here for his view but paid the price in battering winds. I sometimes wonder how his Louise created her garden till the trees grew.'

Enchantment swept over Monique ... Henriette was speaking of *her* great-great-great grandfather. Some day these two dear ladies would know it. But there was more than enough excitement for them right now, besides, it had to be proved. It wasn't enough to announce it on the strength of a scribbled note in a book that tallied with something her own grandfather had told her long ago, or on the fact that Belfield was probably an anglicised version of Beauchamp. No, birth certificates of three generations would have to be produced, and proof of a change of name by deed poll.

Suddenly, she thought of something. From the upper story of one of the outhouses, she'd noticed some straw sticking out from the eaves of an angle of the roof that jutted over the outside staircase leading to Mac's room. She'd been through that room only once, from the inside when Henriette and Thérèse had taken her through.

She'd felt that with the farm owner away, a kindly

man evidently, who wouldn't allow two elderly ladies to sleep in this great house by themselves, it would be an intrusion on his privacy to look around there too much. And on Kevin's, who was taking Mac's place.

She had thought at the time that it was rather dangerous to have such inflammable stuff poked under the roof, and sparrows built enormous nests under eaves. She'd meant to get some steps up there to investigate, but had forgotten. But now she was afraid it had blocked the downpipe; with all that water pouring off the steep gabled roofs and no proper outlet, it would find away down inside. She wouldn't say a word to the old ladies, she'd just slip away.

The rain had stopped, the sun was shining with a scintillating brilliance through a million raindrops caught on leaf and twig and spiderweb. How those same webs had withstood the storm she didn't know, but she'd read once they were miracles of strength, with an enormous breaking-strain.

She took a wind-cheater from a hook on the back porch and a pair of light aluminium steps. They reached all right. The nest was well tucked into the roof and couldn't have blocked anything, but that guttering was a solid mass of pine-needles and sodden rosettes of lichen that had been washed off the old Welsh slate roof and jammed by the force of the downfall at this corner. Good thing she'd come up. She scooped away, regardless of her nails. If she didn't get it out, with water still running, it would force its way inside.

Then, as the water subsided she saw a very ominous crack where the guttering had pulled away. It would be flowing into Mac's room, heaven send not on the bed. No time to be lost. A few more claps of thunder and its consequent rain, and disaster could occur.

She was off the ladder and through the door in a flash. Kevin always left it open till he came in at night. The bed was all right but a dark stain was spreading from the wall above a huge wardrobe, a free-standing one. She'd have to move it. She thought of the slim old ladies; they appeared tough despite their fragile appearance, but it would be risky to let them help her. She flew across and groaned. It was massive and had a huge drawer at the foot. She tried it tentatively, the whole thing. It wouldn't budge. All the contents must be removed, and speedily. She flung open the doors, scooped at the jackets and coats, trousers and shirts and staggered over to the bed to dump them. The bottom was full of shoes. She then tumbled them on the floor. The drawer was a tough proposition. It needed the edges planed off. She tugged at the twin brass handles impatiently, aware of that water steadily streaming down. The drawer would have to be edged out inch by inch ... oh, damn it, the contents seemed as heavy as lead too.

She got it open a foot and it resisted any more effort. Well, she'd just have to draw the things out. Seemed to be heavy books and packages ... yes, like huge ledgers, heavily bound, with wavy multi-coloured scrolls all over them. Must've been there for ages because they were thick with dust and cobwebby. She hoped the spiders wouldn't bite ... she got some out, saw things beneath like huge rectangles of cardboard, wrapped in filthy brown paper, chucked them on the floor, and began to move the wretched wardrobe with the drawer still stuck halfway out.

It adhered to the carpet ... she pushed and pulled, but she managed it. Thank heaven this wasn't a wall-to-wall carpet, just an ancient square. She could fling it back to dry once she got this flaming thing far enough from the wall. She managed it, flew to the bathroom and seized from under the modern vanity unit a huge and valuable old washandstand bowl and dashed back to shove it under the now freely running water. In loosening the blockage she had allowed the drainage from other gutters to flow into it because obviously it must have risen above the crack again. How long would it run? She flew back for the ewer belonging to the basin. She could tip the overflow from it into that and tip it from the landing outside on to the garden.

She thought it would never stop but finally it dwindled to a mere seepage. It was bad enough but not the disaster it could have been had it dripped through these floorboards to the beautiful ceiling below. There was a broom closet on this floor so she sped to it to get a duster. She wasn't going to put those filthy objects back, spiders and all! She supposed they'd been there from the year dot! No woman occupying a room wouldn't have swept every corner of that gigantic wardrobe out before using it. That conglomeration of shoes could've been housed in that drawer more neatly than on the floor of the wardrobe. It was no antique piece, just a monstrosity, though the wood could be used to make a far more elegant cupboard.

The books were account books and given time to study them, they might provide an interesting picture of produce and prices in the late Victorian era here. She flipped through one or two entries. They were in beautiful copperplate writing. François Beauchamp had signed and dated each page. Some were earlier ... Philippe's, bless him. She brushed out the drawer as best she could, with it stuck half open, began dusting off the packages.

She came to some huge unframed photographs and went to pick up three or four at a time, then something different caught her eye. Sketches, surely. She carefully took the torn wrapping right off and her trained eye was riveted. Not just sketches done, as was usual then, by the young ladies of the household ... these were surely of great artistic merit.

She thought they were preliminary sketches for paintings. In the case of famous artists they were only a little less valuable than the finished products. Her pulses quickened, her thumbs pricked, sensations she'd known before on buying trips when she'd come across something rare and lovely. It was wonderful to rescue treasures that would've been lost for ever but for your own recognition.

As she noticed *Novelle-Zelande* above one or two, she knew they went back to the first days of Akaroa. Oh, yes, what was scribbled beneath?

*Etat de la Petit Colonie Francaise*
*d'Akaroa.*

Oh, yes ... View of the little French settlement at Akaroa.

In a flash she remembered the finished etching of this hung in the Christchurch Museum. Oh, surely these must be Charles Meryon's preliminary sketches? She carried them over to the window. The light was brightening all the time as the thunderclouds sailed out to sea. It was very faint, but yes ... oh, yes ...'C. Meryon.'

She leafed through the others. From what she knew of the young midshipman's work, these would be his, too. Some unsigned. But she had read not long ago when she was swotting up the history of the Peninsula, that in the print-room of the British Museum were some very delicate pencil drawings of tiny leaves and creatures he had done. What were they? A sea-horse, she recalled, cabbage-trees, tree-ferns, *toe-toe*. Had he ever, she wondered, visited South America in his voyagings, and likened the plumes of the *toe-toe* to those of the pampas grass? Here was one of gulls, against the background of what she was sure were the very same cliffs opposite. How long had these lain in that drawer? Carefully she laid them back, closed it.

Henriette and Thérèse had had enough excitement for one day. If she told them what she'd discovered they'd never sleep. Besides, she must be sure. She must bring an expert in. Never do to raise hopes only to dash them.

She went down, told them of the leak. They came up with her to view the damage. Thérèse was horrified, 'You never moved that great brute of a wardrobe by yourself?'

Monique waved towards the pile of clothing on the bed, the shoes on the floor. 'Oh, I threw all that out first. I haven't hurt myself.'

Henriette said, 'There's a lot of heavy junk in that drawer, too. It used to have the shoes in it but Mac tipped them out just before he left to stow a whole lot of ancient account books. He found them in the stables. He's got the rooms above there that used to be the coachman's, for an office. Beats me why he wants to pore over those. I told him I'd only be interested if I could find a few bank-notes in the pages, in the old currency, or Father's sovereign purse that we've never been able to find. But he said there was nothing there of any value, but it would be interesting for some journalist comparing present-day prices with those of last century.'

As they finished hanging the clothes back it hit Monique. *Nothing of any value.* But surely no one could've torn the wrappings off those sketches without recognising them as true art? People here were very conscious of the value of antiques, how far could this Mac be trusted? No doubt to buy the farm property he'd had to raise an enormous mortgage. Maybe he wasn't as altruistic as he sounded, protecting the two dear ladies. Perhaps it paid him to be under this roof. How many other things had he assessed and perhaps taken away? Where was he now? The woman had been very vague. Had muttered something about he often went away for courses, and could do it because he had such a reliable man, Kevin's father, on the property. She'd better not raise any questions. Better to wait till this man arrived back and see what she thought of him. They expected him this weekend.

One thing she did ask, during tea, 'Is Mac from Banks Peninsula? Or was he just looking for a farm anywhere?'

'He's from Akaroa, in a way, but through his mother, who was a de Courcy. His father was—is—in banking, so they've moved around a lot. Came to Akaroa as a clerk but finished up as a manager in Christchurch. Mac took after his mother's side. Farming was in his blood and the Peninsula, too. His uncles still farm the de Courcy estate with their sons to inherit it, so he struck out on his own. A piece of luck for us, we'd known him so long. Unlike Kevin he eats with us, says that way he can make sure we get decent meals and don't just live on toast and boiled eggs.'

Monique said to herself, Sounds as if he has really dug himself in. Oh, stop it, you are jumping to conclusions.

Right after the meal the 'phone rang. Monique

answered it and a charming voice, English, surely, came along the wire. 'Oh, hello. You must be Monique. I'm Margot Laveroux of Rossignol Bay. The Beauchamps may have mentioned us. My husband and I run motels but also the Maison Rossignol, which is open to tourists on certain days. We're in a fix. We've a Woman's Institute group coming here the day after tomorrow and we've been flooded by leaks in two main rooms. Couldn't possibly have them walking over wet carpets. Tell me, did you get the hail? No, well, we did. That sort of gully between the gables filled up inches above where the flashing reaches, and went in under the roof when it thawed. Our ceilings are tongue-and-grooved, and the water poured through in thin streams where the boards meet.

'Now perhaps you're nowhere ready, but I heard from Jen Stevens you were getting on famously and I wondered if there's a chance of diverting them to your place? It would be marvellous kick-off because we find word-of-mouth recommendations are the best of all to say nothing of cheaper than advertising, and as these groups always invite pairs of guests from other groups, before you know where you are, you'll be quite well-known. Any joy?'

Monique made up her mind instantly. 'Can do. Margot . . . that's a magnificent offer. We don't have to look on each other as rivals, do we? The Beauchamps assured me there was room for another. There's a lot to do yet before I reach what I'm aiming for, but there's enough to create much interest. I'll rope Jen in to give me a hand. Can't aim for French refreshments of course, no time, but with tomorrow ahead of us, to put the finishing touches on and do the flowers, and set out the identifying cards, I'm sure we could manage pikelets and sandwiches. What do you think?'

'I think you're wonderful and I can relieve your mind there. Do the sandwiches, of course. I'll send the cut bread and fillings over. I never do those till the night before and put them in the fridge in clingfoil, but I've got all the French pastries done. I'll get my brother Jules to run them over in the station-wagon when he takes the carpet squares in to get them steam-cleaned and he can continue on. Don't think you need to keep up the pastries ... it's just something I do for Tante Elise, who is in her nineties. Catering can be a headache. Sandwiches and pikelets would be fine as a regular thing. Only I can't waste these.'

Monique hung up and turned round, eyes alight. 'You got it, my darlings? We're in business. Great! I'd rather take the plunge now than plan an opening too far ahead and get cold feet.'

Never had Beauchamp House looked fairer. Errol got his sign up, complete with *fleur-de-lys*, Margot sent over a dozen filet-edged tablecloths for the small tables on the verandah, Henriette and Thérèse polished the exquisite furniture till the reflections of their ornaments and silver on display reflected back in all their glory. Kevin mowed the huge lawns, and now, at two o'clock, they were standing on the steps to welcome their first guests. Henriette and Thérèse had the dress sense of Frenchwomen for an occasion, one in a lavender silk, with an old-fashioned jabot of lace at her throat, the other in grey with an amethyst brooch and swinging earrings to pick up the purple velvet band across her white hair.

The night before they'd brought out what they wanted Monique to wear. 'You can turn it down, dear child, if you think we are sentimental old idiots, but it belonged to our mother. She wore it for her twentieth birthday. It isn't really too different from garden-party dresses of today. We are sure it will fit. She was Marie-Rose.'

A quiver had passed over Monique's face. Thérèse said, 'What is it, my dear?'

Monique laughed lightly, 'Just that my second name is Rose, too.'

They were delighted. The frock was wonderfully preserved. She slipped her own dress off, standing before them in her plain white silk slip. 'Be very careful, it may be more fragile than you know.'

Henriette shook her head. 'No, this cotton was made

to last. The sash may be fragile, it's silk.'

Monique was afraid it might look too young, but it didn't. White broderie anglaise, with a gathered neck threaded through with pink ribbon. The sash was the most delicate silk she had ever seen, in rose-pink, with fringed ends. It was three-quarter length and felt wonderful. Thérèse had laid a box on the table, now she opened it and drew out a pearl choker. She went to the back of her, clasped it about the creamy brown throat.

Monique was enchanted. 'Oh, I've never worn a choker before. I love it.' Thérèse took out two tortoise-shell combs, swept the browny-gold hair back from her ears, fixed them in place. 'Yes,' she said softly, 'now you look as I thought you would . . . like some of the very young pictures of Queen Alexandra.'

Monique laughed, 'I'm glad you said the *young* pictures. I've no wish to be like the older ones, with my hair frizzed out on my forehead.'

Henriette said, 'Queen Alexandra nothing! Much more like those younger photos of Mother. The high cheekbones, the oval chin, and all. Or am I seeing what I want to see?'

'I expect it's the dress,' said Monique gravely, but someday, please God, she might be able to tell them it was true. How lovely to be in possession of something unknown till now . . . *she was like Marie-Rose, her great-grandmother!*

But now it was two o'clock and their guests were here and were enchanted from the first glimpse. 'To think this has been here all my life,' said one, 'and this is the first I've heard of it. We must spread the word around.' Success was assured.

At first Monique was nervous as she began her commentary, but soon the absorbed faces gave her confidence and she warmed to her subject and all her love for this place of her forebears shone through, though they knew it not. At afternoon teatime one woman said, looking at the glorious gash of the turquoise inlet below the colourful garden, 'I'd love to

see this in all seasons, including winter. Please don't
have a closed season.' The driver came to Monique,
said, 'I'll get my firm to advertise a visit to this
homestead on their leaflets. Okay by you?'

Jen and Monique were still happily serving the tea
when a car came up the drive, stopped short of the
circular sweep in front of the steps, because of the
coach waiting there, and went a short way along a
branching path that went round to the stables.

Monique, half hidden by the wistaria's drooping purple
plumes, looked with interest as the driver emerged from
the path. Then her eyes widened, oh, delight, oh,
happiness at day's end . . . *it was Edouard Fergusson.* He
must have rung home, been told where she was, and come
in search of her. Her lips parted with anticipation. She felt
warmth in her cheeks. Fancy meeting him in front of all
these people! Nevertheless, she took a couple of eager
steps towards him, then checked.

He had looked up, an amazed look on his face as he
took in the busy scene, the hum of chatter . . . then as
he saw her, he looked even more astounded. But why?
Why should he come *here* if he hadn't expected to find
her? He kept on coming, somehow automatically. Then
right beside her was Jen's voice, 'Oh, look, here's Mac
. . . ahead of time . . . what a surprise for him. Just look
at his face . . . the perfect picture of a man who finds his
home invaded by a monstrous army of women!'

*Mac!* Who lived here! Who was knowledgeable about
antiques. *Who had some priceless treasures hidden in his
bedroom!* Who couldn't—after all—have expected to
find her here, by that look.

Monique panicked, turned and fled. She found
herself in the kitchen. It was less than five minutes
before she heard his footsteps coming. She'd been
gazing out of the window over the sink, trying to take it
in. Then if Mac was Edouard, there couldn't be any
hanky-panky over the sketches. *Couldn't.*

A wave of what must be happiness swept over her . . .
this was magic, to have him *here.* She swung round and
the delight faded from her face as he demanded, 'What
the hell are *you* doing here?'

# CHAPTER FIVE

THERE was a sickening moment when it seemed to Monique that the whole room swung from left to right and upside down.

She said, when it had steadied, 'I—I thought you must have found out I was here! That that was why you had come. I—I didn't know *you* were Mac!'

'You didn't know? Oh, come, don't give me that! Henrietta and Thérèse call me Edouard as often as Mac. In fact more. You *must've* known.'

Scarlet surged into her cheeks. She looked the picture of outraged innocence standing there in her white and pink simplicity. 'If I said I didn't know, *then I didn't know*. Had I known I'd have been delighted. We had no chance that day we met of exchanging anything much about ourselves. If you'd told me you were farming at Port Beauchamp I'd have reacted as anybody would and said, "Well, what a small world. I went to Port Beauchamp for the first time ever quite recently." I don't think I'd have told you I was coming here because I wanted to be sure before I told anyone. I had to make sure I could get official permission to open the house like-this. And I hadn't told Henriette and Thérèse I was coming myself. They only asked me to try to get them someone. But why on earth are you flaming mad? Oh, I get it ... it was a fun encounter and you don't want any more involvement than that ... believe me, *I* wasn't the one who followed things up. I'm just not interested.'

His tone was not the tone of one who had been placated by explanation. It was silky with suppressed anger. 'That I *do* know. So it *now* makes two of us.'

She was completely bewildered. 'Point taken. That suits me. But in that case why in the name of heaven send me flowers?'

He shrugged. 'That meant nothing. Just the sort of

75

thing one would do, after, as you put it, rescuing a damsel from a distressing situation.'

She was silent, dumbfounded.

He added, 'But finding you here turning this lovely old house into a sort of beer-garden ... it's beyond bearing.'

Monique had always been told in times of stress, to fill your lungs with oxygen. So she drew in a very deep breath, felt her shaking cease, control take over. 'I think, Mr Fergusson, you'd better get things into right perspective. I was most grateful to you the other day, thought you a chivalrous sort of chap, respected you for your understanding, appreciated your giving me lunch so I could get over that scene in the office ... a scene that meant less to me, however, than you'd imagined because I was on the point of giving in my notice to take on this job. I thought it so sweet of you to send me flowers but I didn't look for anything further, believe me. I had this new, inspiring job ahead of me.

'It *is* extraordinary that the Beauchamps never mentioned you as Edouard but even if they had I'd probably have thought of it as the common or garden kind of Edward, the anglicised name. When they spoke of this Mac, I thought you must be a Macdonald or a Macnab or something equally Scots. Oh, I know Fergusson is Scots ... but Mac as a nickname usually belongs to someone with the right prefix. How could I possibly have had even a remote suspicion it could be you?'

He made an impatient gesture as if cross because it sounded like a red herring. 'It goes back to school days in Akaroa. I got into a fight with a boy who reckoned Fergusson couldn't be a truly Scottish name because it didn't start with Mac and I lost my cool and waded in till he admitted names changed and originally we were called MacFhearghuis.'

She heaved a sigh. 'I can only imagine you're as hot-tempered now as you were as a boy. But let's get down to tin tacks ... can you give me any good reason, why Henriette and Thérèse can't do as they wish with

Beauchamp House? You are not family. It's nothing to do with you.'

'Neither are you family.' (It was a good job he rushed on or she might have been tempted into announcing she *was* family!) 'It seems to me you were carried away by this beautiful home and its contents, and without pausing to weigh up the pros and cons leapt into a business enterprise many an experienced company director would've taken weeks to decide. This is going to cost money. Don't you realise that to launch a thing like this you've got to take out whopping insurances, the public have to be insured against accidents, there will be advertising, the whole house will have to be done up, their whole way of life changed if you're going to keep the rooms we've always used as showplaces? There——'

She cut in, 'Ah, we're getting down to the truth now. You don't want your easy existence here disturbed! Many bachelor farmers have to manage their own pad, cook for themselves ... you've got a cosy niche here, Edouard Fergusson. As for the other things, I attended to them before I left Christchurch. I got permission where permission was needed, went to the insurance brokers Montmorency's have always dealt with, *and*, in case you bring that up too, have had burglar-proof locks, the dead-lock kind, put on all the doors, and a few other safety-precautions taken, fire extinguishers and so on. I'm not a callow eighteen-year-old, I've been in business for years!'

'Well ... I'm glad to know something's been done in those areas but how in the world do you expect Henriette and Thérèse on the strength of a few busloads of visitors occasionally, to pay you the sort of salary you must have commanded at Montmorency's?'

The light brown eyes flashed with the intensity of her feelings. 'I realise you're a very impulsive type, for which I was grateful at our first encounter, but you assume too much. I am taking no salary at all this first year. The only outgoings will be to Jen Stevens, who is helping with commentaries and waitressing, and a couple of women, part-time, from the Port, who are thrilled to have the chance. We haven't leapt before we looked; we were arranging for an opening in a couple of weeks time, but Margot Laveroux rang up to see if we could possibly take a bus-load of Institute members instead of them because a thunderstorm two days ago flooded their carpets!

'In this sort of industry one needs to work in with others to preserve goodwill and Margot sent over the refreshments, and let me tell you this . . . there will be very little disruption to *your* life. The only room you might miss will be the dining-room because that is a real showpiece with the table set out in the style of the old days. But they told me that the three of you almost always used the cosier breakfast-parlour with the round table. The bedrooms we have on display are all spare. And in case you're worried about your dinner tonight, with all these people here, I have a roast of hogget in the oven, with all the trimmings, and Henriette made your favourite steamed pudding yesterday!'

Again he made the impatient gesture. 'As if that mattered. But I *am* concerned about this business of no salary. What on earth can you mean? No one can live without a salary. Or——'

'What can I mean? Just that. That's why I was giving in my notice at the shop. My Aunt Amabel—a courtesy aunt—has gone to Canada with her new husband and left me enough to live on for a year. I'm taking only my keep.'

He stared. 'You're what? Why on earth would you want to do that? Don't you want to spend your windfall on travel? Or a new car or something? I'm sure that's what an aunt would've expected. This sounds crazy to me.'

'Crazy or not, it's my affair. There were strings tied to my aunt's gift. She felt I was in danger of becoming one of the maiden aunts of *her* generation. Her family duties had tied her for years to that sort of existence. Oh, it was different in my case. When my mother died I didn't have to surrender the love of my life. *She* did but he came back, thirty years later. Also I had a career as well. But she thought I was spoiling my sisters and brother. So she made it a condition of the bequest that I got out for at least a year and did my own thing.'

'Can these children fend for themselves?'

She achieved a chuckle. 'For sure they can. The elder girl is nearly the age I was when I gave up my job in Auckland, came down here to keep house for them. Fortunately my firm transferred me. When I met Henriette and Thérèse on a buying expedition and saw and loved this place, I felt I'd met my destiny. And I imagine, Mr Fergusson, that *you* can't do one darned thing about it.'

The grey eyes were like steel. 'It would appear so. But at least I'll be here to keep an eye on things.'

Monique looked at the clock on the kitchen wall, said, 'Good heavens, I thought much more time would have gone by. Doesn't take much time to clash, does it? I'm sorry the even tenor of your ways should've been so disturbed, Mr Fergusson, but that's the way it's going to be. It's a *fait accompli*. And I must fly to speed the parting guests. One thing, your arrival wasn't too badly timed. It might've thrown me had I been in the full flow of my commentary but they were just finishing their tea. A very successful first day.'

No one could have guessed at Monique's turmoil of spirit as she flitted about, from group to group. They waved goodbye and Jen and the others started clearing the tables. Not till all were gone, did Edouard Fergusson come down. The three of them had subsided into easy chairs in the parlour.

Henriette and Thérèse were radiant, saying as he entered, 'Who could have believed our first day would've gone so smoothly and promised so much for the future?'

Monique nodded, seemingly undisturbed, 'Much better not having too long to anticipate and perhaps dread. That bunch is going to spread the word very effectively. We're going to have to make bookings well ahead. Lovely time of year to start, most of spring and all of summer and autumn to come.'

Her heart was racing. What would this unpredictable man say to her unaware great-aunts?

He sat down, ran a hand through the thick fair hair, pulled a face at them, said with mock grimness, 'I don't know what to do with you! I turned my back on you for three weeks and arrive back to find this place a hive of tourist entertainment and I've found out from Monique you had it planned before I left.'

Thérèse giggled, 'Well, dear boy, it was in the melting-pot. Me, I do not like to count chickens before they break the shell and, quite candidly, we did not know how you would take it.'

Oh dear, this was being frank with a vengeance. What now?

He said, with a shrewd glance, 'It would be more correct to say you knew very well how I'd have taken it. I'd have gone into it very thoroughly before——'

Thérèse made a face at him. 'I know. You would've attempted to put your foot down. No one could've gone into things more thoroughly than Monique, dear boy, and besides, in this field she's the expert. In farming you are. This is out of your scope.'

The dear boy looked singularly unimpressed. 'Well, I'll give my opinion of that when I've had proof of it. I hold a watching brief. On your behalf. It will have to be done with approval and oversight of your solicitor and accountant, of course.'

Henriette said calmly, 'Monique insisted on that. She's got things moving there. I don't know how she does it. I've always found it hard to put the skids under that staid firm.'

Monique suppressed a grin. Really, Henriette used such expressions for a woman her age. She began to think the two of them were more than a match for Edouard. What a cheek he had. The farm acres were his. Not Beauchamp House and the five acres surrounding it. He was assuming too much for someone who merely lived in the house, getting his meals in return for his protection.

Edouard was standing in that typically male attitude, feet apart and firmly planted on the hearthrug, back to the fireplace . . . putting three women on the spot. But not succeeding.

He expressed no approval of her businesslike attitude to the venture, narrowed those steely eyes, said to Henriette, 'I've known you too long to be taken in entirely. Especially by the seeming chance that Monique was kept in the dark about who I was. Now, come on, you call me Edouard much more often than Mac, so my guess is that you concealed that fact on purpose. Come on . . . why?'

Monique was startled. 'What would they do a thing like that for? I certainly didn't mention you and our dramatic meeting. No reason why I should. I don't know what you're getting at.'

He compressed his lips. 'No, *you* don't know. I realise that. But *they* do.' He nodded at the two sisters.

When Henriette dimpled she looked like a mischievous child. 'Well, you see, Edouard, we didn't know if you'd paid attention to our suggestion or not, and gone into Montmorency's to meet her. She didn't mention you either, so we kept mum.'

'That's as clear as mud,' said Edouard.

'To me too,' said Monique, 'but I'm hoping all will be revealed.'

Thérèse giggled. 'It's just that we couldn't spring this on him on the eve of his departure on such an important mission. So we didn't say that Monique of Montmoreney's was going to find us someone to help us turn this into a second Olveston House. We had an idea he'd think we were taking on too much. Also that if he arrived back to find Beauchamp House turned into a showplace, he might even get antagonistic towards you. But if he met you first, all unknowing, he wouldn't be as prejudiced because he'd know that you were a simply lovely girl.' She stopped because she wasn't sure she'd made it clear, but Edouard seemed used to following her involved sentences.

He said, grimly, 'You cunningly said that you'd like me to meet the head buyer of Montmorency's seeing I'd missed her the day she was here, and that I could buy my mother another blue plate for her wall, because this buyer had said they had some, so why not call in?'

Thérèse was giggling. 'And you took on the aspect of

a hunted male ... so old-fashioned of you, dear boy, if you don't mind me saying so. Said were we up to more of our matchmaking tricks? So we were all confused. What did you say, Edouard?'

'I said that made three of us. But carry on.'

'Right-ee-ho. So we thought either you wouldn't go in at all or if you did, you wouldn't be at ... er ... your usual cordial self, though of course once you met her you were bound to be disarmed by her, so, oh dear, I've forgotten what point I was making.'

He said sarcastically, 'I *think* you are trying to explain why you didn't mention me as Edouard. Okay, let it go.'

Henriette turned to Monique, 'How was he when he came into the shop, dear girl?'

Monique's tone was purposely cool; she shrugged, 'Definitely on the defensive. He thought I'd persuaded you into selling that French clock to Montmorency's. Didn't approve of valuable possessions leaving the families they'd belonged to. The clock not only belonged to someone else, but had no sentimental value to the woman I bought it off, whatever. Her husband had been a compulsive buyer at auctions and this was his only bargain, which proved a godsend to his widow when in need. We only sold it on commission and she made a tidy sum out of it.'

Thérèse did her clapping. 'Oh, goody. I think it's lovely when someone with plenty of money buys something like that and a deserving case benefits. I hope you really rocked it in.'

Edouard pulled a face and for a moment Monique could see the whimsical guy who had rescued her. '*I* was the mug who bought it so don't look too overjoyed. I hold you two personally responsible. Now, Monique, don't eat me. I know it was worth every penny and will appreciate in value. It's about time I began collecting a few antiques of my own, against the day I can build my own home here. There are a few treasures over at my uncle's place, the de Courcy estate, that are to be mine. Awfully decent of them to house them. They were to come to Mother as her share, but with Dad moving round so much she thought it safe to leave them there, bar the ones she gave to Francine when she married.'

Henriette beamed fondly on them both. 'So you see, Edouard, it was all for the best. You didn't have to worry about what we were doing, when you were on such important business in Australia, and it meant you didn't develop preconceived ideas ... prejudices in fact, against Monique. The dear girl decided to run it herself, not just organise it for us, and our venture is going to be a great success ... Beauchamp House is going to be kept as it deserves to be, and I can see we shall all work harmoniously together.'

The grey eyes met the brown eyes in a telling look, then both looked swiftly away. Later, meeting on the stairs, as he came down and she went up, he put a hand out, stopped her, said, 'We'll play it that way, Monique Belfield, those two old ladies deserve only the best, only a harmonious home-life.'

She looked at him levelly, 'Until today my being with them here meant nothing but harmony. It won't be any different from that if I've anything to do with it. It was you, unknown to them, who introduced antagonism. Why?'

'Because I'm a little more cautious than they are.'

She controlled her temper and said as calmly as possible, 'You seem to be a singularly untrustful person. You can't believe I'm not on the make. It might surprise you to know I entertain similar doubts about you. You can't understand anyone doing a job like this for nothing, which makes me wonder what sort of a man you are yourself. I've found before that people who view other people's actions suspiciously are in reality revealing what they are themselves. You won't find I've any ulterior motive in coming here. It's a heaven-sent opportunity, thanks to Aunt Amabel, to be free for a year, to live exactly the sort of life I regard as ideal, in an old house full of memories and treasures, in one of the most beautiful spots on earth. I don't need any more motive than that.'

She wished he wasn't standing above her; it gave him a tactical advantage. She also wished he'd remove his restraining hand. His touch, seemingly, could do things to her. He looked searchingly into her face. 'I'm so afraid it's a flash in the pan, that you may build up their hopes, then tire of it. You may be doing what you like, but I doubt if that makes you completely free of responsibility. You could think it a great lark for a year, then you could feel just as imprisoned here by Henriette and Thérèse's growing dependence upon you, as ever you did with your family.'

The brown eyes went wide, almost as if she didn't see him momentarily, as if in very fact she beheld an idyll. 'Hasn't someone said, somewhere, that: "The prison into which we doom ourselves no prison is"? That's how I feel about here. And I'm not a quitter.'

He said sombrely, 'As long as you don't find it too ideal. As long as no one else ever turns up feeling they have more right to run this place than you.'

She was startled. 'How could that be so? Henriette and Thérèse are the last of their line. It's a tragedy that neither of them had offspring. All I want to do is to preserve this place for the sake of Philippe Beauchamp who ought to have founded a lasting dynasty, and for the people of Akaroa for whom it ought to be a heritage, part of their history.'

He took his hand from her arm, said, 'It was just a thought that occurred to me. You hear of such things happening.'

A tremor ran over her. It was too near the bone. She said quickly, to change the subject, 'Did they tell you your room leaked the day of the thunderstorm?'

He nodded. 'Yes, and that you coped very well. I'll have my men over to renew the board that is cracked, put new flashing in. Good job the stain's behind that cracking great wardrobe. Not one of the nicer periods for furniture that. I don't know how you moved it, though Henriette said you'd thrown out all the stuff inside it. You'd not be able to get the drawer open to lighten it, would you?'

Did she just imagine he watched her very carefully?

She shook her head. 'I soon gave up on that. Couldn't edge it out more than a few inches. I would've rubbed it with candle-grease or soap if I'd got it out, but it needs planing.' She thought he looked relieved. Definitely Edouard Fergusson would bear watching.

She ought to have been tired to the point of exhaustion with all that had been needed to get the great house ready for their unexpected first day, or happily relaxed with the success of it, but she wasn't. Not now.

Henriette and Thérèse rarely retired early and Edouard Fergusson worked at a report at the French Provincial table in the breakfast-parlour, seemingly undisturbed by the chatter of the two sisters. Monique had said pointedly, 'We haven't done anything to the study yet. Wouldn't you rather be in there?' but he had answered quite naturally, 'No, I often work out here, unless I'm recording tapes, then I use the study.'

She made up her mind swiftly. It was only fair. 'We won't need the study on display. The library is all that's needed. It's a delightful room, opening as it does on to the side verandah, with its glimpse of the harbour. The drapes will need dry-cleaning and every inch of the shelves dusted. Nothing urgent, though, because it needs cataloguing and I'd like to do it myself so I can get expert advice on what's there.'

'Do you mean for pricing?'

She answered the meaning of that promptly. 'For valuing, but not for selling. For insurance purposes. Those books belong to Beauchamp House, gathered together through the years. They belong to everyone of every generation who has lived here, bought them, loved them or detested them. Even the children's tattered books. I'll have to catalogue them myself first as time permits. We couldn't possibly afford to pay anyone to do that.'

'Good. Because I wouldn't consent to one book leaving the property.'

Henriette and Thérèse didn't seem to resent this assumption of authority at all. They must have been used to it.

At last the evening was over and she was sitting in one of the chairs in her tiny sitting-room on the higher level, and the book in her lap was the one that had been such a startling discovery that day, surely her day of destiny, when she'd come here on a buying expedition.

She needed right now to re-read that entry in her grandfather's writing to bolster her spirits. All through this time of change and organisation had been the buoyant feeling that new emotional adventures awaited her. No one, no man, had ever touched her heart, her imagination, as had the surprising stranger who had impulsively rescued her from the humiliation of that overheard situation in the office that day.

He had been debonair, daring, altogether chivalrous. Recalling it now, with its telescopic sequence of events, it seemed impossible her rescuer could be the dour farmer who had confronted her in the Beauchamp House kitchen, obviously resentful that a chance encounter had turned into someone who had invaded the house he lived in.

Well, maybe St George had ridden on after killing the dragon, never as much as looked the damsel up again! She *must* try to see the funny side of it. But her grin stopped before it widened ... *let's be honest, I feel devastated.* She'd certainly built up in her mind a false picture of him. What an immature thing to do! Yet who could blame her? He'd flung himself into it so wholeheartedly, the quick plan, his obvious sincerity when he said he'd like to knock Clint's block off, the extra unnecessary touches, the posy of violets, the audaciousness which he'd shown as he dealt with his sister's bewilderment that he hadn't known Monique's surname, the kiss that had been anything but a peck, the expensive flowers sent Interflora, the card and its message.

Had she just dreamed that message? She went across to where the basket stood on a tiny table. The roses had faded long since, of course, but just yesterday she had filled its liner bowl with rose-pink hawthorn. The card was underneath it. She lifted it up, read it again: 'Till I return. I hope you know your Robbie. Edouard.' Why would a man write that if he didn't mean it? Nothing made sense any more. As for asking her to write her telephone number down!

She pulled herself up. To the devil with moody Edouard Fergusson. She dropped the card disdainfully into the wastepaper basket, then made a dusting-off gesture with her two hands. There! Now she must study her grandfather's writing at leisure, something she hadn't been able to do when first she had glimpsed it. Thérèse had said, in that tiny boxroom, full of junk, 'Well, you've seen what was here, none of it valuable. Mostly just our old school exercise-books.'

Monique had said casually enough, 'Don't despise those, Mrs de Quincey. You know these Historic Places Trust Houses have usually one room that was used as a schoolroom by the pioneers ... they—the people who restore them—often long to have old authentic exercise books like these, but have to resort mainly to getting some that don't belong, from other hoarders, and just say the schoolroom is typical of the period. These have the Beauchamp House children's names written in them. If ever you and your sister decided to run this like the Kemp House in Kerikeri they would be marvellous.'

There and then the great idea was born in Henriette's mind. 'We've dreamed of it for years, ever since we came back here, but we haven't anyone of the younger generation to help us on it. Someone like yourself for instance, young, knowledgeable, mature.'

Something had stirred in Monique, mingled with the knowledge that, due to Aunt Amabel, she could do something like this.

The very next moment it had crystallised into something she *must* do, was *going* to do ... because she flicked open a book on family mottos and crests. This was interesting. She turned back to the flyleaf.

The ink was old and faded, but it reminded her so much of her grandfather, that childishly scrawled name: Hilaire Beauchamp. Only Grandad had been Hilary Belfield. Beau ... beautiful ... Champ ... field ... what a coincidence!

Then her eyes had dropped to the scribbled comment below, 'Father says we haven't got a family motto. Well, I'm jolly well going to start one of my own right now. And act on it. My motto is going to be: "Be not

daunted." And I'm going to go out tonight in the dark,
to try to find that laughing owl. Nobody need come
with me. I won't be scared. I'll go myself. I will *not* be
daunted.'

It had taken her back to Grandad's Sydney garden,
with him sitting in a deck chair and herself a child, on
the grass beside him. He'd mentioned no places, hadn't
given away a fraction of a clue as to that, but had said,
'I was a funny kid, you know, a loner, but I think I
invented a pretty good family motto. I'd like to think
you took it for your own, Monique. Not a bad one for
anyone. "Be not daunted." We can all know fears, some
real, some foolish, but not to let them undermine you
before you tackle them is a fine thing.'

There *couldn't* be two incidents like that. It had been
her grandfather all right. He'd anglicised his name, cut
himself off, disillusioned and bewildered, but had won
through to happiness in his marriage. Sad that his only
child had died so long ago. A wave of grief for the
father she just remembered rose in Monique. Then and
now as her eyes fell on Hilaire Beachamp's writing she
said to herself: 'Be not daunted.'

# CHAPTER SIX

HILAIRE Beauchamp's sturdy motto stayed with her the next morning. What was the use of having a family motto if you didn't stand by it? She still had a piercing sense of loss because disillusioned about the man she'd deemed a chivalrous throwback to his French ancestry, but she wasn't going to let either matter or show. Life was for getting on with. Grandad hadn't allowed himself to be daunted by his father's lack of faith in him. He'd gone into a tough sea-faring life, found satisfaction in it, and skills, met and married Gran, who had been sweet, and settled down to a life he loved, running his ferries on a dream of a harbour.

As she looked out of the window at the little port below she felt a fierce surge of gladness that he had come to safe harbourage in that little bay in the huge harbour where he had built his home and kept his boats. It had been as near to this as he could find. There his son had been born, and when he died, his widow and her little Monique had come to live there with them, till her mother had re-married, this time a New Zealander, living at first in Auckland. Now she was here, and in this very room, at that *kauri* davenport very likely, Grandad had vowed not to be daunted.

When she had showered she slipped into beige trews, donned an artist's smock over it in tussore-colour, splashed with cabbage roses and blue cornflowers, one of Claude's ever-changing fancies for his saleswomen's shop garb. A good opportunity to wear some of them out. It was going to be warm today, so she slipped her slim brown feet into thonged sandals, used make-up sparingly, merely outlining her lips with a pale rose frosty lipstick, went running along the passage, tapped lightly on each door, before poking her head round each to say, 'Good morning, my darling ... your tray will be here in ten minutes,' before running downstairs.

Edouard had informed her the night before that he always cooked his own breakfast and had it early, long before the old ladies were up. Fair enough but there was no sign of him yet. No doubt his flight had tired him, to saying nothing of finding an unwelcome stranger in the place he seemed to regard as his own. She had decided to treat him with polite indifference.

She switched the oven on to crisp lightly their croissants, set out the two trays, delighting as always in the fine china that had been used for generations. She ran out to where an almond tree leaned out below the terrace, reached up, broke off two tiny sprays of delicate pink bloom, sped back in.

As she reached the kitchen door she heard Edouard's footsteps coming from the far door that led in from the scullery. He'd obviously been out and about for some time. How different he looked in his farming clothes, old corduroys, with leather patches on the insides of the knees, which indicated he did a lot of riding, open-necked shirt with a bulky cable-knit sweater in blue pulled over it. The sun from the eastern window streamed on to his fair head putting his face in shadow so she couldn't read his expression.

'Good morning,' said Monique blithely, 'I thought perhaps you were tired after your trip home. Or else you'd washed up after you'd had breakfast.'

'Martlett came and got me. That outside staircase is a boon, saves disturbing the whole household. A lamb had got caught between two wires. Its mother had got frantic and tried to butt it out. Mart and Kevin had rescued it but it had dislocated its shoulder. Devilish painful thing. I know, I once put mine out in the school gym. I managed to get it back quickly but it's swollen, of course, but it'll go down. Nevertheless, it's good to be home. Not for me the corridors of power.' He laughed. 'I was a very small frog in that big pool, believe me. Here, where the pool is smaller, I feel much larger. It's my own niche.'

Pleasantly said but the faint hostility didn't pass unmarked. She must walk warily. She was the incomer. How odd, when none of the people in this bay had made her feel a stranger, but this man had. His eye fell on the trays. 'Bouquets and all ... you *do* do them proud.'

Did he mean she was buttering them up? She felt her hackles rise. She crossed to the warming drawer of the oven, slid out the dish of croissants, put some into each of the tiny roll baskets on the trays. His voice held such surprise that it made her jerk her head up. 'Croissants? Where did you get them?'

She blinked. 'I made them.'

'No wonder you're so popular. I believe long ago, in their mother's time when wages were low and labour plentiful, they had a woman who made them. Till it became a tradition. But there hasn't been any kind of home-made bread for years. Or is there now a short-cut in producing them?'

'No, anything but. Nevertheless, they're worth it. You have to make the dough, leave it two hours, then knead it and chill it thoroughly. Then roll it and butter it and fold it and roll it, then repeat that twice with thirty minutes in between, cut it into ten centimetre squares, then into triangles and form them into crescents and brush them with egg and milk.'

He whistled. 'You'll never keep it up. Not with this great house to care for.'

She said, with asperity, 'It isn't a case of a new broom sweeping clean or looking for approval. I'm well aware it won't be done so often, but a deep freeze makes it easier than in early days. I make a huge batch. That's why I have to crisp them before serving. The thawing softens them.'

'Well, it's over to you. But how come you know how?'

'My grandfather taught me,' she said simply.

'Your grandfather? Was he a baker? Or a chef?'

She laughed. 'No. He'd learned how as a child. It was his only accomplishment in the cooking line. Grandfather was a sailor.'

'Where did he live? On leave from the sea?'

'On a small bay in Sydney Harbour. He ran pleasure boats when he left the sea.'

'Did he teach you when you visited him on holiday?'

'No. I was born in Australia and lived with my grandparents for a while. But my father was a New Zealander and we came back.'

She didn't want to impart more than that.

He said, 'Interesting. And if there are any more to spare I'll have croissants instead of toast. At least not with my bacon-and-egg, but after. Don't be alarmed. I'll cook my own breakfast.'

She took the trays up, came down. He was dishing out two platefuls of perfectly grilled bacon. The eggs were still in the pan.

'Hard or soft, turned, or sunny-side up?'

'Softish, and sunny-side up, thanks. But I don't usually go for a cooked breakfast.'

'Well, you're having it this morning. You must be half a stone lighter than when you were at Montmorency's. Fretting?'

'Fretting? No, this job's in the same line of business and much more satisfying. No trying customers.'

He put the plate in front of her. 'Don't purposely misunderstand me. I'm not naïve. You know perfectly well I meant, have you been fretting after Clint Wood?'

She looked at him witheringly. 'I don't suppose I'll ever convince you that it was a relief to me. You still think I was face-saving. I don't think I'll waste my energies trying to get you to think otherwise. I even managed to shorten my notice because I was so keen to get started here.'

Suddenly he smiled at her and the broad craggy face that had looked so stern was transformed into the dancing-eyed, carefree face of the stranger who'd so enjoyed rescuing her and lunching her. 'Sorry,' he said, and meant it if his tone was anything to go by, 'I had a damned nerve asking that.'

Relief flooded over her. 'I might've resented it had it been true. Let's forget how we first met. I'm not at outs with Clint. I'm even advertising his showroom on the catalogues. I believe in working in with people. So, evidently, do Margot and Pierre Laveroux. They aren't regarding us as a counter-attraction to Maison

Rossignol. When they got flooded she thought only of the disappointed coach-load and was only too glad to send them here.' She hesitated then plunged. 'This enables me to say something else, Edouard. I realise you've taken wonderful care of Henriette and Thérèse, taking the place of the sons they never had. I'm not here to usurp the place you have in their lives, just to run this as a paying concern, give myself a freedom I've not known for long enough and to help them stay here where they belong. I know a small ownership flat in Akaroa would be sensible but their——' She came to an abrupt stop and colour flowed up into her cheeks.

He prompted her, '. . . but their what?'

She looked embarrassed. 'It would sound too dramatic. You'd think me a sentimental twit.'

His voice was quite mild. 'Try me. I mightn't. I know that often things are better left unsaid but occasionally rash speech reveals our true selves. Heavens, I sound like something out of a quotation book! But what were you going to say? Anything that concerns Henriette and Thérèse concerns me.'

'I was going to say that away from here their very spirits might shrivel up and die.'

To her surprise he didn't say, 'Oh, come on . . .' or 'Aren't you being rather fanciful?' He nodded. 'Why else do you think I don't build a house on my own land? I've known them all my life. They've been widows so long it's hard to remember they were once wives, and lived quite adventurous lives away from here, but despite those years, their roots are here. Another thing, though they had no illusions about their father, they gave him tender, loving care, so that he never had to leave this place he loved. *They* deserve that, too. Only just of late there was a development that I—no, I'll leave that. But I wish——'

His sigh was heavy. 'Now that really would be better left unsaid.'

They measured glances, then she said crisply, 'I think perhaps I shouldn't probe that.'

She turned away, began gathering dishes up, and asked herself had he been going to say he wished she'd not come here? Why? Had she been some half-fledged scatty youngster, impulsive and irresponsible, she could've understood it.

Oh, to the devil with this unpredictable Edouard Fergusson. She had enough to do without him getting between her and work. What was it Mother had said once, long ago, when a teenage Monique had asked her how on earth had she coped when Father had died so suddenly?

Anna Belfield had stared out of the window with unseeing eyes as if memory-pictures had taken the place of what was before her and said, 'There was so much to go on with. There was always something that needed doing. I had to earn our living, make sure you weren't too much for Grandad and Gran, make your clothes, bring you up the way Philip would've wanted you brought up, helped with the house, the garden, the boats, supervised your homework, played with you ... kept you from too close a contact with our grief, so you'd have a happy childhood to remember, something that is a child's natural right. So it's a good thing to live by, that saying: "Do with thy might what thy hand finds to do." Somehow it gets you through.'

She came back to the present to find Edouard looking at her strangely. 'What is it?' he asked.

She looked down. 'Nothing I can share. I just remembered something my mother said to me once and she wouldn't have approved of me standing here mooning over the past. I've lots to do. Having that crowd here yesterday doesn't mean we are anything near ready for others. I know you'll be flat out today, having just got back, but if you've known the old ladies as long as you say and have lived in this French-founded colony most of your life, I may have to appeal to you at nights to help me sort out and classify some of the things. Some folk from round here will be bound to visit us and I must be accurate. I've studied up the history as much as possible, but I can't bear to slip up.'

'What were you thinking you might slip up on?'

'Well, there's a lovely collection of Tahitian things in

one of the gable-end attics. I thought at first it just meant someone from here had taken a cruise there or maybe stopped over on a trip to Europe, but they weren't ordinary souvenir things. They were older to my way of thinking. Is there any connection?'

She thought he looked at her with respect. 'You've guessed right. Some of the French left here for Tahiti in the eighteen-forties. Some maintained the links. Not easy to do in those days, with sailing-ships. Some didn't, but the Beauchamps did, and so did the Rossignols. And at Larchwood Vale, in Mid-Canterbury, they still keep in contact. One of the Larchwoods married Victorine Rossignol and somewhere in my mother's bunch, the de Courcys join up with the Rossignols of Tahiti, so I may be able to sort out what belongs to who, for you. It's worried me rather, all that junk upstairs. So much of it is probably not junk, but with no descendants to fall heir to them, I was afraid the old girls would get carried away by some unscrupulous antique dealer and let valuable stuff go . . . saving *your* presence, of course!'

Monique, remembering that priceless bundle of sketches crammed into that drawer in his room, agreed, said quietly, 'Yes, best if we sort it together, unhurriedly, so that the assessment is accurate. So we'll do it at night. Oh, here they are.'

Indeed they were, looking both elegant and eager. Henriette said, 'Monique hasn't a chance of looking round the farm yet . . . how about taking us round in the Jeep, Edouard? I feel no one sees the Beauchamp property as it used to be unless they can take in the whole estate.'

Monique said quickly, 'Another day would do, Edouard, you must have lashings to do after so long away.'

To her surprise he didn't take advantage of that, said, 'I'll get a good overall-picture of what's been done, that way. I don't want Mart and Kevin to think I'm desperate to pitch in, as if I feel things aren't up to standard. I'm lucky in those two. They've done well in what I've seen so far. So, *mesdames*, put on your sunbonnets to protect your complexions . . . it's hot for this month.'

Sunbonnets? She was quite relieved when they reappeared in Mexican-style sunhats and handed one to her. Henriette said, 'I thought otherwise you might be tempted to wear that delectable Leghorn hat. I don't think you've got anything else with you. I got quite a thrill when I saw it. Took me back to the days of my youth. Haven't seen a Leghorn Straw for years.'

'I'm not up in millinery,' said Edouard, 'but I'm going to hazard a guess . . . is it a kind of natural-coloured straw, with a brim bound with brown velvet and a band of it hanging down behind in streamers, and cottagey flowers like buttercups and daisies on it?'

They all three gazed at him in wonder. Thérèse said, '*Mon Dieu!* He's clairvoyant. Who'd have thought it of our horny-handed son of the soil! That's exactly what it is! But it could've been anything else. It could've had sky-blue satin ribbon round it and rosebuds and forget-me-nots. How *could* you know that?'

'Oh, there's more to me than a handsome face,' he said, 'And I never divulge the secrets of my inner resources.' His grey eyes were wide and dancing and Monique saw, with nostalgia, St George challenging the dragon. Oh, how absurd. She jammed the Mexican hat on and they departed.

Monique had thought the Beauchamp House surrounds beautiful but when she saw the estate in its entirety it took her breath away. She'd never been to France but had seen enough TV programmes on it to realise this, with its smaller fields and variety of crops, had a Continental air. It was completely different from the huge sheep stations of the Canterbury Plains or the high-country; or from the lush dairy farms of the Waikato she'd known so well during her years in Auckland.

The land was rolling, sloping down to the sea in the regular flowing contours so typical of volcanic terrain. It made her realise that back in an era so distant in time that there was no history of it, two distinct volcanoes had erupted to form the twin harbours of Lyttelton and

Akaroa, and Port Beauchamp was just one of the small inlets in between on the eastern side, where the softer ground had fallen away between the fearsome cliffs and the sea had rushed in.

The paddocks were seamed with hedges, beautifully kept, and in many of them were copsy triangles of European trees and pines, which must make wonderful shelter at lambing time, especially the macrocarpas. The farm buildings were quite near Beauchamp House behind more trees, native trees glorious in their enamelled evergreens.

They created a rise and instead of the huge paddocks covered with sheep grazing, were smaller fields, newly fenced, that seemed to have notices on posts. Monique blinked. 'They're too far away to read, but what are——'

Edouard's voice had a tinge of pride in it, 'I'm carrying on with experimental work for the Plant Science Department of Lincoln College, in field trial work with Wana Cocksfoot. It's a recent variety bred by the Grasslands Division of the D.S.I.R.'

Monique said, delight in her voice, 'Oh, what a satisfying link with the past. Perhaps it's because I deal in antiques that I like to find these things. Not just ornaments and tapestries surviving into the present day, but the old pioneer striving and achievements still being carried on. Cocksfoot, you said?'

Edouard was so surprised he stopped the Jeep, said, 'So, you're actually knowledgeable about other things than your own specialty?'

She said, 'Of course. When I worked in Auckland I immersed myself in the early Colonial history there till I knew almost as much about it as the Sydney and New South Wales history I grew up with. When I came to Christchurch I studied it from the First Four Ships on I was enchanted to find that the pioneering of Banks Peninsula was even earlier and I swotted it up again when I first toyed with the idea of coming to Port Beauchamp. I was impressed by the success of the grass-seeding experiments carried out here so early. What workers those men and women were! I got fascinated—felt I almost knew some of the long-ago characters ... that "Cabbage" Wilson of Christchurch, who first saw the possibilities of the grass in Auckland called "orchard grass" or cocksfoot, and Ebenezer Hay of Pigeon Bay seeing what it could mean to the Peninsula and clearing three acres of land near his "Annandale" property, of the stumps that covered it, to sow it down. When they reaped it first, didn't they tie it in sheaves, then stook it as in Scotland?'

'They did,' said Edouard, absorbed in the topic, 'and it grew into a major industry, finding it was better to thresh it with the flail from shorter stalks. By the eighteen seventies the cocksfoot trade ranked in importance with the Peninsula dairying, timber-felling and whaling.'

Henriette and Thérèse had kept very quiet, this subject was dear to Edouard's heart. Monique said, 'And what's new in cocksfoot? You said you were experimenting.'

'It's been bred from Spanish cocksfoot, and it's claimed that it is more persistent on dry hill country and stands up well to intensive grazing. It's even better than the original Akaroa cocksfoot. Then over the brow of the next hill we're trying Tahora white clover. That has been developed by the Grasslands Division, too. That side of the hill has low fertility and faces the colder south. It's ideal for those conditions.'

'Do you have field days with farmers from everywhere attending?'

'We do.'

'Good. We can work together on this when you have the next. The wives could attend and be entertained at the homestead. Does it stop there? Just cocksfoot and clover?'

'No, we're on C.G.S. That's Controlled Grazing Systems, a strategy strongly pushed by the advisory services for hill country farms. It's a sophisticated type of rotational grazing made possible by the development of electric fencing. You'll know what that means ... moving fences and stock to allow pastures to recuperate. More than ever necessary now with the rising costs of the aerial topdressing with molybdate superphosphate. My Lincoln College colleagues work with me to see if improved varieties of pasture and more C.G.S. might replace some fertiliser.

'But even there it doesn't stop. In a year or two we're hoping to develop more tree crops. Akaroa walnuts are famous, of course, but we're looking at growing pecan nuts, hazelnuts, grapes, citrus, and even some of the more recent fruits being developed at Lincoln, pepinos for example. There are endless possibilities. One chap at Little Akaroa combines traditional sheep-farming with a thriving spring flower business . . . narcissus. His wife manages that side, employs the labour, etcetera.'

Monique had a vision of the fragrance of narcissi wafting over the hills to mingle with the salt tang of the sea and the balsam of the pines. 'Imagine a field of violets,' she said.

They drove round the entire property with Monique enchanted at every aspect and already planning outside attractions that might interest husbands, if enough of the early Peninsula implements could be found and displayed in the stables.

They came back by the Martletts' house, two-storeyed, French-gabled, surrounded by drifts of apple-blossom, mulberry trees, walnuts. Surely an ideal house for the owner of this farmland.

As if in answer to her thought, Edouard said, 'I'm very lucky to have the Martlett family. It's a large one. The youngest boy is just starting at Lincoln College and will work for me when he's through. Kevin finished there last year, so they're right with me in all my enterprises. The eldest one fishes from the Port, has his own boat. Both father and mother are from established Port families. The girls are at Teachers' College. Oh, someone's waving.'

They all looked up at an open gable-window, where someone was waving a duster. They waved back. 'Marie-Rose,' said Henriette fondly.

Monique turned to them as they drove on. 'Marie-Rose? Was she——?

Henriette nodded. 'Yes, named for our mother. It's

long ago, but our mother rescued Mrs Martlett's mother when, as a child, she fell down one of the cliffs and the tide was nearly to her when Mother saw her. Mother was out riding when she saw the child's doll abandoned on the clifftop and curiosity made her rein in. Then she heard the ten-year-old child calling for help. There she was, petrified with fear, injured, watching the remorseless tide creeping towards her.

'She'd dragged herself as far away as she could. Mother knew there was only one thing to do, send her horse, riderless, back home, so an alarm would be raised, and a search party organised. She turned him round, slapped his rump, and he set off.

'There was a way of sorts down that cliff, one taken by bird-nesting small boys clad in knickerbockers, not in a wide, swirling, riding-skirt. Mother didn't hesitate, she dropped her skirt on the clifftop, her petticoat too, and climbed down, calling reassurances all the time to the little girl, just in her knickers. Must've looked quaint because Mother was very correct in her riding attire, the fitting black jacket, the white stock, beautifully tied. They're still at home.

'It was rough going. Sometimes she had to hang from bushes and firmly embedded rocks, reaching for the next foothold, but she made it, scratched and torn, her nails jagged and bleeding. And all the time she was conscious of the waves coming nearer the child. Veronique's cries had stopped because Mother kept calling to her, saying, "I'm coming, darling, I'm coming. And Big Beauchamp will be here soon to get us. Just hang on, darling."'

'When she reached her she was horrified to find the child had broken her leg above her ankle. She knew that in any case all she'd be able to do was to get her to a ledge out of reach of that ravening tide. But what damage would she do, to those broken bones? The answer lay close at hand. A piece of board. It looked like an old copperstick, and there was another, that Mother thought was the branch of a tree, bleached bone-white by sun and sea. It wasn't. It was an ancient moa-bone, now in the museum.

'Off came her stock. She put the two splints against the leg, fastened it with her pearl stockpin, and managed to drag the child a little further up the fissure before the first wave reached them. Just as well, they were going to be cold enough without being wet. It was almost, but not quite, a blowhole. The tide used to swirl in with horrible sucking noises and fountain up. Still does, but it's well fenced in now.

'Somehow Mother managed to lift the child, her right hand supporting that leg stiffly, and scramble up a sort of slanting ridge. There was slimy seaweed on the lower bit, but then sand and shells where the grip was easier. There was a succession of ridges like shelves but they all sloped downwards and were so crumbly they wouldn't take the weight of two people. So Mother, who was slight but tall, and quite strong, knelt before each one and lifted Veronique on to it, got her to shuffle back as far as possible. She managed six, well up above the high tidemark. It was broader than the others, too.

'Then she set about cheering up the child. Told her the sight of a riderless horse would bring all the Beauchamp House folk and half the population of the Port along these cliffs and they would be guided to the very spot by Veronique's doll and Mrs Beauchamp's skirt. She felt some sort of sound signal should be made but felt the child would fall into despair if they called over and over again.

'And no one came. So she got her to sing. Oh, first of all, she gave her the loaf sugar she had in her jacket pocket for her horse, wrapped the coat about her for fear she'd get pneumonia, which was a killer then, in pre-antibiotic days.

'They sang every song they could think of, over and over, until presently, out of sheer exhaustion, Veronique fell asleep. Our father used to say he would never forget seeing the heap of clothing on the clifftop and hearing from far below, Mother's voice, singing clearly:

"*A le beau ciel ma Normandie* . . . Oh, the blue skies of my Normandy, the country which gave the light of day to me." The song that had come out from Normandy with Marie-Rose's ancestors so long before.'

Thérèse took the story up. 'And Father nearly swooned when on his hands and knees he peered down. It was twilight now ... and saw what his wife had attempted ... and accomplished. He found out the nature of the child's injuries. They knew they'd have to improvise a stretcher for her and some went haring back to get the makings. So he went down immediately. Mother said to Veronique, "Didn't I tell you Big Beauchamp would come for us?" They got a block and tackle to winch her up, the child, then the other two. When Mother reached the top she had Father's trousers clutched round her and when Father was pulled over the edge, he was in his long pink underwear!' Thérèse giggled, then added, 'But *then* no one laughed. They cheered. Poor Father. He used to say the moment when he reached the top from the house, and saw that heap of skirt, used to haunt him for years.'

Monique's eyes were golden-brown in the sunlight and sparkling. 'What a magnificent story. I'm so glad he kept having that nightmare.'

They all stared, uncomprehendingly.

She dimpled. 'Because it showed there was tenderness under the granite.'

Both ladies looked a little abashed. Henriette said ruefully, 'We drew too harsh a picture, didn't we? Such unfilial daughters as our poor papa had. He gave up on us.'

Edouard took them seriously. 'You don't do justice to yourselves. Mother told me you were wonderful in his last illness. That you, Henriette, sat by his bed for six hours, without moving, pretending you were his Marie-Rose.'

She looked embarrassed. 'Only because he took me for Mother. How could I disillusion a dying man?'

Thérèse backed Edouard up. 'And during that time I recall that the only thing that passed your lips was a glass of milk because you thought if you left him it might disturb that comforting fancy.'

Henriette retorted, 'And you, Thérèse, walked two miles earlier that day, to get some of those little sweetheart roses from old Mrs Lemoine, so he could take them to Mother. The ones he always gave her on their wedding annniversary. 'The *Cecil De Brunner* ones.'

Monique spoke before she thought. 'Just fancy, I came here positively hating François Beauchamp, and now he's caught hold of my imagination. I'd dubbed him a true despot.'

Henriette sounded rueful. 'It's like I said. My fault, because on the 'phone I said Father was always saying when things worked out well for him that it was personally arranged by *le bon Dieu*! How naughty it was of me to say he had more in common with *le Diable*! I must watch my tongue!'

Monique's heart gave a thud. *And she must watch hers!* She had hated old François ever since she had been told that her grandfather had left home because his father wouldn't believe him. Now she was in danger of being sorry for the old tyrant. What was Edouard saying?

'Is anyone ever an out-and-outer? Like a true despot, or a hopeless criminal, or desperado? There's nearly always some saving grace . . . or a reason.'

Thérèse looked at him fondly, as he drove on. 'You would find an excuse for *le Diable* himself. And one of these days that same failing will get you into real trouble. You'll dash headlong into rescuing some girl from a stupid situation and she'll imagine there's more in it than there is . . . and she'll have you round to declare your intentions to her parents before you've time to know what's happening to you!'

Monique felt herself growing rigid. That astonishing Edouard put his head back and roared. 'My dear nitwit, you've let *your* imagination run away with you. I'm an adept at extricating myself from such situations. After all, a man needs some defence. If you happen to be around when a girl's out of her depth, you yank her out, sure, but it doesn't mean she henceforth belongs to you.'

Henriette rarely left well alone. She said, 'What about that girl in the hardware shop in Christchurch?'

'I knew you'd bring that up . . . but after all, you

took a hand in that, and managed it very well, at that. Though it was quite unnecessary, I'd have steered myself out of trouble, left alone.'

Henriette said to Monique, 'He overheard a manager absolutely browbeating a girl. Putting people on the carpet should always be done in the privacy of an office. Edouard could stand it no longer. He walked round the display stand and told him off to a standstill. Finished up by saying that if the manager sacked her by way of venting his spleen, the owner would hear from him, that he knew him well. That was masterly.' Henriette chuckled reminiscently. 'Trouble was Edouard was recognised by one of the other employees, and that girl turned up here the next Sunday, complete with family, to thank him personally. She came three times after that, hero-worshipping him, and he was too kind to her for his own good.'

Edouard recoiled, 'Yuk! Spare my blushes. It soon faded out anyway.'

'Only because of us. You said so yourself. We twittered, we asked if she'd like to come across the following weekend and added: "Edouard's fiancée will be here. A dear girl, she'd love to meet you. She knows she's getting a treasure in Edouard, but it wouldn't hurt to underline it." She made her excuses and that was the last we heard. Saved her face and Edouard's. I reckon that lie'll be just one more star in our crowns.'

Edouard was scowling horribly. 'If you don't stop all this tittle-tattling, I'll put you out and you can walk back, so help me. I'm supposed to be instructing your protégée in the layout of the Beauchamp Estate. And I didn't need your help, I'd have been just as subtle and possibly more effective, given a chance.'

'How?' demanded Henriette.

'I'd have sent flowers with a message that had a ring of finality about it.' His voice held a derisive note. The old ladies saw nothing amiss but it got Monique on the raw. Her chin came up a little. She could match him stab for stab. 'It would be interesting to know just how that could be done. You could hardly say: "Glad to have been of service . . . see you no more." But perhaps you could use some apt quotation ... I'm sure you can reel off quotations at the drop of a hat. Like: "From a ship that passed in the night and spoke to you in passing," but tell me, surely *all* the damsels you rescue don't pursue you? Some might even *dodge* you!'

She sensed rather than saw the look he gave her out of the corner of his eye. 'I'm sure that's true. Balances things nicely, doesn't it? Some make it very plain they're grateful for the service but don't want you to presume on that. I can get that message very easily. I'm not exactly slow on the uptake.'

Henriette said fondly, 'Edouard, you do talk a lot of rubbish.'

He grinned, 'I know, and after all the high romance of the past we've been talking about, it's a comedown.'

They breasted another rise, saw below them the rest of the acreage, rolling emerald turf, cropped by snowy Coopworth ewes, their now sturdy lambs, dock-tailed, at their sides. For leagues to the lavender horizon stretched the Pacific, sapphire blue this morning, breaking into scallops of white foam nearer the shores. Far out was a container ship coming up from Port Chalmers and an oil tanker turning into Lyttelton Heads to discharge its cargo. Small local trawlers were busy, scattered widely. Overhead swept a fish-spotter plane, ready to indicate where the shoals were and what they were. Further out still, beyond the limit, would be the Japanese and Russian trawlers, and that other immense plane above them would be making its way from Christchurch to the still mysterious South Pole area.

Suddenly a wind off the sea stirred a row of Australian gums, bringing to her the aromatic, sense-stirring pungency of the seawinds of her childhood ... and here she was, where her loved grandfather had spent his childhood, done his bird watching.

Monique experienced a wave of unbelief. It seemed incredible she should have survived twenty-seven years without really losing her heart to any man, without being swept off her feet; then in a wild plunge of action and impulse, Edouard Fergusson had flashed into her life, capturing her imagination, stirring her pulse, wakening her to all manner of dreams . . . red roses he had insisted on from across the Tasman, and there had been no message of *finality* with them. No . . . anything but. *'My love is like a red, red rose.'* It had seemed like a promise of seekings-out to come. Instead he had been furious to find her here. But he was being mellow now for the sake of two old ladies he dearly loved. Oh, St George, ride on! I will not care. *I will not be daunted!*

# CHAPTER SEVEN

DAYS flowed into weeks. The venture was a great success. Margot and Pierre Laveroux had begun recommending that their stream of visitors went the extra kilometres to visit Beauchamp House and came themselves to see it, to offer suggestions, to exclaim in delight over all that Monique had accomplished.

On their second visit they brought Madame Rossignol, in her nineties now, and still beautiful, and old Clothilde Larchwood and her granddaughter, Susannah Hervington-Blair, with her husband Morgan. It wasn't a public day but Henriette and Thérèse called it a red-letter day. They were so proud to introduce their protégée, Monique, to the two old ladies. Edouard took a day off from farm duties. It seemed they were vaguely related. Edouard's eyes danced, 'The relationships round Akaroa are many and varied. We won't take you through the family trees, Monique, they are too tangled in the branches for anyone not related. You'd only get confused.'

How she would have loved to say, 'But I am Hilaire Beauchamp's granddaughter, the sole representative of this generation.' But of late, as she assessed the treasures of Beauchamp House, she had wondered if she would ever be able to announce it. It was claiming to be heir to it all. Oh, what a stumbling-block money could be.

Madame Rossignol said gently, 'But it does not seem to me at all that Monique is a stranger amongst us. Just as I felt Margot was no stranger when first she came to us from London. It was as if her place had always been here, awaiting her. And when you came into the room just before, *chérie*, I had the oddest feeling. Perhaps because she walks like a Frenchwoman. Me, I notice these things. I said to myself, "Why, she holds herself like Marie-Rose."'

Monique's lips parted in delight, colour flowing into her cheeks, eyes astar. 'You—you really thought that? I'd love to think I resembled Marie-Rose in the slightest way. She has come alive for me as if I'd known her in another world. Oh, perhaps that sounds stupid, but since they told me of her scramble down the cliff to rescue Veronique, she lives for me. I daresay it's something to do with dwelling on the past so much in this lovely old historical house, using her cups, her silver, polishing her lamp-bowls.'

Madame nodded her head. 'It is natural, *petite*, because in Akaroa the past is only yesterday. We have no skyscrapers rising where once the Nanto-Bordelaise Company settlers mended their *seines* on the beaches, or tended their five-acre sections. So the past is always with us. Sometimes at a dance the young girls are seen wearing the black ironwork earrings that were all the jewellery allowed in post-revolution days in France. Some have even been unearthed from the tip, because these things were, earlier, despised as of no value. In the main we have to thank the antique dealers for teaching us to value our possessions . . .' She laughed. 'Henriette and Thérèse, your protégée is inspiring me to reminisce, which is a habit that becomes a fixation in old age. One has to curb it, but those shining brown eyes, her listening quality, do inspire me.'

Margot said softly, 'And your own skill as a raconteur, Tante Elise, makes us want to listen. You know what our little Elise says: "No one tells stories like *Grand'tante*."'

'I'll second that,' said Morgan Hervington-Blair. He turned to Edouard. 'Perhaps you and I could have a look at that stuff now?'

They went out. Morgan, like Edouard, was a sheep-farmer, but out on the Canterbury Plains against the foothills. Monique supposed they were going to the farm office, to pour over wool samples, or, as Morgan, too, seemed to have experimental paddocks, compare seeds, herbicides, pesticides.

Thérèse asked Monique to slip up to her bedroom to bring down a miniature of their mother, from the wall.

As Monique passed the room Edouard occupied, she was startled to hear a strange noise from in there. She stopped, held her breath, listened. There it was again, almost like something being moved. But everyone was downstairs! Her heart gave a thud. There was that outside staircase leading from the stable courtyard. It would be so easy to enter by it, if anyone had felonious intent. It was locked only at night.

She didn't hesitate. If she ran back down, an intruder could escape. She went quietly to the door, put her hand round the handle, turned it silently, then flung it open. The two men bending over the bottom drawer of the wardrobe positively jumped.

Monique hardly knew how she recovered herself. She had a hand to her chest, then said, 'What a relief! I thought you were housebreakers! I imagined you were in the office. Thought someone was moving furniture around ... which seemed odd unless they were searching for something.'

Edouard was quick to reply. Too quick? He laughed, 'Sorry, it's such an anti-climax. I'm merely trying to get this wretched drawer out! Morgan was helping me. Tell you what, Morgan, when we get it out, I'll get my plane and take a chunk off.' Then to Monique, 'Morgan's interested in these long-ago account books I unearthed when I set up my rooms in the loft. He's writing an article on prices in the last century. We wondered if the prices on the plains differed from those here. Theirs went by bullock wagon, through riverbeds, to market. Ours went by whale-boat to Lyttelton, Port Cooper as they called it then.'

Monique looked vaguely interested then said, 'No doubt that drawer being almost impossible to open is a nuisance, on the other hand, no burglar would be able to get at it without making the dickens of a din. A sort of built-in security measure.'

Edouard again rushed in quickly, 'A few old account books wouldn't interest a burglar. He'd take one look and leave them. We'll be down soon.'

Uneasiness over the incident stayed with Monique during all the happiness of the succeeding hours. She tried to tell herself she was being foolish, but when she saw from the drawing-room window, Morgan crossing the lawn to the drive where the cars were parked, with a suitcase in his hand that hadn't come with him, she felt decidedly worse. But what could she do?

It seemed impossible, in a sort of extended family circle like this, that any skulduggery could be going on.

In the next few days she almost put it out of her mind. Edouard was less strange in his manner towards her she thought, more like the man she'd first encountered. It still hurt when she remembered the revulsion he'd shown when he found her here but perhaps that had been due to the inborn masculine dislike of change, suspicion that she might have entered in on this in a grand burst of enthusiasm, then could let the old ladies down. He might also have thought that here was another girl he'd played knight-errant to, who would stick like a burr. As far as that might go, she'd certainly show him he was entirely mistaken!

Four days after the visitors from Rossignol Bay had come, Henriette asked Monique if she'd vacuum Edouard's room thoroughly. 'Mrs Bullen just skims it, I know. We always seem to be around when she does the other rooms, so they're all right, but she takes far too little time with his. As she's not coming today I thought it'd be a good opportunity.'

'Very well, as long as Edouard doesn't mind. I'll go over to the paddock and ask him if it's okay.'

Thérèse looked staggered. 'He won't mind *you*. It's no intrusion on his privacy, my dear, he has all his private papers in the coachman's quarters over the stable. Have you never been up there? We turned them over to him. We felt his work for Lincoln College was mainly confidential, and that in any case he needed somewhere of his very own away from two old ladies. Besides, you can't ask him, I saw him ride off in the direction of the Port. Just do it, love. I'd feel so happy to know it was done thoroughly for once.'

Monique obeyed. The whole time she was vacuuming her eyes kept straying to the drawer. She finished, took first a feather duster, then a cloth damped with furniture cream, and meticulously rubbed at the furniture. She lifted the books from his bedside table, put them on the bed, polished, went to put them back ... an Alastair McLean thriller, a farming journal and ... a book of Robert Burns poems, a complete set, beautifully bound. She dropped it on the table as if it had stung her.

What was the next one? A book of clans and tartans. It had a bookmark in it. Curiously she opened it there. It was marking the Fergusson page. She read all about that clan, smiled over the MacFhearghuis, concerning which a small Edouard had fought in schooldays, thereby earning a nickname. Then her eyes picked up the motto. 'Dulcius ex asperis ... Sweeter after difficulties.' A good motto, one to encourage.

Then she found herself saying to herself quite fiercely, 'But the one my Grandad made up is better still: "Be not daunted." and I won't be daunted! That does it, Grandad darling, here goes!'

She marched to the wardrobe, yanked at the drawer. It came out so easily she went flying back on her heels. She had to grin at herself. So Edouard and Morgan really had planed the edges down. Then the grin faded. They had been very thorough. The cobwebs were gone, the account books had been dusted off and lay in neat piles. Three piles, *and there were no packages of drawings. Meryon's priceless sketches were gone!*

She felt sick. Would she have to say something? Do something? How could she? What if her suspicions were unfounded and some explanation could be forthcoming? What would happen if there was skulduggery? If it were revealed, how would it affect life as it was lived here? It would just about kill those two dear ladies to be disillusioned about Edouard. And she would be the cause of it, the girl they had welcomed into their home, delighted in. She knew by now that they loved her as they might've loved a granddaughter of their own.

But what of those sketches? What was happening to them? She thought she was going to *have* to ask Edouard. But how could she introduce the subject? And where?

The thought hung over her all morning. It spoiled the pleasure of all she did, the things she usually loved doing. It was no good going on with the cataloguing. That needed full attention. Instead she went on doing the things that the women of this household had done for more than a century ... she filled the vases, polished that elegant stair rail that owed half its patina to the generations of hands, large and small, that had run over it lovingly as their owners tripped downstairs or steadied themselves going up. She even scrubbed the long tiled verandah by hand, bringing Henriette and Thérèse out in protest.

She laughed. 'I just feel in the mood. I know we have that marvellous Mop-o-Matic, but every now and then I feel it needs hot suds and a scrubbing-brush! And it works off one's energy.'

'How lovely to have it to spare. Ah, to be that young again! But you are scrubbing as if you were blue-devilled, as a cook in my mother's day used to put it. She used to beat the eggs with a fork as if she was whipping the britches off a Highlander ... another of her sayings. You aren't mad or unhappy about something, are you, *petite*?'

She managed to laugh, to say gaily, 'I am not, and because I'm a bean-pole, I love it when you call me *petite*.'

That was the way to treat it, the two darlings were always ready to be side-tracked. Thérèse said fondly, 'We use the diminutive out of love, Monique, as one does.'

The colour of pleasure rushed into Monique's cheeks, 'Oh, you say the nicest things. My Granddad was like that. He believed, he said, in saying what was in his heart. That it was a pity not to, because the opportunity might never come again.' She was wringing her floorcloth with great vigour and did not see the suddenly startled look that passed between the other two above her head.

Edouard's voice broke in, 'Well, well ... such philosophy uttered over a scrubbing-brush and a floorcloth! I hesitate at such an exalted moment to ask when lunch will be ready? I know it's early but I wanted to be around; I'm expecting a 'phone-call within the next half-hour.'

The two old ladies moved off. 'We'll start now. We're having a salad. Those lettuces are perfect for cutting. Edouard, would you prefer cold pork, or cold mutton?'

'Both, thanks, and if you liked to add some of that chicken, we could call it a cold collation.'

Chuckling, they moved off. Monique wished he'd follow them. She said, 'Don't you want to be within hearing distance?'

'Not yet. You heard me say half an hour. They'll feel bustled if I stand over them.'

She wrung out the cloth again, mopped up the last square of soapy surface, pushed herself up on her kneeler and stood upright. He came close to her. 'Monique . . . I was watching you for some time. *Were* you blue-devilled about something?'

Her eyelids flickered and she looked swiftly away from him towards the drive, bordered by dozens of lilacs in full bloom. 'No,' she said. He stepped close, turned her chin round so she had to look at him. 'Meet my gaze . . . and try to tell that lie again.'

She looked down, the dark brown lashes on her warm cheeks, very conscious of the feel of his fingers, cool, rough. Then she said, 'Edouard, everyone has their less bright moments. It doesn't mean we always look for a shoulder to weep on or for someone to tell.'

'No, but sometimes it's nice if there's a shoulder around.'

She nodded. 'But very foolish. One spills out more than is wise. And words can't be taken back, or even said differently. I'm all right, Edouard. Please don't probe. I was just trying to decide something. So my thoughts tumbling round must've made me go for my life with the scrubbing-brush.'

'You don't want to tell me, do you?'

She shook her head vigorously, 'No, I don't. But I may have to.'

'Then try me now. It may ease your mind. Oh, look, Monique, I can understand this reluctance. I was rough

on you when I arrived back from Australia. Forgive me
for that. I was raw about—well, I was raw. Can you forget
that and tell me what's causing you this turmoil of mind?'

'Not now I can't. Not when you're expecting a ring.
It would take time and very delicate handling. Not to
be rushed. Please wait till I find I can. *If* I can.'

'All right. But for now, don't give yourself too much
heart-burning over it. Oh, my God, you don't mean you
want to tell me you can't carry on here? It will break
their hearts and—Monique, if it *is* that, tell me soon,
and frankly.'

Her surprise convinced him it wasn't that. 'Oh, no,
wild horses couldn't drag me away from Beauchamp
House. I'm doing something very dear to my heart. But
I think I will tell you soon, Edouard, when I find the
courage.'

At that moment Thérèse appeared. 'Edouard, your
call. It's Morgan. He hoped you'd be in, he had to ring
a bit early. He's in Christchurch.'

Edouard took off. Monique stared after him.
Morgan! Oh, dear. She took her bucket, fished out the
soap, poured the suds carefully round the roots of an
*Etoile de Holland* rosebush. Its buds were just opening,
showing dark red tips. She put out a hand to one,
caressingly. Red roses! She pushed a wispy piece of hair
from her eyes, went round the back with her bucket and
into the downstairs bathroom to wash her reddened
hands with scented soap and run a styling brush
through her shoulder-length hair till the ends curled
forward. Quite a morning.

She found lunch an ordeal. Edouard seemed in high
spirits. Why? Morgan's 'phone call? Her thoughts
scurried about like a nest of baby mice in a haystack.
She'd committed herself to the extent of promising
she'd tell him something.

Thérèse said in surprise, 'Monique, you once told me
you couldn't stand dry lettuce and you've eaten almost
all that without mayonnaise.'

Monique said hastily, 'Must be because you tossed
that bean salad in oil and vinegar, so I didn't notice. I'll
take a spoonful now.'

'She's not with us,' said Edouard rather indulgently. 'She has things on her mind, not blue-devilled, she tells me, but anyway, she's promised to unburden herself to me later on.'

Monique felt dismayed, now Henriette and Thérèse would want to probe. And they *mustn't* know. What *had* got into Edouard, anyway? He had a queer quirk in his character ... if he thought anyone was in a fix, he had to butt in. Then he lost interest. A sort of St George complex! The psychologists would have a name for it ... a schizophrenic knight!

Instead of looking curious, the two of them looked delighted. Thérèse said, 'And you couldn't tell it to a better person. How nice that you feel you can confide in Edouard. That makes us more of a family, yes?'

Only Edouard laughed. Then he turned to Monique, said, 'You know what your trouble is, Monique, you're absolutely slavish in your devotion to this cause, restoring Beauchamp House to its former glory. You know the old saying: "All work and no play ..." Well, I'm taking you out tonight to cure that. I've got the tickets for a play. Time you were off the chain.'

Monique boggled. 'You—you've got the tickets?'

His eyes danced. 'I know it's no way to ask a girl but I was quite ready to have them transferred to my sister and her husband if you wouldn't play ball. Remember Francine?'

She swallowed. 'Your sister? But—but she lives in Christchurch!'

His turn to stare. 'Of course it's in Christchurch. I didn't mean just a little local play. It's in the Town Hall. Wish I could've given you dinner there first, and watched the fountains play, but we'll do that another time. It's an overseas company doing *She Stoops to Conquer*. You'll come?'

The two ladies looked anxious. A thought flashed into Monique's mind. Fifty miles there and fifty back ... surely in that distance and darkness she could bring up what was troubling her. She dimpled, 'I'll accept your outrageous invitation, kind sir,' she said.

Henriette and Thérèse looked most relieved and said in duet, 'What'll you wear?'

Monique pretended to consider, put a fingertip to her mouth, pursed up her lips. 'Well, either my midnight blue velvet with my mink stole, or my gold lame and the sable cloak.'

They all laughed indulgently, then. Thérèse said, 'But seriously?'

She looked at Edouard. 'Do you want to dress up? Is it a first night?'

'It is, and I do. And I would like you to. In lime green for preference. Can you?'

She looked puzzled. 'Why lime green?'

'Because the first time I met you, you were wearing lime green.'

Monique's voice was brittle with surprise. 'You're mad. I was wearing rose-pink. With enormous white buttons from shoulder to hem. One of Claude Montmorency's famous ideas. We never got tired of our uniforms, if you could call them that. He had new inspirations so often. So what's this nonsense, Edouard Fergusson?'

'Oh, unbeliever! I said the *first* time I met you. Not the time I thought you'd bought the Beauchamp marble clock and had probably diddled them.'

She looked him straight in the eye. 'You *are* mad. We hadn't met before that.'

'Oh, yes we had, Mademoiselle Belfield. One hot February day in Christchurch. You were wearing lime green, sort of a gauzy frock, with satin spots on it in the same green. It was almost noon and you looked dressed up for some occasion. I mean your dress was more like a dinner-dress. Longish. And clasped against you, you carried a Leghorn hat, with buttercups and daisies round it, and I'm almost sure you had a brown velvet sash. You came round the corner of Armagh and Madras Streets like a tornado, and went slap-bang into me. You hit me with such force it dented the crown right in and you cried in absolute fury, "*Now* look what you've done!" and you drove your fist into it and the dent popped out. I'd steadied you with both hands or you'd have gone for a purler, but you didn't even stop to thank me. You tore on, running diagonally across the road in the most dangerous fashion, and went flying round the corner where that church with the pillared front stands opposite the river. The fire station's just past there but I never saw anyone dress up like that for a fire! I was flummoxed that morning in Montmorency's when it turned out this super-saleswoman these two here had wanted me to meet was none other than the hoyden who winded me and fled. What *was* happening that day?'

Monique's disbelieving eyes had gradually become credulous. 'I never even saw your face. I only hit your solar plexus. You were just one more obstruction in a chain of disasters. I was being a bridesmaid at the Oxford Terrace Baptist Church. First of all I was held up at home because my posy hadn't arrived, a Victorian affair of yellow daisies with brown centres. It was a working day so to save time I didn't dress at the bride's house; she lived in the country. I rang the florist. His van had broken down, so they'd get them to the church.

'Even while I was on the phone the taximan was hissing at me, "Lady, this is zero hour, come on!" Then, believe it or not, the taxi broke down. If I'd waited for him to call another one up, I'd have been late and I was supposed to wait for the bride in the vestibule. So I took off. That stupid hat wouldn't stay on, not in a Canterbury nor'wester. It blew into a basket of oranges outside a fruit shop. I was only glad they weren't big red juicy plums. I grabbed it out and rushed on and crashed into a man. You, apparently. I got there, jammed my hat on, praying my hairspray had lasted the course, a split second before the bride arrived with her father, *and* the florist's van! No bride's knees ever shook as mine did as I walked up the aisle behind them.'

When they'd stopped laughing, Edouard said, 'I thought that was going to remain one of the unsolved mysteries of my life. I got quite a shock when your eyes flashed with anger that morning in the shop, because you thought I was accusing you of being a shark! I

thought: Heavens, I've seen this girl in a temper before!'
He jumped up. 'I'm wanted on the wharf at half-past
one. How about if I come in early for a sort of high tea?
Oh, Monique, have you that dress with you? You have?
Do wear it.' He went out.

Henriette looked thoughtful. 'Quite arrogant for him.
For a fleeting moment he reminded me of Father.'

Monique looked startled. 'Is that a compliment or not?'

Henriette considered that. 'Dear girl, tell me truly?
Did you really resent him ordering you to wear a dress
that remained in his mind so vividly?'

Monique's eyes met the faded blue ones squarely and
found herself unable to prevaricate. Her face broke up.
'No, I rather liked it.'

Thérèse said, 'I'm so glad you could admit that.
Don't we all like the masterful touches?' She began to
laugh. 'My Robert liked pretty clothes for me but never
anything outlandish. Now, when was that fashion in? In
the forties, I think. Just after the War, anyway. Things
were getting less scarce and more lavish. Some hats
came out that were sort of Dolly Varden, you know, up
on one side on a bandeau, covered with masses of tiny
flowers. There was an elastic under one's hair to hold it
on, and an eye veil. Mine was extra lavish, with the
edge of the veil sparkling with outsized sequins.

'Rob had seen it lying on the bed but had said no
more than wasn't it a bit overdone, but when I came
out in it the sequins *tinkled* and he said he for one
wasn't going to enter a church with a wife sounding like
walking wind-chimes! I couldn't believe he meant it.
Finally, to convince me, he sat down and said he wasn't
going to the wedding. We glared at each other and
raged at each other for twenty minutes before I went
and got my only other blue hat which was decidedly
shabby. I said nastily I hoped the other guests would
take him for a skinflint of a man who was too mean to
buy his wife a new hat for the occasion.

'We never spoke all the way in. When we got to the
church door I pinned a smile to my face, ear to ear, and
got to our seats. When the minister said, "For better,
for worse," Rob and I glanced at each other and

dissolved into silent giggles. Rob had to make a speech at the breakfast and I terrified he'd bring in that story somehow as an instance of being master in your own house. But he didn't. And he took me to town next day and bought me a most beautiful and expensive hat, a silent one.'

Monique got up, went to stand between them, where they were still sitting at the table, slipped an arm about each, said, 'Darlings, I do love you. I don't know how I existed before I knew you.'

Henriette choked a little as she patted Monique's hand. 'Dear child, if only you knew what it means to us. Our youth has been revived in you. Now dear, we're going to wash up. You go and have a rest after all that scrubbing. Paint your nails and cream your face and neck . . . lie down and relax. Don't fill every moment to the brim as you usually do. Will your frock need pressing? If so we'll do it. And Monique, you must wear our mother's choker. If it will suit the neck of the dress.'

'It would, but——'

'But me no buts.'

She lay on her bed for half an hour thinking, thinking. How *was* she going to enquire about the sketches? She suddenly remembered that he'd thought she'd bought that clock for a song. He'd admitted misjudging her. She could do the same. Certainly this was a more serious suspicion, but perhaps if she took it lightly, it mightn't sound too bad. She could say it had been worrying her . . . that the day of the leak in his room she'd had to try to open that drawer, and when she was frustrated had thrown everything out. She hadn't had time to look closely, but it had seemed to her trained eye that some sketches in it might bear closer scrutiny in case they were valuable. What did he think? Yes, that would be a fairly innocuous approach. It would allow for an explanation. If there *was* one.

She got up and showered, still apprehensive but not nearly as much as when she had been scrubbing. The Edouard who had asked her was she indeed blue-devilled had seemed much more approachable. Heaven send he stayed that way and didn't take offence.

They had their high tea, boiled eggs, tiny radishes fresh from the garden, some of the Peninsula's incomparable cheeses, hot scones that Thérèse had made, a large pot of tea. Then Edouard and Monique disappeared upstairs.

She looked at her reflection in the cheval glass in her room, and decided she looked too excited. She must subdue this sparkle. She told herself it was simply because it had been all work, that they were too isolated for many outings, that it had nothing to do with the fact that today Edouard had seemed more like the man who'd swept her off to the airport, had kissed her goodbye, promised to ring on return. But ... well, it had been rather ... rather nice to know that in their very earliest encounter this frock had made such an impression. But oh, Monique, don't look so starry-eyed. You aren't sweet seventeen ... you're twenty-seven!

She'd left her door open. She was suddenly conscious of someone standing there. Edouard ... smiling. Her eyes met his in the mirror, she blushed. 'Stupid to be standing gazing at one's reflection, but——'

He waved that aside, came in, stood looking into the mirror too. 'I like what I see,' he said. 'Why shouldn't you? Or is there some detail bothering you that only feminine eyes would pick up?'

'How astute of you. There was—but no, it doesn't matter. Only——'

'Only what? Is it something a mere male could solve?'

'It is, probably, only it's something I can't change, I couldn't hurt them.'

The grey eyes narrowed, gained their blue glint. 'I know ... you'd rather have worn something more simple than the choker, wouldn't you?'

She felt a rush of gratitude. 'I would, but I can't. They neither of them ever had a daughter. I'm a substitute. If we were going to a formal ball I might've worn it happily, but just a first night ...'

'Monique, since Christchurch has had this superb Town Hall, it has made more of such occasions. You won't be in the least over-dressed. What did you wear with this when you were bridesmaid?'

'A plain gold locket, a family one, threaded on brown velvet.'

He nodded. 'A nice effect. Would you like to slip it into my pocket, wear the choker downstairs and change it in the car?'

She considered it. 'I would like to, but somehow it would seem like cheating. I think I'd better keep faith with them.'

The corners of the mouth that could look so unyielding, quirked up. 'Good for you. I like that sort of integrity. Bless you.'

He bent his head swiftly, touched his mouth to one side of hers, not to disturb her carefully applied lipstick; not a kiss exchanged or with any hint of passion, but a kiss of tribute.

He said, 'Come on. Don't forget we're going to stop for a few minutes on the way so you can tell me what was blue-devilling you.'

The brown eyes met his frankly, 'I—I don't think I need to any more. I think it's something I can work out for myself.'

'If I let you. Ah ... there's Henriette calling. Coming.' He had hold of her hand. She scooped up a pearl-covered evening bag, and had to follow him down the stairs.

Her thoughts were chaotic. He'd said, 'I like that sort of integrity.' Would a man whose own integrity could be questioned, have said a thing like that? Suddenly she was sure there was an explanation about the sketches. She mustn't let herself be stampeded into telling him what she'd suspected.

Henriette gestured Edouard to the 'phone. 'It's Morgan. I told him you were just going out. He said, "Thank goodness I've caught him." What's going on?'

Edouard positively bounded to the phone, said quickly, 'Yes, Morgan?' then, 'Are you sure? I mean beyond all shadow of doubt? My word, that was quick. This special service is magnificent, isn't it? Well, if the British Museum says so, that's it. No, we won't say a word yet. What a thrill. And the subsequent publicity ought to really put Beauchamp House on the tourist map! Yes, I'll just tell the three women. They're as safe as houses. Morgan, they're dying of curiosity this moment. I'll ring you again in the morning when I've simmered down. Right now I'm taking Monique into Christchurch to see Goldsmith's play at the Town Hall. Yes, a fitting celebration. It would be interesting to know how they came to be here. Right. Goodbye for now, and thanks.'

The receiver was positively crashed down and he turned to them. 'I found some old sketches one day, up in the stables in a box. I was practically certain they were Charles Meryon's, but they could've been fakes. So I consulted Morgan. He knows a lot about such things. Thought he was far enough off from here to stop any hint getting out locally. The Christchurch Museum used this new swift service the Post Office have set up, to get photocopies sent off to the London Museum. They *are* genuine. They are very valuable, and what is to be done with them will have to be gone into most carefully. The fact is we've unearthed a treasure and a bit of the earliest history connected with the French settlement. Monique, what on earth's the matter?'

He caught her arm, guided her to a chair, said in a bewildered tone, 'You've lost all your colour. How could this news affect you like that?'

She pulled herself together. 'Sheer stupidity. I have the most odd reactions. Fear makes me angry, not nervous. Joy makes me weep. And now at this most thrilling moment I get the vapours. Take no notice of me!'

To herself she was saying: Edouard's integrity *is* above reproach!

# CHAPTER EIGHT

Monique recovered her poise in a moment and was laughing at herself in a way that reassured them all. She waved away the brandy Thérèse wanted to give her. 'I don't even need a drink of water. I'm just stupidly mercurial. Oh, I do wish you were coming with us. It would be a celebration for us all then, even if it's hush-hush for now.'

She'd never heard the two of them laugh like that. They let their mirth gradually subside into giggles that were positively girlish. 'Monique, dear child, you're so naïve. Edouard is very good with the pair of us, but we can imagine his reaction if we took you seriously! Besides, at our age a fifty-mile drive before and after the theatre is just not on. Now, be off with you and we can twitter to each other for hours after this. Edouard, even if you have supper out, you'll need something when you come in. We'll leave something out for you. Darling Monique, you look a dream, no wonder Edouard remembered that frock. And that short honey-coloured coat with it is perfect.'

They were past Duvauchelles Bay before Edouard brought up the subject of what she was going to explain to him. 'We're going into the Lookout at the Hilltop Hotel. It's a glorious twilight and a dream of a view. It may soothe your troubled breast. Just right for confidences I think. It's no use your telling me it doesn't matter now. I think it was—or is—something that mattered very much and that's why you got all dewy-eyed and shaken at my news tonight. Good news like that shouldn't have knocked you off your pins, so you must be in a state of tension. I feel somewhat responsible. I was too anti when I came home and found you there, scared for the old girls' sake that you might make a terrific upheaval in their lives, then skip it. And a bit mad on my own account. I'd like us to get back on a better footing.'

If only she hadn't given away her feelings this morning. Then again when Morgan rang. Then she need have said nothing about her doubts. This could rupture the new trust that was growing between them. But Edouard was the sort of man to see through any feeble excuse she might offer.

He swung up to the Lookout, a little away from the other cars parked there. She looked down at the exquisite contours of Akaroa Harbour through the shimmer of unshed tears. Oh dear, she must get a grip of herself. Otherwise she'd make too much of it.

She hadn't put her jacket on. It was too mild. The short cape sleeves of her frock flared out about the shoulders. Edouard looked down on her, glimpsed the downbent profile, sensed rather than saw the threat of tears. He put a warm hand on her arm just above the elbow. 'I'm no ogre, apart from my surly treatment of you that first day at Beauchamp House. Come on. Give.'

She looked up with a defenceless look that, had she known, caught at him. 'If only I hadn't given myself away to Henriette and Thérèse and you this morning, Edouard. That I was worried. Then no questions would've been asked. Nobody would've been hurt.'

'Hurt? Why, who's going to be hurt?'

'You, I think. I mean if—if you had thought such a thing about me I'd be hurt ... and flaming mad ... why, that morning at the shop I was ready to be hopping mad with you because you thought I'd bought that clock for a song and was selling it at a handsome profit, yet what I thought about you was a thousand times worse. Oh, I'm making a dreadful botch of this. I was going to treat it with a light touch, but oh, Edouard, it's all gone haywire and you *will* be hurt. You'll positively eat me. I don't know how to tell you—'

He gave a great guffaw and brought his other hand across her to grasp that arm too as if he'd like to shake her. 'You *are* botching it. You're floundering, my girl. You'll hate me for saying this, but I'll risk it ... I'm almost enjoying myself. You're so poised as a rule, at least that was the impression I got at the shop at first, till suddenly things happened, and you were just like any other girl needing a hand. I rather like you this way.'

It flummoxed her, side-tracked her. She forsook her jumbled utterance, said, in a most accusing tone, 'It's this St George complex! You're so unapproachable sometimes, even dour and forbidding, but let a girl be in trouble and you're altogether different. You must be some sort of schizophrenic!'

He guffawed even more. 'Oh, poor Monique, she can't quite tape me so she's falling back on that sort of psychological jargon. Come on, idiot, what am I going to be so flaming mad about? Out with it!'

To his immense surprise, two big tears overflowed the brown eyes and dropped on the green satin spots of the curve of her bodice. She said bluntly and miserably, 'You were getting the Charles Meryon sketches valued *but I thought you'd pinched them.* I was sick to my soul. Then tonight when you said you liked my sort of integrity, I knew you couldn't have, that I'd have to trust you, that I needn't tell you what I'd thought. But you said you were going to worm it out of me.'

He sobered up immediately, gazed at her blankly. She thought, trying to be brave enough to hold his gaze: Now the vials of his wrath will fall upon me!

He said, the grip of his fingers tightening, 'You clever little devil! You knew all about them! Well, I'll be damned. No one could ever get the better of you.' Then his look changed as did his voice, 'And you're brave enough to confess it. You didn't need to after Morgan rang me. But I'm glad you did because I was determined to find out what on earth was bugging you. I don't like to think of bottled-up cares and sorrows under the Beauchamp House roof. Oh, Monique!' His lips twitched, 'Only for heaven's sake don't tell Henriette and Thérèse. You may be the apple of their eye, and the daughter they never had, but they're also quite fond of me, forbidding, cross-grained and all as I am.'

Monique sniffed. 'I didn't say cross-grained.'

'You would've if you'd thought of it. Darling girl, mop up those tears. Good job you don't use mascara or it would've run all over the place by now.'

'How do you know I don't use it?'

'Because your eyelashes intrigue me. They're streaky like your hair. Darkish with goldy streaks. I've never seen that before. Oh, what an inadequate hanky, here, have mine. I picked a clean one off that pile of ironing. There, isn't that better? You'd made up your mind to tell me you'd found the sketches had gone, before Morgan rang to break the good tidings, I take it? Well, that was even braver and sensible too. Half the misunderstandings in the world wouldn't exist if only people came outright with things that puzzled them. You were going to risk my being offended and self-righteous if I had an explanation. Good for you. Then your relief made you throw a wobbly when I broadcast the good news. Now tell me how you found out, then we'll get going.'

She told him. He heard her out, uninterrupted, nodded. 'It added up. Now, have you got make-up in that pearly bag? Then use it. A trace of powder, a brush or two of colour . . . am I right? And you have smudged your eyebrow line this side.'

'And lipstick,' she said, blowing her nose.

'Not yet,' he amended, 'Repairs to lips come *after* this.' He bent his head, his hands left her arms to slide about her, to draw her close, the laughing eyes looked down into hers in a long look first, and they were the daring eyes of the man who had rescued her at Montmorency's and at the airport. She was aware of the warmth of his breath, the cedar-sharpness of his aftershave, the wholly masculine strength of the arms about her, then his lips found hers in a kiss that held nothing of the goodbye brevity of the one at the airport, or the light blessing of the one at the side of her mouth an hour or so earlier. This clung, sought, found, both gave and received. Her response was quite instinctive and held nothing in reserve, a moment when time seemed suspended for two people. Then their lips released each other's, they drew back a little, breathing deeply, unwilling to quite relinquish the moment and the magic.

Then a voice said, through the open window at the side of Edouard's head, 'And very nice too. Just as well I came out of the hotel ahead of my wife or a description of that would've been all over Akaroa by tomorrow. But it's your close-mouthed cousin, so you're damned lucky, Ed!—And if you introduce me to the lady, I won't breathe a word to even my nearest and dearest!'

Edouard let Monique go with a 'Hell . . . what are *you* doing here?' which was mild to what he might've said, and swung round. 'André! Trust you to pick a moment like this! Monique, this is my graceless cousin, André de Courcy. André, this is Monique Belfield, the expert who is turning Beauchamp House into one of the show places of the Peninsula. I guess you've heard of it. She used to be at Montmorency's.'

André was every inch a Frenchman. 'Expert, eh? In many fields an expert, I'd say. Aren't you the lucky one? Well, about time we saw you getting involved. Are you coming or going? Is it a celebration? Are you having dinner here?' His eyes narrowed, roved over Monique's garb, 'Not an engagement party, is it?'

Monique waved expressive hands, a typically French gesture had she but known it. 'It was nothing like that. Please don't jump to wrong conclusions. It was just . . .' She came to a full stop and neither man helped her out. For a moment both cousins looked alike, which was astonishing, with Edouard so ruggedly a Fergusson, André so elegantly a de Courcy. Their eyes brimmed with mischief. André waved a hand, 'Proceed, *Mademoiselle*, we are intrigued!'

Edouard said, 'Yes, do, Monique. I'd like to hear your definition of what that *just* was.'

Monique said feelingly, 'You utter devil! You know exactly what it was . . . just relief at—at—at something being cleared up satisfactorily.'

Both men gave way to mirth. André said, 'And I couldn't think of a better way of relieving feelings at that. That's what these misunderstandings are for.'

Edouard gave a quick look at the door of the hotel. 'André, we're going to Christchurch to a play. I dare not stay to get involved with the family. Bring Jill across to Beauchamp House one day soon but dodge the public days. Goodbye for now.'

The engine sprang to life, he reversed, headed out and took the road again. 'You can make your running repairs as we go,' he said.

Monique said, 'How safe is the volatile André?'

'Not safe at all, but who cares? Though he may keep it just to Jill.'

'You'd better be more circumspect. We can't explain to all and sundry how it came about.'

'Could *you* explain how it came about? Honestly? It just happened, didn't it? Inevitably.' She wouldn't deign to answer so he just patted her knee.

The night continued to have a magical quality all its own. Perhaps it was stupid of Edouard to lengthen the trip by running through Gebbie's Valley and cresting the Cashmere Hills above Governor's Bay so that the huge sprawling city below was revealed to them as a blaze of lights as they drew in briefly at the Sign of the Kiwi, the lonely resting-place on the summit.

The pool of lights gradually dwindled towards the west till just a few pinpoints marked solitary homesteads on some of the huge sheep-stations and wheat-belts of the plains, till every light was lost against a huge nothingness of darkness that ran from north to south and beyond that only starlight, gleaming on eternal snows, showed that this was the mighty backbone of the Southern Alps.

They purred down the tussock-clad untenanted hills till the climbing Cashmere suburb met them, then took the long straight line of Colombo Street north till, skirting Cathedral Square, they came to the complex of the Town Hall buildings, saw the lights of the restaurant, the silver spray of the fountains rising from the shallow ripples of the Avon River.

Goldsmith's comedy was exactly the sort to appeal to two people whose lives were so intermingled with those who had lived before them, other generations, other ways. To Monique's relief, she had no reason to feel over-dressed and in fact was femininely pleased with a few admiring glances and took delight in her broad-shouldered, well-groomed escort.

It wasn't till they rose to leave that she looked across and saw Athol with a companion. She turned to Edouard, 'Oh, Edouard, how lovely, there's my Dad. He's seen us so they'll come to us when we reach the foyer. See . . . a tall, fair-haired man going a bit silver. He's with a lovely looking woman in a kind of ashes-of-roses colour. Dull pink to you, I suppose. She's got dark brown hair and what I think is a moonstone necklace. Oh, I do so hope this is the Board member he's been going out with lately. He's been keeping her quiet . . . when you have three teenage children as well as one as old as me, I guess you don't want any brash teasing to rub the bloom off a belated romance!'

They met in the foyer and drew aside into a small alcove. Monique kissed her father and said, 'How lovely to see you, Dad. This is Edouard Fergusson who runs the Beauchamp Farmland. My father, Edouard . . . and this is . . .?'

She turned smilingly to the woman who'd stood a little aside during the embrace. Athol, after shaking hands with Edouard, drew his companion forward, said with a hint of pride, 'Monique, this is Beth Harding, who's very interested in what you're doing at the Port. I was going to ring soon to ask might we come over as a family, but Kerry didn't seem to have a free Saturday in the offing. Beth, you've heard a lot about Monique.'

Monique was sparkling. She gave a saucy look at Athol, said, 'Tell me, Dad, is Beth on the Hospital Board with you?'

He looked surprised, 'Yes, but why?'

She dimpled, 'I was beginning to have suspicions about this Board member you were always meeting. Thought it sounded more like dating. I did hope it wasn't some stuffy-minded old wallah.'

At that Beth Harding's face relaxed and she joined in their laughter. Edouard said affectionately, 'It's

Monique's night for plain speaking but she gets away with it every time. Her charm of manner, I believe.'

Athol's eyes rested on Monique's face with fondness. 'We've missed you horribly, of course, though we've appreciated the way you've kept in touch by 'phone, love. It's really going well? Oh, good show. It's what you should've been doing years ago, but you had too big a sense of duty and looked after us too well. It took Amabel to shake us up to awareness of how we were leaning on you. I say, you aren't going right back to Akaroa tonight, are you? Plenty spare beds at our place, you know.'

Monique was amazed to find herself offering up an instinctive prayer ... oh, please no, please no, dear God? Don't let Edouard accept? It would rub the bloom off. Please let me have that lovely long drive home?

Edouard was prompt in reply. 'Sorry, that's a kind offer, but we have to be back. I'm loading at the harbour early tomorrow morning. But I hope you'll make it soon to Beauchamp House; why not a weekend?'

Monique added, 'Don't wait till everyone can come, Dad. You know what it is, they never seem to have a Saturday free all together. Besides, I'm sure you'd enjoy it more if you aren't cluttered up with family. Beth, could you and Dad make it pretty soon? We have lots of room.'

Athol turned to Beth as eagerly as a young man. She nodded, 'I'd love that, Athol.' What a serenity this woman had. How she suited Dad. She added, to Monique, 'Let us know when you've a weekend free of the visiting public and we'll fit in. People often think widows are lonely, but I'm the other way, I find. I never seem to be without family. Both my daughters have too much conscience about me and make sure I've got one or other of my grandchildren staying. I love them all dearly but sometimes I don't feel I'm a person in my own right any more. Athol, may we go as soon as they can have us?'

'Of course, Beth. Look at Monique's face, she can't

believe you are a grandmother. Monique, she was married quite young and so were both her daughters. Give me a ring, preferably at the office, when you're free to have us. Are you having anything at the restaurant before you take off? If so, let us take you.'

Edouard said quickly, 'I think we should be on the road. We have one of my men staying in the house tonight, but the two old ladies could get nervous about us if we're late. And Monique ought to be tired. Isn't she a tiger for work? Scrubbed our huge verandah by hand this morning, daft creature. Sounds a bit of a contrast with the way she looks tonight. A Cinderella at home and a princess tonight.'

'Sounds like our Monique. Glamour *and* practicability. Just like her mother. Well, you've quite a drive ahead of you, so we'll let you go. Take care. We'll see you soon.'

As they walked away someone going past said quite clearly, 'Oh, hullo, Mr Lethbridge, good show, wasn't it?'

Edouard swung round, looked over his shoulder, said, 'Who on earth is that chap talking to? There's nobody else within coo-ee.'

Monique looked amazed. 'He was speaking to Dad of course. Oh, didn't I say my stepfather's name? Don't believe I did. He's Athol Lethbridge. What a poor introduction I must've made. I didn't realise you didn't know his name.'

'I didn't even know you had a stepfather. Good job I didn't make an ass of myself by saying you were like him. And what's his address?'

'Avon Eastbank. But what's that to do with it?'

'I'll tell you on the way home.'

How mysterious. When they were in the car she said, once they were free of the theatre traffic, 'My own father died when I was very small. I can just remember him. But Dad—my stepfather—has been all I could wish for in a parent.'

'What did your mother do, at first I mean?'

'We went to live with my father's parents in Sydney. My Grandad ran pleasure boats, little ferries, on the harbour. And Granny was sweet. Mother took a job and managed very well. Then when she married again, they became very fond of Athol. Doesn't always work out but this did.'

'Perhaps that's why you've fitted in so well with Henriette and Thérèse. You've always lived with older folk.'

'Possibly. Gran and Grandad were like Henriette and Thérèse, all super kind of people. They were sad when my stepfather moved to New Zealand, but they made the best of it and spent many holidays with us in Auckland. Later Dad was transferred down here, then when Mother died I got a transfer so I could keep house for them. I'm so glad you backed up the invitation to Dad and Beth Harding, Edouard, and the fact they can come alone ought to give them a chance to get to know each other better, though perhaps they get some time to themselves at her place.'

'Yes, but it sounds as if it gets cluttered up with grandchildren. Not conducive to romance. I take it the others in your family are half-sisters or brothers?'

'Yes, Noel would be sweet about this, I think. He's at Varsity and his girlfriend is a dear. Sylvie's quite adaptable but Kerry, I'm afraid, is rather selfish. Not altogether her fault. In fact some of the blame could be mine. I was so much older I spoiled her when she was tiny till Mum and Dad realised it and nipped it in the bud. So I always feel a bit responsible for her faults. As if I owed Kerry something.'

His voice was harsh. 'How surprising! Then you mustn't think that any longer. Look, I'll draw in, just past the next gateway.'

Monique said diffidently, 'Won't it make you too late? You have such long days. Can't you explain as you go? I can't imagine what——'

There was a faint radiance raying up over the high-rise buildings that indicated the moon was at last rising. Two Lombardy poplars in some city garden stood in blacker silhouette against the nearer greyness, and the Avon near by sang its endless and gentle song. Even here, in the city bounds, there seemed just themselves and the world of night.

She turned to him, 'Yes, Edouard? What has Kerry to do with you? Can you have met her? But——'

He put his right hand across and laid it on both of hers as they lay in her lap, loosely clasped. That brought his left shoulder against her. She wished his nearness didn't make her so breathless.

Edouard said, 'We had so little time that day at the airport. It was telescoped into so short a space. I naturally expected your father to be Belfield too. You scribbled your telephone number down. I don't usually ask girls I've just met for their numbers. I was rather surprised at myself that day. I kept on leaping in.' He gave a strange little laugh. 'You'll think me crazy but the day you went thump into me and yelled at me for denting your hat, you made quite an impression. Oh, sorry, a bad pun, but not intended. Never mind. It seemed like a moment suspended in time . . . a girl all goldy-brown hair and velvet and lime-green and buttercups and daisies sort of thrown at you one moment, then gone forever. It seemed idyllic.

'Then suddenly, Whang! She's back in my life again. I felt off-balance. Thought I'd come to my senses on the plane, especially with the prosaic tasks ahead of me, all speeches and reports, facts and figures. Should've brought me down to earth. Didn't. So on a mad impulse I sent those roses. Monique, you did get the card, didn't you? I rather let myself go. Did you have a glimmer of which of Robbie's poems I meant?'

She was silent momentarily. He was going rather too fast for her. He heard her gulp, then she found the courage to say, 'Yes, I don't know many of his but— but did know that one.'

She heard the smile in his voice. 'Good. We'll leave that for the moment. I couldn't get you out of my mind. The time stretched like an eternity before I could return and seek you out. I so wanted to hear that husky voice of yours again.'

She couldn't help but laugh. 'It was nothing less than a yell the day I was rushing to the church.'

'Granted. But at the airport, your voice got me.'

Monique felt bewildered. She'd known unhappiness

ever since that day Edouard had returned to be
furious at finding her installed at the place where he
lived; she couldn't believe there was anything to
explain. What——'

Edouard said, 'I just *had* to hear that voice again. I
even slightly panicked thinking you'd said you were
leaving Montmorency's, and I'd no idea where you
were going. I was sure I ought to have insisted on
knowing. I could hardly barge in and ask your boss and
ex-boyfriend where you'd gone, when I'd been calling
you darling in front of him and showering you with
violets and sweeping you off to lunch! I thought if I
rang you from Canberra, you might be able to tell me
by then what job you were moving on to.

'So I 'phoned. It was one of those calls that took a
little time to connect, because of course I had to make it
person-to-person. I knew you might be anywhere but at
home. I heard someone answer, and the operator ask if
that was the number? Then she said, "Mr Edouard
Fergusson is calling Miss Monique Belfield. Is she
available please?" I thought in a moment I'd hear your
voice. Then the voice at Christchurch said, "Miss
Monique Belfield? There's no one living here of that
name. Perhaps it's a wrong number."

'The operator checked with me, then with the other
number, even asked was she sure no one of that name
lived here, was it perhaps a guest-house? The voice said,
"No, a private house," and it sounded very final. I
managed to get in to ask could I please speak to the one
who'd answered the call. I told her this Miss Belfield
was going to a new position, though didn't know where,
but she had herself written her number down. There
was a pause then a voice said pertly, "I'm afraid that's
an old dodge. It sounds as if you didn't know this
woman well. So she didn't tell you where she was going,
and deliberately put a wrong number down. It's well
known and it works if you don't want a new acquaintance
following you up. She's probably got a jealous boyfriend
or husband. Sorry to be so blunt, but I can't help you,"
And she hung up. Until now I hadn't a glimmer of what
had happened, though even now it beats me why.'

Monique said, 'But what's it mean? You seem to have a glimmer now. I certainly haven't. I *must've* copied the wrong number down. It's possible. That's all it could be.'

'Listen. In the first moment of that incident when the person at the Christchurch end answered the ring, I heard her say her name. She wouldn't dream I'd heard it or she wouldn't have taken the chance. She said: "Kerry Lethbridge here." Darling, I don't want to make trouble in your family but that's what happened.'

There was a moment of stunned silence. He increased the pressure of his hand upon hers to give her a moment to take it in. He said, 'I was sure there was some mistake. I had to wait till I got back. Straight off the plane I went to the Christchurch directory. There wasn't a Belfield in it. So I went to the Chief Post Office. They have a directory of just numbers, you know. I found the number and instead of Belfield, that number had A. M. Lethbridge against it. So that was that. I concluded you *must've* taken that way of brushing me off just as Kerry had said. Perhaps because I'd been a witness to your boyfriend plotting with another woman to jilt you. I'd like to tear Kerry's liver out. She's going to know it didn't work. She'd never dream I'd be at Beauchamp House, any more than you did. But don't get upset about it. That was sheer malice or jealousy or something. But please don't let it spoil our night.'

He felt her move a fraction nearer him. 'Oh, Edouard, it hardly matters ... not against the devastation I felt when you didn't want me at Port Beauchamp. This doesn't matter alongside that. Kerry has an awkward nature. She's her own worst enemy. But oh, I felt so bewildered, so hurt, Edouard, when you let fly at me. I thought you were angry at having your own domain invaded. And I loved Thérèse and Henriette so much I couldn't bear to leave them, but I didn't know if—if I *could* stay if you hated me being there. I felt a real cuckoo in the nest. I——'

All of a sudden there was a hand covering her mouth. 'Quiet, Monique. It's always horrible to think you are

living in the same house as someone who resents your
being there. I hate to think I made you suffer that. And
of course it was unthinkable to let the two dear old
ladies down. In fact you couldn't have. The wheels had
started to turn. But . . . but was that the only bugbear?
Was that the only hurt?'

His arms came about her the way they had at the
Lookout above the Onawe Peninsula, but this time he
had to slip them under her fleecy jacket. He put his chin
against the side of her head, 'Monique, I asked you a
question. Look, I've told you I felt devastated when it
seemed as if you'd given me a false number to brush me
off. How about you? How did you feel about *my*
apparent change of feeling?'

She found courage then, moved her cheek against his
caressingly. 'It's a moment for honesty, isn't it, Edouard?'

He was smiling, she knew. 'It is. So . . .?'

'I couldn't credit you wouldn't follow up your
flowers with a 'phone call. That was the only thing
about being able to leave the showroom early. But I left
messages with the family, that if you rang, they were to
give you the Beauchamp House number and address. I
must admit I rang Noel one day, asked had there been a
ring. He's a darling. He said no, but he'd make sure the
others were reminded about this. I looked for your
name in the Akaroa telephone listing but you weren't
there, and though I knew your mother's address from
sending the clock there for you, pride wouldn't let me
ask for you there.

'Then came the opening day at Beauchamp House
and it had been such a success and you suddenly
appeared on the drive. It was like a mini-miracle. I
thought you'd got my address from home and had
come to seek me out. Then Jen Stevens said, "Oh look,
here's Mac . . ." at the very moment I saw your face
change from surprise to wrath. I panicked and fled to
the kitchen and you——'

He filled in for her, 'And I, great stupid hulk that I
am, said, "What the hell are *you* doing here?" Oh,
Monique, forgive me. But my stupid pride had suffered
a setback too.'

This time she was the one to stem back the words that were spilling off his tongue, 'Edouard, don't. It wasn't your fault. Kerry made the mischief. It wasn't my fault either. Let's be glad about that. It was horrible to have disharmony and distrust in that lovely old house, but none of it had any real foundation. And ... and in spite of everything we——' She realised she was giving too much away and turned against him, and his mouth moved swiftly across her glowing cheek till it found her mouth. And stayed there.

No wonder she'd decided to end things with Clint. When had she ever known rapture like this? This was what the poets sang about. How odd that one could know so suddenly. Strange that sometimes, because she'd never felt stirred to her depths like this, she'd wondered if she was slightly cold in her emotions. It had taken Edouard's touch, his nearness, his seeking, to bring her to full existence. And with it all, more than that, there was a kinship, a sharing of things loved and enjoyed by both, even a mingling of buried racial memories, somewhere back in Europe. She wondered if he, too, during the long sweetness of this kiss, was thinking conscious thoughts? But one couldn't ask so foolish a thing.

Gradually Edouard came up for air. She could see the outlines of his face faintly. He said, 'Know what I was thinking?'

She could have laughed. 'No, but I'd like you to tell me.'

'That you were meant to bump into me that day and make such an impression that your image stayed so clearly with me. Otherwise I don't think I'd have lingered so long in the shop. One moment I was thinking that this girl I'd been asked to look at, to meet, had probably diddled Henriette and Thérèse out of a valuable possession and I'd jolly well clear out without meeting her, and the next *you* were there ... the girl in the lime-green dress. Who could've thought we'd have so much in common. As we have.'

She stayed against him, well-content. After a while he said, 'What a day. First the news about the sketches,

though that matters very little against this ... getting
our lines uncrossed. Now we can start again.' His hand
rubbed against the back of hers.

She said, 'Edouard, we must stir. We have a long
drive home.'

'Yes, I know, and I'm going to love every metre of it.
But——'

She sensed reluctance in his tone and was glad he
didn't want to move. But she was wrong.

'Monique, I don't want to introduce a jarring note
but there's something that must be straightened out,
otherwise Kerry will feel only that she didn't succeed
after all, in keeping us apart. Your father was taking
his lady-love to supper so won't be in for a while. I'd
like to go to your house and tell Kerry that I know
she deliberately tried to stop us meeting again, and
that she must never again try to make mischief
between two people. She may resent your father
marrying again, and anyone capable of what she did
to us, might try something there. She must know that
spite doesn't pay off. It will spike her guns in that
other direction.'

Had he not put it that way, Monique might not have
consented, but Dad deserved his second chance of
happiness. He was surprised she didn't argue. 'I think
that's fair enough. I know you won't bawl her out.'

He burst out laughing. 'How can you know that? I
bawled *you* out, that's for sure.' Monique said nothing,
and he added, 'Of course that was because I cared so
much.'

She told him the way to Avon Eastbank. They had
luck with them. Noel was out with Merle, and Sylvie
was spending the night with a friend. Monique used her
key and before she could call out, Kerry sung out 'Is
that you, Dad?'

'No, it's Monique. I want you to meet someone,
Kerry,' and opened the door into the lounge. Kerry
uncrossed her legs from where she was relaxing on a
couch with a book and stood up. Her eyes widened as
she took in her sister's elegance, and the undeniably
good looks of her escort.

'Why, hullo, Monny. What brings you here at this time? Do you want a bed for the night? Have you——'

But Edouard got in, 'No, we're going right home to Port Beauchamp.'

Kerry looked surprised, Monique could imagine the thoughts flitting through her mind, probably, 'My, my, Port Beauchamp must be full of surprises,' or some such thing.

She said swiftly, 'Kerry, I want you to meet Edouard Fergusson. You heard about him before I left home. When he sent me those roses. You were in the shop when they arrived, remember? Edouard, this is my young half-sister, Kerry Lethbridge.'

Kerry recovered herself after a moment of surprise. 'Oh, so you live at Port Beauchamp too, how strange, I hadn't known that.'

Edouard's face set itself into grim lines. 'Neither did Monique, come to that. Of course you didn't know, Kerry, or you'd never have pretended that no one called Monique Belfield was known at this address when I rang from Canberra.'

There was a moment of complete silence and shock. Kerry's nonchalance deserted her, her mouth fell open, her eyes became slightly glazed, her skin went a queer mottled hue.

Then she closed her mouth, swallowed, said feebly, 'I—well—I——'

His voice was gentle, but somehow frightening. 'There just aren't any words, are there? No excuse possible. And your suggestion that this girl you pretended never to have heard of, had given me a wrong number as a brush-off, was one of the most despicable things I've ever heard of. I can only conclude you were jealous of Monique having been left this money for a year of freedom. I think this Amabel must've been a very astute woman when she decreed just that. But for the fact that unknown to Monique I was farming the land round Beauchamp House, it could have made permanent mischief.'

Kerry had to say something. Edouard waited meaningly. She swallowed again, said, 'That seems very strange to me. I mean one hears of coincidences but——'

'Oh, it was no coincidence. Henriette and Thérèse asked me to go into Montmorency's to make the acquaintance of this girl who had visited them about antiques. I did, got bowled over by her, but had no idea that she was thinking of offering her services to Beauchamp House. It was a wonderful moment when on my return from Australia I found her graciously conducting a coachload of sightseers round our stately home!'

Monique saw Kerry bite her lip. It served her right, yet Monique knew a pang for her, the little sister she'd loved and looked after. What could she do? She knew Edouard was right, this could check Kerry making mischief for anyone else, especially for Dad.

Kerry said stiffly, 'How did you find out?'

His voice was smooth. 'Your father was at the theatre tonight. Monique introduced us. Till then I'd no idea she had a stepfather. Even then she just said Dad.'

Kerry's mottled colour ebbed. 'Then . . . does Dad know?'

'No. You were fortunate. But any hint of further mischief, say between your father and the woman he was with tonight, and I'll see he does. Just as we were leaving them a passing acquaintance said, "Hullo, Mr Lethbridge." I instantly connected it with the voice I'd heard answering that ring from Canberra. It had said: "Kerry Lethbridge speaking." You hadn't realised the caller was already on the line. It gave me a nasty jar tonight. I don't like to think Monique was exposed to such malice. Well, it was a petty bit of feline spite, so best forgotten, but it gave both Monique and myself some painful moments till we got it sorted out.'

Monique caught Kerry's eye and threw everything she had into an appeal to respond to this gesture.

Kerry drew in an uneven breath, said, 'Th-thank you. I—I'd been upset that Monique was leaving us. About her aunt thinking we were leaning on her too much. I— I apologise.' She gulped, 'Thank you for not telling Dad. C-can I make you a cup of tea or something before you take on that drive?'

He smiled, quite nicely considering the circumstances.

'No, I guess it would be tactful for us to take off before your father gets home. If we run into him on the way, Monique will say she remembered something she wanted to pick up. By the way, Athol and Beth are coming for a weekend soon. Let them come by themselves. I'd like you and the others to come another weekend. Nothing will be said about this. As far as I'm concerned it's wiped clean.'

As they drove off, he sensed Monique was restraining tears. He touched her hand. 'No tears, only fair skies are ahead, girl.'

She took his hand, rubbed it over her cheek in gratitude. She agreed. Neither of them could know that across the Tasman where most of the bad weather came from, clouds were gathering.

# CHAPTER NINE

EVERY mile home had been a happy one. No definite
words were spoken to confirm the relationship that
must surely be theirs from now on, but the whole
atmosphere was one of trust. There was a magic about
this night that Monique knew she would remember and
treasure all her life ... and when they began to climb
the hills that formed the Peninsula she knew them in
very truth for the hills of home, the hills of her
ancestors, the hills of a future shared with Edouard.

Tonight was theirs, a world of two. Now wasn't the
time to tell Edouard who she was. But she would be
able to, soon. Perhaps she would tell him first, and
together they would tell Henriette and Thérèse. For
now, the delights of hovering on the brink of falling in
love, were enough.

Henriette and Thérèse had left them their sandwiches
and thermos jug of coffee in the room Philippe and
Louise had called The Little Salon, more than a
hundred years ago. It was set out on a small round
table, with violet-sprinkled china, and the fire they had
lit had burned low, quite an unnecessary luxury on a
night like this, but endearingly intimate, and a curved
sofa was drawn up and a tablelamp lit. 'Bless their
romantic old hearts,' said Edward. 'Let's not disappoint
them, let's make the most of it.' He kissed her.

She was shaken with delicious laughter. 'How absurd
... you can hardly give them full details of this.'

'I could, you know. Not a blow-by-blow description,
but kiss-by-kiss. I wonder if they are blissfully sleeping,
or lying awake, wondering if I'm taking full advantage
of this.'

They weren't, had Edouard and Monique but known.
They were finding it very hard to sleep, or to lie
thinking pleasant thoughts. ...

Downstairs, all unaware, Monique said finally and

firmly, 'Edouard, it's not far off dawn, and you have a big day tomorrow, starting with the loading. It's time we said good night.'

Where the big passage joined the little one he whispered, kissing her again, 'Good night, Monique, and God bless.'

She slept dreamlessly, sure that for them now was a pathway uncluttered by misunderstanding.

They both slept in, rose guiltily and found the two old ladies down before them and with breakfast prepared. Kevin had gone across to his mother's early and would be out in the paddocks now.

Henriette and Thérèse were delighted to hear about the play, interested to know that Monique's stepfather and his new romantic interest had been there.

Edouard said, 'So you knew she had a stepfather, I didn't. Thought he was a Belfield too. They're coming over one weekend soon. Beth Harding is a charming woman. What sort of an evening did you have? Uneventful?'

It was an idle remark but had quite an effect. Henriette and Thérèse were rarely lost for words but they appeared to be struck dumb. Then Thérèse got up, snatched up the toast-rack so quickly the unwanted slices skittered to the floor. She said, 'No matter, they were going on to the bird-table, anyway.'

Henriette rushed to help her pick them up, said, 'Well, you're late enough now, Edouard, don't let us delay you any longer.'

He stretched his legs out, said, 'Come on, you two. Spill it out. Something happened last night. What was it?'

Henriette said, 'Nothing that needs be gone into now, dear boy, we'll see you later about it.'

Edouard looked bland, and implacable. 'I said come on. If it's bad news let's get it over. Facial eczema broken out among the sheep?—Not likely. A stoat got into the hen-house? Or the sketches are fakes after all? Or something personal?'

Henriette said reluctantly, 'There was this ring from

Australia. Someone you met over there. A girl called Emilie.'

Monique saw a tinge of colour rise above Edouard's open collar. She said hastily, 'Look, I've got things to do. A group wanted me to let them know what time next Saturday would be convenient. I'll go into the study and ring their secretary.'

Edouard spoke quickly, 'Don't go. I've been meaning to tell you about this ever since I got back. Only I thought it might come to nothing. I was going to tell you last night, in fact, Monique, but it got overlaid with other things.'

Monique breathed a little easier, though she still thought Edouard looked a little apprehensive. Oh, sheer imagination.

Henriette said flatly, 'Where and how did you meet her, Edouard?'

He said, easily enough, 'Result of a talk they got me to do, not on TV, this one, just radio. In Sydney. The interviewer got interested in the French connection of the Peninsula. Naturally I talked of my own farmlands and how it was once part of the great Beauchamp estate, and this girl's aunt got in touch with me. Rang the station as soon as I finished and gave me her address.

'You know how people like to visit the spot their forbears come from? ... like us going to France as a family once ... it's only natural.' Monique felt Edouard didn't realise how much on the defensive he sounded. He went on, 'I called to see them. This girl lives with her aunt, her parents are dead, and it seems Emilie's grandparents or some such, come from round here. The aunt was keen for her niece to visit here.'

'She certainly was,' said Henriette, with some asperity. 'The girl wasn't pushy but her aunt certainly was. Said you'd invited her niece to come any time and stay with you. I felt I couldn't commit you to that, so I said very coldly, when the aunt got too persistent, about dates and so on, that there were some very good hotels in Akaroa, that it was no distance to this Bay, and I was sure the people down in the Port would help her trace her forbears. But that wasn't the end of it as it should've been. The aunt said she thought I didn't understand, that it was a personal invitation. She actually took me for your housekeeper! I got rather uppish, I'm afraid.'

Edouard grinned, 'I can just imagine it. Wonder you didn't freeze the marrow in her bones. Poor girl, she's not a bit like her aunt, thank goodness. Her aunt embarrasses her. She needs rescuing from her. Go on, my darling warhorse!'

Henriette looked relieved rather than insulted. 'I worried after, in case I'd offended someone you really wanted here.'

'So what did this uppishness consist of?'

Thérèse giggled reminiscently. 'She said: "How extraordinary when Mr Fergusson doesn't even have a house of his own but is a paying guest in ours." You sounded like a squatter, Edouard.'

Henriette said, 'Thérèse, be quiet! I've a feeling it's no laughing matter. This dreadful woman said, "I've no doubt that Edouard will make his own arrangements for Emilie!" Incidentally, she then in a strange voice said, "I should tell you her name is spelt E-m-i-l-i-e." As if I cared how the wretched girl's name was spelt!'

Edouard said rather quickly, 'Perhaps she was stressing that Emilie has French forbears. That's the French spelling, I suppose. And, darling, she isn't a wretched girl, she's really rather sweet. Don't make too much of it. She's not expecting to stay here. That would be her aunt's idea. I'll get someone at the Port to put her up. Or perhaps Mrs Martlett. Anyway, I don't think Emilie even wanted to come. She'll probably refuse and it'll all fade out.'

'That's just it. She's arriving today. The aunt said she had booked her at a hotel in Christchurch and you were to pick her up there this afternoon. She gave me the name. I said tartly that you were in Christchurch at the moment, *with your young lady*, wouldn't be home till the early hours of the morning; would be busy here with shipping all day, and I was quite sure your work programme would preclude you from taking another trip to Christchurch for most of the week! Whereupon the woman said her niece would give you a ring from there and she was quite sure you'd be only too eager to call for her.'

Monique expected ... hoped ... Edouard would swear but he didn't. He merely said, 'Poor Emilie. We must give her as nice a time as possible. She may blossom away from her go-getting aunt. Not to worry, my dears. We'll give her a chance to see where her ancestors came from, then wave her back to Australia from Harewood Airport. It's nothing to worry about.'

Nevertheless, Monique didn't think he had the true ring of confidence in his voice.

'It mightn't be anything to worry about,' said Henriette darkly. 'But you've got involved before and it's led to complications. You let your sympathies run away with you, Edouard.'

He got up, went out of the room whistling, looked back over his shoulder and said with a grin, 'Know what? This is something quite different,' and was gone. Monique thought bleakly, *How* different?

She had a feeling Edouard wouldn't want to discuss Emilie with her. She was wrong. When he knew Henriette and Thérèse had gone out of the room he came back, said hopefully, 'Monique, how about if you picked Emilie up? Say the day after tomorrow? I've got some urgent work to do on the experimental stuff, besides a lot of stock work.'

Monique was surprised at the mean gladness she felt at being able to say with perfect truth, 'Out of the question, I'm afraid. Have you forgotten? That's a big day for the women of this household. A special tour coach. We're opening the house to the Lovers-of-Antiques Society.'

'So you are. Say I ask her to stay another night in Christchurch and you can——'

She said quickly, 'That's out for me too, sorry. No tours, but some folk from the Eteveneaux Museum in Akaroa are coming here at one-thirty to identify some pieces for me. More for dating the probable time of their arrival here. It looks as if you've saddled yourself with one rescued damsel too many, St George!'

If there was a faint asperity in her tone he didn't take offence. He came across, tilted her chin, dropped a quick kiss on her lips, said, 'I'm sure only one particular damsel meant very much in that gallant knight's life . . . but you'll like Emilie. I've a feeling she deserves a good break from that domineering aunt of hers.'

'You must've spent some time with them to have summed her up like that, surely?'

'I did. Accepted a pressing invitation and got really involved. Mind you, I mightn't have done had I not been blazingly mad with a girl I thought had taken a very mean way of seeing I didn't follow her up.' He laughed. 'I had a bit of time to kill before another assignment over there and the redoubtable aunt latched on to me.'

She shrugged, 'So you rode off looking for a dragon and found one. You really need a nanny to keep you away from them, which is most surprising, a great big hulking brute like you!'

He chuckled. 'Methinks the lady doth woo me with tender speech! You're almost shrewish this morning, my love. Perhaps late nights don't agree with you. And I don't need a nanny to protect me . . . a wife would do. Think on that!'

She laughed, 'What I really think is you'd better be off to your cocksfoot and Tahora white clover. I can't spare any time this week worrying over your clinging vines.'

Henriette was inclined to be grittily annoyed about the visit. 'That woman! I thought I was sparing Edouard a rather presuming result of a chance encounter and she reacted as if I was a jealous mother-in-law trying to stop this niece re-uniting with her true love! I'm pretty sure that when it was mentioned the girl's forbears came from here, Edouard would only say, "Why not come across some time and see the place? You could look us up."'

Monique felt she must be fair. 'I daresay there's more to it than that. I don't think anyone would've picked him up on so casual a reference. And from what Edouard told me just now he spent some time with them and thought the girl needed a spell away from aunty!'

'Then he's a bigger fool than I took him for. And it's decidedly odd when it's our house he lives in.'

Thérèse said, 'Henriette, what's got into you? You asked Edouard to look on this as his own home. He asks Eugenie and Francine and her family over here quite often. You were even disgruntled when he took that rather ugly room of Emile's, thought he should have one with a better view.'

'You know quite well that's entirely different. That woman was no class at all.'

Monique laughed, came across to her, put an arm round her, said, 'Now, now, Henriette, snobbery rears its ugly head and that's not like you. This Emilie may be an engaging little thing, needing a break, interested in a family background and she needn't disturb us, she'll be just a ripple on the surface, soon here, soon gone. Let us not be daunted!'

The moment she said that last bit she wanted to snatch the words back. But that was silly. It wasn't as if it was in truth the motto of the Beauchamps. It was just something a little boy had written in the front of a book. He'd lived by it all his life, and had been an exceptionally happy man, which was something to be thankful for, remembering. His young sisters may never have known of that boyhood fancy.

At lunch Edouard announced that Mrs Martlett would put Emilie up and that furthermore, as Kevin wanted to go to Christchurch, he'd pick her up, though not till Friday. Mrs Martlett was interested, wondered if her own old father might've known the family. 'But I had to tell her they're very vague about the connection. Evidently Emilie's grandparents died young and had never said very much about their early days. In fact it might've been a great-grandparent who was from here. The aunt is on her mother's side and knows the family tree there from A to Z and feels Emilie should know both sides.' Monique thought he then went very quickly over to farm topics.

They were terrifically busy the next day or two which was as well. One moment Monique felt it was just as well she hadn't let Edouard prolong that sweet hour in the Little Salon when she'd felt he was rushing things too much, in the wave of joy at knowing they had cleared up their misunderstandings, the next moment she longed to have him declare himself. Yet she felt as if she had known him for ever. In one of her grandfather's poetry books, tucked into a drawer of the *kauri* davenport she loved so much for his sake, a short poem said it for her.

'It cannot be that once there was a time
　When you, my love, had dawned not on my world,
My second self, past reason and past rhyme,
　You came so secretly, like grass dew-pearled
To add a lustre to the earth I love,
　To so enhance each step upon my way,
Until it seems to me that heaven above
　Fashioned you for me out of yesterday.'

It expressed exactly her feelings, as if he'd always been in the wings, waiting. That was why no other man had really stirred her, caught her imagination, wholly possessed her, body, soul and mind.

If they could have spent more time together it might have been easier, more reassuring, but it was hideously busy. As it was, Edouard wasn't only engaged on his own farming work, he was writing reports at night, keeping in touch with Lincoln College by phone. Sometimes he shut himself into the study and talked for ages there.

Twice he asked Monique to keep the other two women away, he didn't want to be disturbed. She thought his manner strange when he said, 'Henriette bursts in you know, eager as a schoolgirl, talking before she gets the handle turned.'

Monique thought it rather engaging that someone Henriette's age could still be eager, even naïve. But then Edouard added, 'In fact for the next hour I'd be glad if none of you interrupted.'

She was careful not to sound resentful, said, 'You're

quite safe, mate, we've got so much on our plate preparing for tomorrow we won't want to be bothered with mere men! Short of fire or haemorrhage we'll not disturb you. With us, too, business must come first.'

A pity then that Smoke, the big grey cat, who loved the wing chair in the study above all chairs, started to scratch at that door. Monique pounced on him to carry him off and heard Edouard say clearly, 'I hope you'll love it here, Emilie. It may lack the excitement of Sydney, but it is very beautiful. Casts a spell on people. They never want to leave it.' Didn't sound like business! And the 'phone hadn't rung, so it wasn't as if Emilie had rung him. Was this the call he'd wanted such privacy for? The shining beauty of the day dimmed for Monique. Why did this girl have to appear here now? Would life ever be the same after she came? A strange tremor ran over Monique.

Oh, stop it. It was stupid to think the magic of the hours they had known the night of the play could carry on at that pitch. There had to be ordinary moments sandwiched in between the peak times. But they'd been so busy since, she almost felt those transports were being erased.

It mightn't have mattered if Edouard hadn't been so preoccupied, so withdrawn, except when he made a conscious effort, like at meals; if Henriette hadn't been so crochety, unable to keep from returning, mosquito-like to the subject of That Girl who'd be arriving soon, and Monique was sure she wasn't just imagining that Edouard evaded the issue every time Henriette raised it. Only once was he definite and said irritably, 'Henriette, I agree the aunt is impossible, but is that Emilie's fault any more than it was your fault your father was harsh and overbearing? Wait till you meet her. Emilie would disarm a saint *or* a despot!'

He'd gone out immediately. His horse was tethered just outside and it looked to the three women as if he wanted to ride his temper off. Thérèse said mildly, 'Henriette, that's the wrong technique. Much better to welcome the wretched girl here. If she's shoddy it'll show up; no entertainments, everyone busy, nothing to do. You are only antagonising Edouard.'

To Monique's surprise, Henriette took no offence, shrugged, grinned, said, 'Maybe there's more of Father in me than I thought. I'm quite surprised at the enmity I feel towards that woman who rang.'

Monique hugged her. 'Henriette, you old humbug. It's no use you pretending to be a dragon . . . you've a heart of butter. At present it's in deep freeze, but it'll melt. Edouard thinks Emilie will disarm you. You'll see.'

She dropped a kiss on the crêpey old cheek and went out. As she shut the door she heard Henriette say to Thérèse, 'She ought to be jealous!' Monique continued upstairs, a hand to her throat to still its throb. She *was* jealous.

Edouard came in at ten, no hint of anger or strain about him, chaffed Henriette, who looked relieved. She had made his favourite ginger gems for him in case he had time for coffee. He had. He sorted through his mail that Monique had collected from the gate, then said, 'Nothing urgent. I'll attend to it tonight. Girls, I'll be in sharp at twelve for lunch. I'll just *have* to pick Emilie up today. I've neglected her long enough. I'll get her myself. She's such a shy little thing she might find it a bit of an ordeal driving eighty kilometres back with Kevin, a stranger to her. I'm off now to move those electric fences a bit nearer the headland. The men are busy in the yards. See you at noon.'

He'd been gone twenty minutes when the 'phone rang and a voice that could only have been Emilie's, asked for Edouard. Monique felt her pulses quicken. The voice faltered a little. 'Is—is that Beauchamp House? Is—is Mr Fergusson there, please?'

There was quite a pause so that Monique said, 'Are you still on the line?' The voice had a distinct wobble now, 'I—yes—oh, dear, I wish he was there, just when I've made up my mind. I—don't know what to do.'

Monique couldn't help responding to the childish quiver. 'I think you must be Emilie. Look, if it's any help to you, before Mr Fergusson went out after morning-tea, he said he really must go in and get you this afternoon. We've been frantically busy or one of us would've been in for you before now.'

Another pause, then words tumbling out. 'I realise it's been inconvenient, that's the whole trouble. I just don't want to come, now. I wouldn't dream of foisting myself on strangers. I never did want to come, only my aunt got a bee in her bonnet about it. I don't care where my forbears lived. I don't even think the ones who lived there were any great shakes. I'm just being a nuisance and Edouard was so sweet about it. He was even nice to my aunt and most people don't even like her. He—Oh, I've never met anyone like him before, so kind, so chivalrous. But I'm not going to be hung round his neck like the albatross in that poem. It's not fair to him. Aunt will be furious but I just don't care.' There was a distinct sound of a hiccupping tone, then, 'Anyway, she can be furious all she likes because I'm not going back. I'll stay here and get a job. I like Christchurch. I'm sick of being pushed round and foisted on to people. I think I can get a job in Heathcote. I saw some advertised for there. So—so will you please tell Edouard he doesn't need to bother about me any more? I'll be fine. Everyone thinks I'm not capable of standing on my own feet but I am, if I ever get the chance. Will you tell him that, please?'

Monique's feelings underwent a complete change, an instinctive response to that forlorn, desperate voice. She said quickly, 'Emilie, don't disappear. Please don't do that. Stay right where you are and wait for Edouard. We feel so badly about not getting to you sooner, but there were things we couldn't postpone. You see we now open this old French Colonial home to the public on certain days. Not like a private house any more. That was the only reason for the delay.'

'Who are you? Are you his sister? But you sound Australian?'

'I am Australian, but my mother married a New Zealander and I've lived here for years. I gave up my job quite recently to run this place. I think you ought to come to see where your forbears lived. It's different from any other place in New Zealand, with its French connection. I haven't known Edouard Fergusson long, but I know he'd be really upset if you didn't come. Now please, don't do anything foolish. Edouard specially asked for an early lunch so he could get you. Don't, what ever happens, leave the hotel. I promise you he'll be there.'

'All right ... only please tell him if he'd rather I didn't come, it doesn't matter. I'll just get myself a job here. I've got quite a bit of money with me. I'll get board that's cheaper than this. But if he does want to come ... oh, dear, I can't convince myself he does. Aunt was just awful doing this. I say, if I do wait, would you come too? You sound nice.'

Monique hesitated, 'If it's okay with Edouard I will. I can't say more than that. But promise me you'll wait, Emilie.'

Emilie promised. Monique put the 'phone down, stared at it, then jumped as Henriette's voice said behind her, 'I can't believe what I've just heard. It sounded as if she'd changed her mind about coming here and you've changed it back! Have you no natural feelings at all? You ought to be jealous.'

Monique took Henriette's hands. 'Darling one, you're matchmaking. You're sweet to want it, but it can be embarrassing. Edouard and I got off on the wrong foot about something very early in our acquaintance. But the night we went to the play it got all cleared up when he met my stepfather. Earlier, in Australia, Emilie's aunt got in touch with him when he talked about this property. When he visited them and saw what a thin time Emilie was having, all his chivalrous instincts were roused. Now Emilie's got out from under the dominance of her aunt, she doesn't want to go back. Thinks she'll get a job in Christchurch. We must bring her here first. Jobs aren't easy to get. How about putting lunch on, and I'll get Edouard?'

Henriette said slowly, 'Monique, be careful. We don't want any more spanners in the works, but if you must be as tender-hearted as Edouard, I suppose I can't stop you. Remember, this might be just another way of appealing to Edouard, threatening to run away. Thérèse and I have plans for you that are nothing to do with matchmaking. We don't want them to come to nothing because you, like Edouard, let your sympathies run away with you. Go and find him and Heaven help you!'

Monique ran her car out and took the hill track. Edouard was just coming away from moving the sheep on their next rotational grazing. He dismounted, waited for her to come up to him. She told him. He looked appalled. 'That's the last straw. She mustn't disappear. Her aunt would raise hell and hold me responsible. I want her to see this place anyway. She must.'

She *must*? Monique felt as if someone had stabbed her. Why did it matter to Edouard that Emilie should see this place? She felt as if those few words had nullified all that had happened between them the night of the play. What had happened between Edouard and Emilie in Australia? She thought she knew. She owed all this to Kerry. Edouard had admitted he'd felt very sore that Monique had, apparently, deliberately given him a wrong telephone number. This Emilie had then come into his life, exactly the type to appeal to this modern man with the St George complex, when his masculine ego and pride had been bruised. He had promised her hospitality, yes, but had it been more than that? Had he hoped she might fall in love with the setting here?

Monique felt a bitter taste in her mouth. Oh, Kerry, Kerry! She said crisply, 'Of course she mustn't be allowed to disappear. I felt dreadful. There was something so lonely and lost about her. I'd have promised her anything just to keep her there till you can get to her. I hope this suits you, Edouard, but she begged me to come, too. So you're stuck with me. I couldn't let her down.'

To her surprise his face cleared. 'Thank heaven. Emilie is like a badly broken horse. Shies away from any hint of disapproval. If I arrive and browbeat her into coming here, she'll give any onlookers the impression I'm kidnapping her. At least you can appear in the guise of a chaperone.'

'Now that's a role I really fancy,' said Monique in a tart tone which wasn't lost on Edouard.

'Now don't *you* go all up-stage on me, I've got enough troubles with Henriette. I didn't mean you were dowager type, nit.'

'Well, don't try your luck too far.' She was surprised to find a tide of real anger rising in her. Edouard made an exasperated sound, grabbed her by the upper arms in a grip that hurt, said, shaking her, 'Stop it! Temper doesn't suit you. Where's the girl I took to the play gone? What do I do to get back on that pliable, co-operative footing?'

He laughed, a laugh she thought positively arrogant, bent his head, kissed her in a hard, taking way. She was strained against him, resistance in every fibre of her being. He took his mouth from hers, still holding her tightly, demanded, 'Well . . . any go?'

She couldn't help it. Her right hand clenched itself into a fist and she beat it against his chest. 'The lordly male! That's more likely to make me refuse to come with you. This situation's got nothing to do with kissing. Besides, I'm not worried about *you*. I am about this Emilie. She sounded such a child, and desperate.'

He looked rueful immediately. 'She is. She's twenty, but could be fifteen. Very appealing, in an old-fashioned sort of way. Not a modern self-sufficient girl at all. We can't even talk it over on the way, because I met Kevin and he's changed his appointment with his friend to this afternoon.'

Monique said urgently, 'Stop holding me, Edouard. For one thing I'll be bruised. For another Nicko is trotting away.'

He shrugged. 'I'll ride back with you. He'll chase along after us once you start up. Come on.'

All of a sudden the rage left Monique. She wouldn't admit that Edouard's touch, his nearness, his lips had done this to her, left her with a delicious weakness.

She started off. Edouard wasn't looking at the track ahead, he was studying her, perhaps calculating how much help she could be to him in a ticklish situation. Just let him try! Apart from feeling on the 'phone that here was a distraught, bewildered child, she wasn't going to be drawn in too far. He could jolly well get himself out of any fix his quixotic nature had led him into.

She embarked on small talk, said, 'When I get those old photographs and portraits I found in the lumber-room cleaned up, and their frames re-gilded, I wondered what you'd think about putting them all along that wide passage at the front stair-head? I feel they'd lose their effect scattered through the house, but together, they'd make a portrait gallery effect, and if in chronological order, they'd be a potted history. Some of them must have been done in France, because there is one of Louise which must have been done long before she married Philippe. They aren't masterpieces but they aren't flops, either.'

Edouard said, 'That's the eye of the expert picking them out. To me they'd probably be just a bunch of old photographs. I think it's a splendid idea. I do remember one of Helmut Schmidt, the son-in-law of Philippe. A fine-looking man.'

'Yes, I thought that too. I haven't quite finished them.'

'I'll give you a hand with them, Monique. When we've restored them, I'll hang them for you. After Emilie gets here.'

*After Emilie's coming.* But how much would her coming mean to them?


Edouard drove much faster than usual. She was glad when they dropped Kevin and reached the hotel. They parked at the rear. Edouard said, 'Come on . . . I have a feeling she may have changed her mind between speaking to you and now.'

'Your imagination is running away with you. She's probably making up her face right now, all eagerness to meet you.'

She was wrong. The receptionist said, 'Miss Emilie Fairlea? I'm afraid she booked out less than five minutes ago. What a shame. You've just missed her. She got us to call a taxi.'

'Where to?' demanded Edouard. The receptionist looked surprised. 'I've no idea. We rarely know a destination, unless they call for a taxi for the airport or station. I'm——' but she spoke to empty air. Edouard had grabbed Monique's arm and was rushing her outside.

As they descended the steps at a rate that was positively dangerous, he said, 'Look up and down the street . . . if a girl's getting into a cab, yell and grab her. I'll go back and ask which company . . . we might trace it that way . . . oh, there she is . . .'

A girl had emerged from behind a pillar, a case in her hand, just as a taxi drew up. For a man who'd said earlier he didn't want to look as if he were kidnapping someone, Edouard appeared completely oblivious to public opinion. His bellowed: 'Emilie!' stopped all passers-by in their tracks. He took the last two steps in one bound and got there as the driver got out to open the door for his fare.

Emilie dropped her case, swung round. Monique stood transfixed, as Edouard grabbed her, barked out, 'You little idiot! Where do you think you're going?'

The taxi driver rushed round said, 'Hold it, mate. Maybe the lady *wants* to go where she's going!' The passers-by decided to stay to watch. Edouard became aware of how it sounded, said in a different tone, 'Darling girl, you promised to wait till Monique got here . . . here she is.'

Monique decided she must save the split-personality knight from himself, rushed up, said, 'Emilie . . . here I am . . . did you think we were never coming?' She turned to the burly, belligerent driver and said with all the charm she could muster, 'It's all right. This is my shy little cousin from Australia. We live way out in the country and got prevented from coming here for almost three days. No wonder you began to think we didn't want you, Emilie. She finds the thought of meeting dozens of strange relatives most daunting, but I assure you, Emilie, they're right now getting the fatted calf ready.'

The taxi-driver, having heard this mixed-up speech, turned to Emilie, and said, 'Is this true? You just got tired of waiting for them? I must make sure it's on the level, I've got a daughter your age.'

Monique's eyes lit up, 'How lovely to find someone who cares about what happens to other people. I think we ought to identify ourselves in case you feel uneasy. I'm sure my friend here doesn't carry cards, farmers, as a rule, don't, but I do.' She flicked open her bag, drew out one of her business cards. Claude had always done his employees well, the card was artistic, almost ornate. It bore Monique's photo and announced: 'Monique of Montmorency's, our authorised buyer of antiques.' Monique turned, said, 'And this is Mr Edouard Fergusson of the Beauchamp House Estate, Port Beauchamp. It's just past Little Akaroa. You may have heard of it.'

The passers-by decided it was a tame affair and moved on. The taxi-driver's face cleared, 'You mean that property that featured in last Saturday night's paper? Why, there was a photo of you in it, with two old ladies.' Monique beamed. 'Yes, and this is my cousin from Sydney, who is going to assist us. I wonder if you'd like to come to see the House sometime? Bring your family.'

She surprised a slightly staggered look on Edouard's face and had to control a surge of laughter. Edouard wasn't used to being rescued ... he usually played the role of rescuer. However, he came to himself, pulled out his wallet, said, 'I'm most grateful to you for your concern, sir, and of course you mustn't be out of pocket because of a wild goose chase. No, no, keep the change ... and we'll be delighted to see you any time you can make it.'

The cab drove off and the three were left looking at each other. For the first time Monique took stock of Emilie ... a cloud of dark hair, the deepest of blue eyes, an exquisite mouth, a matt-white skin tinged now with a wild rose colour, an oval chin with a faint cleft ... not quite the childish figure she had imagined, rather an elegance that spoke of breeding. Not what one would have expected as the niece of the woman Henriette had described. In fact she was quite too tiresomely lovely.

Oh, what an awful thing to think! What on earth was the matter with her? Monique hardly knew herself.

Emilie wasn't looking at Edouard, her eyes were fixed on Monique. She stammered a little. 'F-fancy you being as quick-witted as that. Oh, how I wish I could do things like that. B-but I can't. I panic.'

Monique took hold of the outstretched hands, said, 'So did I at your age. Not to worry. Like blushing, it passes as the years go by.'

Edouard said, 'I feel quite eclipsed. I had a frightful feeling that taxi-driver was going to say it was a matter for the police.'

Monique said severely, 'No wonder. It was your own fault. Grabbing her like that. A runaway wife and an angry husband was written all over you. You're usually far more in control of your wits when you're rescuing damsels. And no one could say you lack practice!'

Emilie stared, then said, 'Aren't you fun? I'd never dare speak to Edouard like that.' She giggled, the look of strain on the small face breaking up.

Edouard said, 'I should think not. There wasn't time to be subtle. Emilie, you speak balm to my soul. I get no respect from this jade at my side.'

Emilie giggled still more. Perhaps that was what Edouard wanted. '*You* make everything sound fun, too. I'm so glad you caught me.'

Edouard's face softened in a way Monique had never seen. This girl made him feel all protective. Monique felt that way towards her too, but she didn't want Edouard to look like that for another woman, so she said crisply, 'We're not meeting Kevin till three-thirty, what shall we do till then?'

'Well, seeing we're picking him up at Francine's, we'll go there now. That's my sister, Emilie. You won't be able to feel shy with her. Kevin was delivering some tools he'd borrowed to a friend of his who lives in the next street. Right, let's go.' He picked up her case, 'This all you've got? Now, I do like a girl who travels light.'

Emilie said to Monique, 'I saw that article and photo too, that the taximan saw. It made me more scared than ever. You all looked as if you'd stepped out of yesterday. And belonged. I don't know a thing about antiques.'

Monique shrugged, 'It was just because of our clothes. That dress I wore belonged to the old ladies' mother. It makes me feel like that portrait of Lawrence's ... do you know it? It's called *Pinkie*. *You* probably have other interests about which *I'd* be dumb. What do you like doing best?'

Unexpectedly Emilie answered, 'Bird-watching. I've read up about New Zealand birds. You have a lot of English birds here, too, don't you?'

Monique nodded, 'Some we don't have, like robins or wagtails or jays, but we're getting swallows now. And our native birds are lovely.'

Edouard said with enthusiasm, 'Then you'll love the Peninsula. I know all their haunts. We'll love showing you. Kevin, too, is fast becoming an expert, with a special interest in sea-birds.'

'He can have that on his own,' said Monique. 'I've no head for scaling cliffs.'

Edouard looked down on her, his mouth softening, 'What a relief to find something something at which you don't excel, Monique Belfield.'

Emilie said immediately, 'Belfield? ... You said you were from Australia ... there used to be a lovely old man who ran pleasure boats at a little bay on Sydney Harbour. He once——'

Monique's eyes were starry immediately, 'Emilie ... what a surprise ... that was my grandfather. My mother and I lived with him. How did you know him?'

'He once gave me a free ride, and all my friends. In fact we were on the boat with him most of the afternoon. He went close in shore to show us the sea-birds. He knew a lot about them.'

'About all birds,' said Monique softly, 'Oh, Emilie, you've made my day. I love coincidences like this. Since my mother died I've no one to share my memories of Grandfather with.'

'And I feel less strange now,' said Emilie happily. She was sitting between Edouard and Monique. Edouard patted Emilie's hand.

They found Francine playing hide-and-seek in the shrubbery with the children, so Emilie had no chance of retreating into her shell. Francine said Kevin had rung to say not to wait afternoon tea for him, he'd have a mug of coffee with his friend while they tinkered with his motorbike. 'So if Edouard and Emilie keep these two amused, Monique and I will make ours. I've got it spread out on the patio.'

She needed no help, it was only a matter of making the tea. She said sharply to Monique, 'What's my brother up to now? Why is this girl here? All he said to me on the 'phone was that he'd met this girl in Sydney and her grandparents or some such were from the Port, so he'd asked her over for a holiday. Trust Edouard. There'd be some hard-luck story connected with it . . . and he'd be in over his ears, and out of his depth probably! Don't let him make a fool of himself this time, Monique.'

Monique said slowly, but not resentfully, 'It really isn't any business of mine, Francine.'

Francine said scornfully, 'Don't give me that! Mother and I both agree you're the very one for Edouard. Even in just two visits we could see that. Of all the things to happen *now*.'

Monique looked at her with eyes of love. 'Francine, that's sweet of you, but don't *you* start matchmaking too. It's bad enough coping with Henriette and Thérèse. They're very much against this visit and there's something pathetic about Emilie. It was her aunt made her come over. She heard Edouard on the air talking about Port Beauchamp and got in touch with him. That poor child is so embarrassed about it, she was on the point of running away when we got to the hotel. She'd rung me earlier and said not to come, and that she wasn't going back to Australia. She was going to get a job here. She's so young for her age, Francine, we just can't let her run loose.'

'Trust Edouard,' said Francine bitterly. 'This has been the story of his life. And of *our* lives. She *seems* sweet but if she's anything like the others, she'll cling like a limpet. If only he was different!'

Monique didn't mean to say what she did but the words spilled out. 'I wouldn't have him any other way!'

Francine's mouth fell open, then delight succeeded the surprise. 'Good for you . . . then all isn't lost! And listen, oh dear, they're coming. I'll just say this. Don't you let *your* sympathies run away with you. One in the family's enough. Mother will be delighted.'

Kevin was a boon, he got Emilie into the back seat so he could point out the landmarks. 'Better than the driver doing it,' he said. He knew nothing of the situation, so talk became more relaxed. Scenery and birds seemed to be the subjects in the back seat. Then Monique and Edouard caught Kevin's voice saying, with a quickening of interest, 'Do you mean you actually work for a nursery firm?'

'Yes, quite a large one. Aunt had me trained in office work but I loathed it. This is next best to being outside all the time. I do a lot of the pricking-out of small plants. Fiddly but really fascinating.' Emilie spread out her narrow hands in an expressive gesture.

Kevin said, 'I'll take you over to Little Akaroa, they're growing narcissi for the flower-markets there. I'm trying to kid my mother into starting a few plots, but she says she's more than enough to do already. I'd like not just bulbs, all kinds of flowers. Mrs de Quincy and Mrs Olivier have still got more land than they need. They said I could rent some if I wanted to try it in my spare time. Don't know why they didn't sell this lot when Edouard bought the rest, except that the older one said to me once that that plot of land was a sacred trust, for them to follow out their father's wishes. Beats me, from all I hear he was a crusty old devil, although my grandfather says yes, but he was a *fair* devil. But they would be willing to lease it to me. You might be able to give me some hints.'

Edouard said in a whisper to Monique, 'Good therapy. Might give her some badly needed confidence. Perhaps I've done the right thing in getting her to stay at Martletts'. I told Kevin's mother I'd have dinner with them tonight. I owe it to Emilie not to dump her among perfect strangers. I won't bring her across to meet Henriette and Thérèse till tomorrow morning. What did Emilie say when you said you might be able to use her on the public days?'

'Said she'd love to help as long as it was in the background, that she could never conduct people around, talking to them. But we'll see. There's something a little old-fashioned and sweet about her; she might go well with antiques.'

Edouard said, 'Thank you, Monique,' and touched his hand briefly to hers. 'It's important she should fit into the picture at Beauchamp House, though I didn't dare instal her under that roof to start with.'

Monique felt her spirits slump. *How* important? And why *to Edouard*? He said, extremely low-voiced, 'You see, the old ladies fair dote on you and that aunt of hers put them against Emilie to begin with. But you can do no wrong in their eyes. Your sense of values, your efficiency, the way you've made it possible for them to stay on in their childhood home, solving their problems of maintenance and making it financially viable ... well, it would be too cruel a contrast to bring Emilie up against, but taken in small doses, they could get reasonably fond of her.'

Monique's heart felt like lead. That didn't sound like a brief holiday. Under her depression a spark of resentment was stirring. It didn't pay to be too efficient, then. Was this where equality led women? Did men still like the helplessly feminine types? All right, Edouard Fergusson, I wish you well of her!

Some sense of fairness made her report to the two old ladies that she had found Emilie appealingly sweet, rather pathetic, but exquisitely beautiful, with a cloud of dark hair and the deepest blue eyes. Henriette nodded, 'Sounds like Highland colouring. Has she Scots ancestry, do you think? Quite a few of the Port folk were Scottish, far back. That was how Philippe's son married Morag Macdonald. Has she mentioned who her folk were?'

'I did ask, naturally, but she said she thought they were called Robinson, or it might've been Tomlinson, but that they weren't Port people; she thought they were here a very short time, working for someone. Perhaps in fishing. She thinks her aunt was mad wanting her to come. She gave me quite a thrill. Kevin is going to take her bird-watching, but she mentioned it to me earlier and said her first interest was stirred by an old man who ran pleasure boats on Sydney Harbour. It was my grandfather.'

Henriette unbent a little, 'Sounds as if she may have possibilities . . . not that it matters. I suppose she'll just have two or three weeks' holiday. Thought she might've been a real city type.'

Monique chuckled. 'Darling Henriette, *I'm* the real city type, born in Sydney, brought up there, and in Auckland and Christchurch.'

'Rubbish, just as you inherited your love of the sea from your grandfather, I'm sure from the way you've taken to the life here you had generations of country folk in your blood.'

'Perhaps,' said Monique lightly, 'but I don't really know much about them. Talking of families, you know those portraits I was cleaning? Edouard and I thought about making a small gallery of the upstairs landing for them. Okay by you?

Thérèse did her soundless clapping. 'Henriette, we must bring Hilaire's portrait down for it.'

Monique caught her breath. 'I didn't know there was one.'

Thérèse brought it down. 'We found it hanging behind the clothes in Father's room, after he died. We think he kept it there to look at. When Emile died and he found his confession, he burned *his* portrait to ashes.'

Monique got a firm control of her tear-ducts. It had been done by a Christchurch artist and Hilaire had been eighteen. The painter had caught his spirit in a way no photo could have done . . . he was at the wheel of his launch, in a turtle-necked sweater in just such an attitude as she'd often seen him, fair hair lifting from his forehead, brown eyes looking over the aquamarine waters of Beauchamp Inlet, a hint of dark cliffs beyond.

There were no sad lines grooved into his cheeks, no furrowed forehead, yet this was still her own dear grandfather. 'This shall have pride of place,' she said. Then as if she must ask, 'Was his brother like him?'

Henriette shook her head. 'No, completely opposite. He had the dark hair and blue eyes of our father. Hilaire was like our mother.'

Edouard brought Emilie over next morning. Monique went to meet them, Emilie needed the support of someone nearer her own age. She stood back as they went into the room so saw the full impact Emilie made.

She was simplicity itself, in a blue frock sprinkled with white daisies that had a collar like an old-fashioned fichu. The cloud of dark hair had been caught back and tied with a blue ribbon and the severity of the style showed up the exquisite clarity of her features. The sun from the far windows struck full on her.

The two old ladies looked up from setting out the morning-tea table and the look on their faces was identical. It was like seeing a movie turned to a still. Monique knew what had happened. Despite her description they'd been prepared for someone in a coarser mould, not this shy, lovely young creature. But suddenly Emilie lost that shyness, she came forward, held out her hands, said, 'Mrs Olivier, Mrs de Quincy, it's so good of you to let me come. I realise you're just getting this project underway. I hope you'll let me help, even if it's just washing dishes, or weeding the flowerbeds.'

It was nicely said and brought Henriette and Thérèse out of their trance. Monique saw the tension go out of Edouard. Oh, it mattered to him, mattered greatly, that they should like Emilie.

Evidently he felt he could safely leave her here now, said, 'Well, I must be off. We're drenching ewes this morning. See you later.'

# CHAPTER TEN

MONIQUE showed Emilie over the house. Henriette and Thérèse came on part of the tour with them and Monique knew they were watching most keenly Emilie's reaction to the beautiful possessions. Not once did she ask the value of anything, only the histories of most pieces. When it came to the top floor, Henriette and Thérèse left them.

Monique hesitated but just for a moment, when Emilie asked, 'Where does that door lead?' She pushed it open. 'Edouard sleeps here, so there's a man in the house. It has an outside staircase which makes it easy if his men want him.'

Emilie said, 'This belonged to the bad egg of the family, didn't it? The one who let his young brother bear the blame for what he did.' She waved towards the far door, 'That's the staircase he used to slip out to conduct his secret affairs, isn't it?'

Monique got a shock. Edouard must've seen quite a bit of this girl in Australia, to have imparted so much family history. He'd never have brought that old scandal into a radio talk. She felt a little annoyed ... after all, it wasn't Edouard's ancestor who'd blotted his copybook. She felt she must temper that. She said gently, 'He had a very harsh father. Who knows, he might've been so scared of him that he got into the habit of telling lies. He could've been genuinely attracted to that girl and because she wasn't what François Beauchamp would deem top drawer, knew he ran the risk of being disinherited if he married her. There are two sides to every story.'

Emilie turned to her eagerly, 'I never thought of that.' Then her face darkened. 'But letting his brother take the rap for it was unforgivable.' She whirled round. 'I'd rather see the brother's room. He was bookish and loved bird and forest life. The man who slept here ... and at times didn't sleep here ... robbed his brother of his birthright. Took from him everything that mattered ... I tell you ever since I heard that story it's haunted me.'

Monique said, 'Oh, Emilie, don't let it do that. If he had as lovely a nature as his sisters say, it wouldn't take from him all that matters. He may have found great happiness elsewhere.'

She longed to tell this sensitive girl the truth, that he had, plying his boats on one of the loveliest harbours of the world, marrying a woman as fine as her grandmother. But she couldn't, she had known for some time that if Edouard asked her to marry him, she wanted it before he knew she was the last of the Beauchamps. She was sure Edouard was the sort of chivalrous chap who wouldn't want the girl he loved to wonder was she loved for herself alone, or for what she would inherit. Not that she any longer dared think on those lines. She wasn't sure where Emilie fitted into his life.

She swallowed, said, 'Hilaire's bedroom is my bedroom. Come.'

Emilie was enchanted with it, the drawings of the birds, framed on the walls, his books on the shelves he'd fashioned from timber milled on the estate, the old-fashioned fretwork letter-rack, and the two glass cases, one holding shells and fossils, the other stuffed birds. Monique said, 'It was Emile who made his young brother the glass cases, and his father, Big Beauchamp, who had the birds stuffed for him by a Christchurch taxidermist.'

Emilie looked at her curiously. 'The way you said that, "Big Beauchamp," sounded as if you think he wasn't a bad old guy, after all.'

Monique laughed. 'I loathed him at first, but I keep on finding out more endearing things about him. Like Mrs Martlett telling me her old dad says he was wonderfully tender with animals, as good as a vet. There weren't any vets then on the Peninsula and he'd go any distance at any time of night, in any weather, to an injured animal.'

'I'm glad of that,' said Emilie. Then fiercely, 'But nothing can whitewash what Emile did to Hilaire . . . I can't bear to think that because of his brother's actions, Hilaire was never able to return.'

Monique knew a pain almost beyond bearing. She, too, living among the reminders of that little boy of long ago, had agonised over this, yet here was a stranger feeling it almost as deeply. That stranger added, 'It makes one long to be able to undo yesterday.'

Monique said, 'Emilie, I'm sure you could be coached to conduct tours here. You are already absorbing its history. But of course we don't display this room, it's one of the private ones.'

Emilie nodded. 'This belongs to family alone. Oh, Monique, look at the sunlight . . . it's casting dancing shadows up on to this ceiling. Little Hilaire must've lain in bed many a time and watched just that, bless him.' Monique felt a wave of love sweep over her for Emilie. A kindred spirit. And more mature than at first thought. Succeeding that came another thought, would Edouard too find her kindred? *Irresistibly* kindred?

In a month's time it seemed as if Emilie had always been here and as if Henriette and Thérèse had never known antagonism towards her coming. Emilie herself was a different person, there was a spring in her step, a confidence in her voice that hadn't been there before. Henriette and Thérèse delighted in being in the garden with her. Though the New Zealand shrubs and flowers were, in the main, so different from her own Australian ones, Emilie had an affinity with all growing things. She and Kevin went over to Little Akaloa to visit the bulb farm there, inspected the land he might lease, poured over flower catalogues, talked glasshouses, heating, drainage. Mrs Martlett said, 'Normally, I can't be bothered with another woman in my kitchen, but that lassie's like the daughter I was never lucky enough to have. Would you believe it, Monique, her second name is the same as mine, Rose? Of course it's a common enough name round here. I was named for Marie-Rose Beauchamp, of course, because she saved my mother's

life when she was just a child, but she was such a
wonderfully kind person half the older folk at the Port
bear the name of Rose.' Monique kept her own counsel,
didn't say she bore that name, too. Not yet, not yet.
Mrs Martlett added, 'That aunt of hers wouldn't even
teach that child to cook . . . and she's just delighted in
having me show her how. She's got a natural flair for it,
too. Edouard thought her bran muffins were mine the
other day when he dropped in for morning-tea.'

Monique came back to the house, riding. She often
rode now. She was becoming quite proficient at it.
Henriette seemed to be in the study, must be using the
telephone. She thought she'd go up and do a bit more
work on the portraits. She had a fancy she'd like to pick
out the scroll work on Morag Macdonald's picture
frame with a touch of gilt. At that moment it hit her . . .
Morag, the Highland lass with the black hair and the
blue eyes . . . it could have been a picture of Emilie!

She positively sped upstairs, where they stood against
the walls of the lumber room. She drew it out, carried it
to the tiny window so the light could fall directly upon
it. That was it! *That was it*. Given that white frock, the
tartan sash, it could have been Emilie standing there
with her cloud of hair, her sapphire eyes, the hollow
cheeks, the tiny ears. Morag had handed her colouring
down to Big Beauchamp, and to his son, Emile. Emilie
*had* to be Big Beauchamp's descendant, just as she was,
but one generation further away, because Emile had
been so much older than Hilaire. And Monica's second
cousin.

Emilie wouldn't want to claim that relationship, she
so hated Emile for what he'd done to his young brother.
But the aunt knew, oh, that was obvious. And Edouard
knew. That was why he had longed for Henriette and
Thérèse to like Emilie. Another thing hit her. Emilie
*Fairlea*.

Just as her own name was an anglicised version of
Beauchamp, so was Emilie's. The Fair Meadow. Very
clever. Emilie's grandfather, who had been Emile's son,
born out of wedlock, would have no name save his
mother's, so perhaps this new version of the French

name had been made his by deed-poll. That would be it. Why hadn't she seen it before? But then when she first met Emilie, she'd thought the name would be spelt the same as that South Canterbury township, Fairlie.

Well ... it was up to Monique now to see that her little second cousin was acknowledged, welcomed, loved. And she must do it soon or that go-getting aunt would do it and antagonise everyone. Oh, if only Henriette and Thérèse would see it that way. But they were close on eighty and belonged to another generation.

Monique knelt there, frozen into a shell of indecision. *How* would they react? Would they hate this reminder of their elder brother's treachery cropping up? Would they want to banish Emilie? But she so loved it here! By all the ties of blood, if not legality, she belonged here, even as Monique did. That aunt would have an eye to the main chance. That was why, too, Emilie had so hated the room that had been Emile's.

Emilie loved every other room in the house, every picture, every figurine, miniature ... everything in the garden, too, especially those that had an association with France ... the gilly-flowers with their spicy perfumes of stock, carnations, pinks ... the walnuts, the Normandy poplars, the Bourbon roses ... Emilie must never leave this spot.

Monique had the maddest desire to rush across to Martlett's, to embrace Emilie, to cry, 'We're cousins ... well, second cousins ... I'm Hilaire's granddaughter,' but she mustn't, oh no, she mustn't let on that she, Monique, had the legal right to inherit this.

She couldn't do that to Emilie, Emilie who had not only inherited Morag's colouring, but also Hilaire's love of birds, his ability to sketch. She was more like Grandad than Monique herself! No, Emilie must be revealed as one in whom the Beauchamp blood flowed strongly, before Monique revealed her descent.

Meanwhile she must subdue her air of excitement. She wanted time to decide. Should she consult Edouard? At the thought she flinched. She wasn't sure of Edouard's reason for getting Emilie here, for not wanting her staying at the big House to begin with; not wanting Monique's efficiency contrasted with Emilie's diffidence. But he'd been wrong there ... away from her aunt's dominance Emilie had come into her own. No, she wouldn't consult Edouard.

It was a little awkward. Henriette and Thérèse had invited Emilie and Kevin for the evening meal. A nice thought, including him. Of course, they were greatly interested in Kevin's plans for growing flowers. Monique rose from her knees, tore her eyes away from that picture, went downstairs.

She bumped into Henriette coming out of the study. She had a most becoming flush on her cheeks. Monique said, 'Oh, Henriette, that colour suits you. You look excited. What have you been up to?'

Henriette shrugged in the French fashion both sisters had. 'Nothing really exciting, love. I've just been talking to our solicitor, that's all.'

Monique laughed. 'That's all? I must meet this solicitor some day if he can make you look like this! Is he an old beau?'

'Absurd child! He's no more than forty-five. But he's just made a dream come true for us. No, you aren't to ask what. Time enough for that. Suddenly time isn't getting away from us any more and a lot of it is due to you. Last year we both felt really old, but not any more.'

Monique glowed, kissed her. 'You mean because Beauchamp House has come into its own again, as a showplace? Oh, Henriette, how glad I am you both feel that way. Is that it?'

Henriette looked mysterious. 'More or less. But I must go and help Thérèse. Emilie loves her butterfly cakes, and I promised to chop the red jelly for them, to decorate the cream. Come on.'

Monique's head was whirling. She must have time to think. At their age, she must be gentle. Would it be better if she wrote it out for them? Should she ask Emilie's permission first? For instance how shocking it would be for them if Emilie's aunt got impatient and rang up and blurted the whole thing out? At that

moment the 'phone rang. Monique jumped, gazed at
the instrument, with dire foreboding ... had she
mesmerised the thing into a ring from Australia?
Henriette answered it, listened, said, to Monique's
dismay, 'Yes, I'll accept the call. Put her on please.'

Monique held her breath. Surely the woman wouldn't
have the effrontery to make a collect call? Then she
could've laughed. Henriette said, 'Oh, Pinkie, how
lovely to hear from you, back in New Zealand. No, of
course I don't mind the reversed charges. But isn't it
just like you to find you haven't got the right currency!
You haven't changed a bit. I'm so glad about that. If
you had, I'd feel old indeed. You're coming down this
way? And staying at *Maison* Rossignol? Lovely. Margot
and Pierre will bring you here.' They chatted on with a
blithe disregard of the minutes ticking away, and by the
time Henriette put the receiver down Monique had
made up her mind. She wouldn't risk that aunt
bludgeoning these two dear women with news that
might take some assimilating.

She gave Henriette time to report on it to Thérèse.
Then the two of them went on with the cake decorating.
Monique took the whipped cream from the one sister,
the jelly from the other. 'There's something I want to
ask you, my dears. I don't know how to put it, so I'll
just have to plunge. Have you ever thought how tough
it must be for someone to find out they belong to a
family by every tie of blood and kinship, but can't claim
it because one's great-grand or something was born the
wrong side of the blanket? I—I—it sounds strange
but—I mean——'

She stopped, because Henriette had held her hand up.
She had a mischievous smile on her face. 'You mean,
dear child, that Emilie is our brother Emile's great-
grandchild!'

Monique looked hastily around for a chair, seized it,
and sat down. Thérèse clapped her hands, 'It looks as if
we can still, at our age, take the wind out of the sails of
the younger generation.'

Monique boggled at them. 'But—how did you find
out? I mean I'm the one who's been dusting and

touching up the old portraits. She's the living image of Morag. It suddenly swept over me.'

Henriette said, 'In my father's day they hung in the downstairs hall, so Morag's picture was part of our lives. But she is not only like Morag, she's Emile in the feminine form. And the same colouring as Father, though not in features. But that's not all she's inherited—she's been given Hilaire's love of birds, his gift for sketching. That is very wonderful to us. It's given us the chance to carry out a wish of Father's that was dear to his heart. It weighed on him so much. Will you think us foolishly dramatic if I say we feel now he will rest easy in his grave? You won't? Good.

'So many young things these days are afraid to display emotion. We're going to tell Emilie we know tonight, at the end of the meal. That will make it semi-public so she will be sure we welcome her into the family. She knows, of course. That was why that aunt of hers made her come here, but Emilie would never tell us, we know. I've asked Emilie to wear white but wouldn't tell her why. I'm going to put that tartan sash of Morag's over her white frock, then compare it with the portrait. Now, run off, and dress up for the occasion, too. To do us all honour.'

Monique heard Edouard come up the outside staircase, dash to the shower. She wondered what she'd wear, flicked at the hangers in her wardrobe . . . ah yes, she'd wear the lime-green frock she'd worn when, unaware, she'd bumped into Edouard. Why did she want to remind him of an encounter he'd called tantalisingly idyllic? What was it going to mean to him, this surprising way the old ladies had taken this relationship? And how far, in Australia, had he committed himself to Emilie?

She wished now she hadn't been so sure Edouard would propose to her before long. That night they'd returned from the play and had an hour in the Little Salon before retiring, she'd said to him, 'Don't rush your fences, Edouard, let's get to know each other more.' Pity. And she'd thought later she'd wait till he did declare himself before revealing who she was. Again pity. Yet in some ways, for Emilie's sake, it was just as well. This must be Emilie's supreme moment. What an anti-climax it would've been in the very hour of her recognition, if the legitimate heir to the property had turned up, the granddaughter of their dearly loved and long-lost brother, who'd suffered so badly at the hands of Emilie's forbear!

Kevin and Emilie came in together. She hadn't seen Emilie in this before, a simple white frock, a wide oval neckline that complimented her matt-white shoulders, a wide black patent belt about her slim waist, rose-pink lipstick, the cloud of hair caught back each side and held there, above each tiny ear, with white bone clasps. Oh, that lovely line of chin. In her hands she carried a spray of the first of the roses from Marie-Rose Martlett's garden. They were still in bud, apricot roses that were called *Vesper* she said. She presented them to the two ladies. They put them in a slender silver vase with a fluted edge.

'Louise was given this by Philippe to celebrate their silver wedding,' said Thérèse. 'I'm sure Louise would love to know we were using them this night. On occasions like this, one is always conscious that those who lived in this house a hundred years ago are here. As if they listen in and are glad.'

'Occasions like this?' asked Edouard, 'Is today something special?'

Henriette laughed mischievously, 'We're the only ones here to know. It's Emilie's twenty-first birthday!'

No one was more surprised than Emilie. 'How could *you* know?'

Thérèse said, exchanging a glance with her sister, 'We have our sources,' and refused to be drawn.

Emilie went pale, 'Aunt didn't ring to tell you, did she?'

'No, dear child. We'll tell you how we found out, when we've had our meal.' Emilie's colour flowed back.

Edouard was in high spirits. Monique wondered was this because he thought Emilie was on the way to being accepted? But he didn't know the aunts knew, they'd told Monique so. He wore a cream turtle-neck pullover, above light trousers, the ends of his fair hair were still damp from his shower, the small scar at the side of his mouth showed faintly white against his tanned skin. Monique thought with nostalgic longing: 'I've kissed that scar.' She caught the tang of his cedar-sharp aftershave. He was sitting between her and Emilie, Kevin on Emilie's other side.

Thérèse slipped out and brought in a beautifully iced cake with twenty-one candles. Monique said, 'Oh, you clever girls, how could you ice that without us knowing?'

Thérèse grinned in a way that made them see the small Thérèse who'd been such a tomboy, riding her pony bareback, getting up to all sorts of devilry, 'It's wonderful what you can accomplish if you slip downstairs in the early hours of the morning,' she said.

Emilie looked enchanted. 'I've never had a birthday like this.' She gazed at the delectable concoction, edged with tiny forget-me-nots and silver cachous, and with a tall slender silver vase of blue cornflowers set in the ring of candles.

When the birthday honours were done, Henriette said, 'Now for our present,' and she went away to return with what looked like an ornamental scroll, tied with blue ribbon. She laid it beside Emilie.

'I feel I'm being given the Magna Carta,' she said, untying the ribbon. She rolled it out, gazed at it mystified ... some sort of legal document ... she just couldn't take it in. But there was a card with it, beautifully executed in the Gothic lettering Thérèse excelled at. It said:

To his great-great-grand-daughter
From
François Beauchamp
With Love

Emilie gasped, paled, then flushed, said: 'I—I—don't quite understand. What is it?' She spread the document out and realised it was the deeds to the land she had advised Kevin to lease for his flower experiments. Kevin and Edouard each leaned over it to see better.

Emilie let it roll up, gazed unbelievingly at the card, her passport to an acknowledged relationship to his family.

Edouard said, 'How in the world did you find out? I've been trying to work out how to tell you, and I didn't know how . . .' He floundered and stopped.

Henriette chuckled. 'Didn't know how we'd react. I don't blame you. But you see Father left us a splendid example. Old despot as he was once, he did try, at the last, to retrieve the mistakes he made. He felt that if he hadn't dealt so harshly at times, with Emile, that he'd never have been so afraid that he shifted the blame on to his brother. He felt that somewhere Emile's son would be growing up, not knowing the stock whence he'd sprung. He tried to trace Muriel—whom he'd treated quite generously financially, and failed. But in his will that patch of land was left in perpetuity for that child's descendants. It's been a tricky thing to administer over the years. Father tended that patch very lovingly. He planted those trees. They'll make a splendid shelter-belt for your flowers. So it's your inheritance, Emilie . . .' She paused and Thérèse said, 'Go on, Henriette, go on. The next bit!'

Henriette nodded, 'So, Emilie, you needn't go on refusing Kevin. Your secret's out, this is your home . . . the income from that land, leased over the years for stock grazing, has been held in trust and by now should be enough to build you and Kevin a fine home on the Beauchamp Estate.'

Monique felt a singing in her ears, a thudding in her breast, Emilie and Kevin! Not Emilie and Edouard . . . oh, dear God in heaven!'

Emilie's eyes were astar with tears and wonderment. She said, 'But—but nobody but Kevin knew he'd—he'd——'

'Proposed is the word you want,' said Thérèse. 'Emilie, eavesdroppers are supposed to hear no good, but there are exceptions to every rule. Henriette was in the big hay-barn. She heard a chook come clucking from the top bales at the far end. You know what she is, can't realise she's nearly eighty, climbed up on them. She heard you and Kevin coming, Emilie, thought she'd get scolded for doing it, so sat down, right up near the roof.

'Evidently you'd proposed some other time, Kevin, but you were trying to batter down Emilie's defences. We'd known from first meeting her she was one of us, and we were sure that was why Edouard brought her here, but we didn't know what he was up to, so we bided our time. Henriette heard you tell Kevin that you loved us all so much you couldn't revive for us all the old sadness, that you were going to go away soon to make a new life for yourself, despite pressure from your aunt. We had already set the wheels in motion, making sure you were Emile's and Muriel's descendant. Our solicitor in Christchurch handled it. He even flew to Sydney to make sure of everything.'

Emilie did the only thing possible, dazed and all as she was. She got up, went to them at the other side of the table, put her arms about them. 'You have been so wonderful. I feel I belong. And now I have a family behind me, I shall be able to tell my aunt that no more mischief must be made.'

Henriette said shrewdly, 'You mean about trying to make out that there was a secret marriage between Emile and Muriel?'

Emilie nodded. 'How——?'

'You asked if she'd told us it was your birthday, had she 'phoned? Well, not lately she hasn't, but she did earlier. Oh, it was all right. As I said, we already knew. But she got impatient about you not making yourself known, and rang. She tried to make out that that was why your name is the anglicised version of ours, but we found that your grandfather's name had only been made Fairlea when he was an adult. Before that, naturally and sadly, he'd had to bear his mother's name. We would have been happy either way, but had to make sure. That's how we knew it was your birthday, we got a copy of your birth certificate.'

Kevin said, 'And *I* didn't know when your birthday was! And I'm engaged to you! But all I can say is thank goodness I proposed to you before you got that land deeded to you.'

Edouard burst out laughing. 'I take your point, Kevin. How devilish awkward that would have been. I'm sure *I'd* never find the courage to propose to an heiress. Now look, I must go and get your parents. They must know about this, and stay to celebrate. We mustn't let them feel they're left out. But who could have dreamed Henriette and Thérèse knew?'

'Well, Monique did, but only just. She went upstairs to paint the frame of Morag's picture, and came rushing down here to tell us. And, Emilie, she was prepared to fight for your rights to the death, if we'd been hidebound and prejudiced about legal aspects.'

Emilie leaned over to kiss Monique's cheek, said, 'Thank you, Monique. I've never had a sister but if I chould choose one, I'd choose you.'

Monique longed to say, 'How about settling for a cousin?' but held her peace.

It was a small community and there was the usual grape-vine. They were content to have it so, letting it seep into the life of the tiny fishing-port, without causing more than a ripple. The people already knew and liked Emilie for herself. And it had been so very long ago.

They were frantically busy with two public days and with Edouard preparing to go off to Lincoln College beyond Christchurch for three days, and he was also planning for a return visit here from his fellow experimentalists. Life as always in New Zealand was hotting up towards the end of the school year, in early December, and the holiday season following, and already preparations for Christmas were going ahead.

Monique longed for the tempo of the earlier season when they had long, quiet evenings. Well, she'd asked Edouard to mark time, and also she was still marking time to spring her own surprise on them all. Emilie must be able to enjoy her family atmosphere till after Christmas. Once she and Kevin were married it wouldn't matter so much. She would have her own home, land, husband. Thérèse and Henriette had touched Monique to tears when they told her, on the quiet, that they had made provision for her in their wills. 'No one knows but us, but it means you will never have to leave Beauchamp House. We want the home we love left in your hands, my dear.'

While Edouard was away they had a magic moment. Emilie came running from the Martlett's house, a box in her hands. It was rosewood, and exquisite. Henriette and Thérèse and Monique were all in the kitchen. Emilie put it down on the table reverently.

She said, 'It's your mother's handkerchief box. Mrs Martlett's father gave it to me. Your mother left it to his wife, who was Veronique, in her will.'

Thérèse nodded. 'Yes, I remember. And her handkerchiefs were in it.'

'They still are,' said Emilie. 'There was a little note with them from Marie-Rose to say the one with the cross-stitch was the very one she used to dry Veronique's tears that night at the foot of the cliff. And there are rose-petals there. Kevin's mother said they would be from the sweetheart rosebuds. But—best of all, under the tissue-paper at the bottom is a letter to Marie-Rose from Big Beauchamp himself. I love it. Can I read it to you?'

She said, 'Your mother was evidently staying in Oxford in North Canterbury, convalescing after an illness. Listen . . .

'"Marie-Rose, my dearest,
    That was a wonderful letter you wrote me. It was almost worth while enduring your absence to read that. And it gives me the chance to tell you how much you mean to me. I'm not always an articulate man and on the rare occasions I am, I don't always express well the things that are in my heart.
    I know I'm not a particularly understanding father. I'm clumsy and impatient with the boys so they are reserved with me. I sometimes envy you your shared laughter with them. I'm trying to do better with the girls. But if you can say what you did of me as a husband, then my cup is full and brimming over. And

it *is* true, we've known many moments of rare delight in each other, as you say. I thank *le bon Dieu* that you were sent into my life to leaven my crustiness with your joyous spirit. Here are some petals from the last rose on the *de Brunner*.

Do you know what I miss most, Marie-Rose? That last hand-clasp you always give me as we settle down to sleep.

> Yours now and always,
> François.'''

As Emilie finished, there were four pairs of wet eyes. Henriette said shakily, 'What a wonderful year this has been, it brought Monique here, then Emilie, and now a love-letter from yesterday to sweeten our memories of Father. I wish Edouard was here to see it, but he'll be back on Sunday. Oh, I forgot to tell you girls, Margot and Pierre will be here on Sunday afternoon, bringing Madame and Pinkie over. Pinkie will love to meet you.'

Always crowded with people, thought Monique despairingly. Edouard and I never seem to be alone these days! She had a white night on Saturday night. Would she and Edouard ever get back to the magic of that night of the play? Would he want to? Has everything changed?

At last morning came. Had there ever been a fairer day? The sea from her window was the colour of a *paua* shell, iridescently blue and green, with here and there those odd streaks of pink and burgundy that seemed copyright to the waters around Akaroa. Monique thought she must ask Edouard did he know what caused it ... some trick of the sea-light? Or some sort of sea-growth? Oh, what an unimportant thing to be puzzling over, instead of dwelling on the fact that Edouard would be home today. She hoped he'd get here early to add to the joy of the morning.

The bell rang out across the inlet waters, striking as always an echo from the dark cliffs opposite. It had rung there nearly a century and a half, as silver-tongued as when it had been sent out to Louise and Philippe from the village they had left in France.

They walked down from Beauchamp House, entered the little white picket gate, and Monique saw Emilie detach herself from the Martletts, and walk towards her, ready for something they had planned to do together. The others waited for them.

They walked round behind the white vertical-timbered church, till they came to the family plot. Monique unpinned the spray of sweetheart roses from her frock, Emilie opened her bag, took out a tiny vase filled with a compound well moistened with water, took the roses from Monique, carefully pushed the stems into it.

Monique took it from her again, both girls knelt on the low coping, and Monique said, 'For the two of you, Marie-Rose and Big Beauchamp, Emilie's ancestors.' And in her mind she added, 'And mine.'

Emilie rejoined the Martletts and Monique knew that by Easter Kevin and Emilie would be walking down this aisle, husband and wife. A wave of envy swept her. Their house would be built among the larches and pines Big Beauchamp had planted in the hope that some day a descendant of his might farm it. How would Edouard feel about that? Had Edouard, seeing Emilie in this setting, been drawn to her, only to find she, in turn, was irresistibly drawn to Kevin?

They came into church, sat down. Sunlight sifted through the rose window, spilling a shifting mosaic of colour on Monique's white dress. She'd tied her hair back from her ears with a piece of crisp rose-pink gauze to match the necklace of rose-pink quartz Thérèse had insisted on her wearing.

Someone came into the pew from the far side, sat down beside her, Edouard. He knelt, resumed his seat, smiled across her at the old ladies, turned to look down on Monique. Their eyes locked, she knew a surge of joy out of all proportion. It was just as if the intervening time had been swept away and they'd been transported back to that magic evening before she'd even heard of Emilie.

He held that look. The corners of his mouth tilted up, the sunlight lit up the grey eyes. He said in a whisper so low it isolated them from every other worshipper in the church, 'Ah . . . here I am where I've longed to be.'

Her eyes dazzled. His hand dropped to hers where it lay between them, touched it briefly. He said, 'I tried to get back last night. I knew we were having visitors today. Pierre rang me at Lincoln. I'd worked out that there was a full moon. I thought that it would be perfect for us. That after all the hoo-ha of the past weeks, trying to stop Emilie's aunt rushing over to new Zealand to claim what she said were her niece's rights . . . oh, the telephone conversations I've had with that woman! But I had it planned that at last you and I could get on with our lives, that we knew each other well enough by now. So everything was set fair, moon and all, and what happened? There was a lecture I didn't have to attend . . . the lecturer went down with flu and *I* got roped in! So there I was, babbling about the effect of aphids on crops, instead of walking under that moon asking you to marry me! Will you, Monique?'

She felt laughter welling up within her. Oh, he was absurd. She said on the same thread of a whisper, 'Edouard . . . you can't possibly propose in church . . . *in a whisper*!'

His eyes danced. 'Can't I? I just have. Would you like me to shout it out from the steeple? Come on, jade . . . put me out of my misery. The vicar will be coming in at any moment. Will you?'

'Too right I will,' said Monique, and right then Henriette leaned forward across Thérèse and hissed at them.

'Ssssh! I'm surprised at you!'

They subsided, then rose as the vicar entered and exchanged only a telling look. She went through the entire service in a daze, telling herself she'd only dreamed it. But there was Edouard's bulk beside her, solid and reassuring, his baritone matching her contralto in the hymns.

At last it was over. They came out, chatted to the usual groups . . . there was hardly a person there not known to her . . . *my* people, Monique thought, I need never go away from here. I'll just let Emilie have a little longer, but I'll tell Edouard tonight!

They went home in Edouard's car; he said he had just made it in time, he'd been up at the crack of dawn. He looked blandly at Henriette, 'That's why I talked in church. There was something I had to tell Monique right away, but I won't do it again, promise.'

'I should think not,' said Henriette.

He chuckled, 'In some ways, you know, you're a chip off the old block, old François.'

Thérèse said, 'Our visitors are coming early, so we'll serve dinner as soon as we get home, then we can be all washed up and ready. I want Emilie to come to meet her, too, she'll be so interested. But I'd like to explain fully first. She was very fond of Hilaire. He *was* good to us. Some brothers so much older wouldn't have bothered with a trio of little girls, always giggling, but he never minded.' It gave Monique a queer feeling. This woman would have known her grandfather as a child. Oh, what a pity she hadn't told them yet who she was. She wondered how long the woman would stay with the Rossignols.

Henriette said, 'How about just popping a pinny over your dress, Monique, and doing the Yorkshire pudding right away? Don't bother to go upstairs first.' To Edouard she said, 'We left a corner-cut of topside of beef roasting and if she does the pudding now, it'll be just right.'

Monique caught a resigned look on Edouard's face. He'd hoped to get her alone upstairs! She donned the apron, made a face at him, began dropping oil into the patty-pans, opened the oven, slid the tray in, gave a quick whip to the batter she'd left standing while they were at church, gave her Gallic shrug, as Edouard said, 'Now, damn it, I share you with roast beef and York-shire pudding! It's enough to take a man's appetite away.'

Her eyes brimmed with mischief, 'But it's glorious fun, isn't it?'

Edouard said, 'That moon will still be pretty full tonight and no matter who is here, tonight is ours.' He cut off as he heard voices approaching.

*     *     *

They washed up, and Monique got pressed into making pikelets. She said over her shoulder to Edouard, 'I seem to have been doing nothing but spooning batter out. Oh, bother, I've got this griddle too hot. I'll have to drop the heat.' He stood watching her flip the small pancakes over, spoon more out, turn them on to a snowy tea-towel on a grid. She said, 'You're making me nervous. It does nothing for the pikelets to have you so near.'

She could hear the smile in his voice, 'Doesn't it, love? Well, I'm not moving, suppose you burn the lot. Somewhere in this interminable day I might get a chance to kiss you! Is that the lot? Good. Come on.' He untied her apron, took her hand, whisked her out of the door towards the stairs.

They were halfway up when they heard a car door slam and voices in greeting. Thérèse and Henriette had been sitting oin the verandah, waiting for their guests.

'Let them wait,' said Edouard, hurrying her towards her room. He thrust her in, slammed the door, turned the key. The sun was streaming through the latticed casements, shining on Hilaire's davenport, on the bed her grandfather had slept in, had dreamed his boyish dreams; on the window-seat where he'd sat on moonlit nights listening to an owl hooting. Where he'd sat in misery, hurt and bewildered that his father wouldn't believe him. The room from which he'd stolen out, leaving a note behind, to join a ship at the wharf below that was sailing with the dawn tide and carried him out of their lives forever.

But he'd been a happy man, never daunted; happiness had been born in him, a great joy in the beauty of the earth and all its creatures ... all this flashed through Monique's mind as Edouard crushed her to him, looked into her eyes in a delightful moment of anticipation, bent his head, touched his lips to her cheek in a way he had before, trailed them across her face till he found her mouth.

At last it ended. She turned her face against his chest, the top of her head against his chin, and said, 'Oh, Edouard, Edouard,' on a happy sigh. His fingers

slipped beneath her chin, tilted it up, he said, looking
down on her, 'Let's keep this to ourselves till after
tonight, sweetheart, I can't bear to share it yet, dearly
as I love Madame Rossignol. And there's this visitor
with her. It'll be all schoolgirl reminiscences and giggles!
Oh, blast, they're calling us.'

They came down the stairs side by side to the group
below, so it was quite an entrance, the man in his grey,
chalk-striped suit, the girl in a plainly cut white dress,
the rose-pink quartz necklace about her throat, and a
carelessly tied pink sash about her waist. She was
enchantingly flushed.

Madame said, 'This is this young friend of
Henriette's and Thérèse's,' to her friend. 'The one who
has wrought the transformation here, Monique Belfield.
And this, Monique, is——'

She got no further, because the woman beside her,
tall, white-haired, with glowing dark eyes, broke in,
said, '*Monique Belfield*! Then *two* descendants of the
Beauchamp family have come home! Elise, why did you
not tell me? Oh, Monique, how wonderful! It's just like
seeing my own dear Hilaire all over again ... your
golden hair, your brown eyes ... my dear, *dear* girl!'
She stepped forward and took Monique into her arms,
folded her to her.

Monique was frozen, immobile. Then the woman
held her away from her, searched her every feature
lovingly, said, 'But why ... why did no one say?'

Monique swallowed yet she managed to say.
'Nobody knows ... nobody knew but me. I—I wanted
to prove myself first, so they would know I had no
ulterior motives. I wanted to get Beauchamp House
able to support itself for all time. And then Emilie
came, so shy, so diffident, so aware she had no legal
claim ... I couldn't take from her the joy of being
welcomed, loved. She is entitled to be one of this family
just as I am. She's my little cousin and I love her. I was
going to tell you all after her wedding. Just letting a
little more time pass. But ... how did *you* know? It was
my name you recognised, wasn't it?'

Henriette, tears in her eyes, said, 'This is the woman

who met Hilaire in a Sydney street. She didn't tell us he had changed his name. I suppose he asked her not to. I know he met Father under the name of Beauchamp in that hotel. This was the dear friend who arranged that meeting with Father. No wonder *we* couldn't trace him. We tried now and then through the years. He must have called you Monique after her. Or got his son to. Pinkie was her nickname.'

Henriette took Monique in her arms, kissed her, said, 'This is the happiest day of our lives. Beauchamp House is come into its own this day. Thérèse, this is our dear, dear great-niece!'

Nobody thought anything about Edouard kissing Monique too; after all, so did Pierre and Margot and Madame. Thérèse said, 'We did notice certain things, I realise that now, but the likeness isn't as strong as in Emilie's case. Some of it, we thought was wishful thinking . . . when you said your grandfather believed in saying what was in the heart—that was a constant saying of Mother's. Then another day you said, "Let us not be daunted." But we thought it just marked you as akindred spirit.'

Monique then told them of the wonderful moment when she had, on her first buying visit, opened the book on heraldry and family mottoes and had matched up Hilaire's childish scrawl with the story her grandfather had told her long ago. 'It was so unbelievable . . . to see it written in his own handwriting. My dears, give Emilie a little longer. It's the first time in her life she's felt so much part of a family, so surrounded by love. When she has a home of her own, she'll have such security, it won't matter so much.'

They heard a sound at the door and all swung round. Framed in it stood Emilie in her blue, daisy-sprinkled dress. 'It won't keep till then,' she told them clearly, her head held high as she stepped into the room. But she didn't look dismayed, she was sparkly-eyed. 'Oh, Monique . . . I've just realised something. The old sea-captain I loved, Captain Belfield, . . . he's related to me too . . . no wonder he said——' She stopped, a peculiar look crossing her face.

Monique came forward, 'Emilie. What did he say?' Emilie hesitated. 'He said I reminded him very much of someone he had loved dearly when he was just a little boy. But—but that must've been——' She couldn't go on. Monique nodded. Henriette said gently, 'He meant his brother, Emile. Hilaire worshipped him as a youngster. The big brother who was so good to him. Who taught him to walk, to swim, to ride, who gave him his first cricket bat, his first football . . . nothing can take away those things.'

Emilie said, 'And you were willing to keep the news to yourself, Monique, till we were married. I'll never forget that.'

Edouard said clearly, 'But she wouldn't have been allowed to, I would've forbidden it.'

Emilie looked at him in puzzled fashion. '*You* would have—why?'

Monique put out a protesting hand, which he caught. 'Because it's going to be a double wedding, but I'm not waiting till Easter. Monique promised to marry me just this morning. Sorry, love, but I just can't keep it.'

When the surge of delighted congratulations had died down, Henriette said, 'But when? It was all pikelet-making and Yorkshire puddings. Edouard, you didn't propose to her when she was wearing my pinny?'

Edouard looked at her sternly, 'When? *In church.* I was in the middle of proposing when you shushed me down, you unromantic woman! It was going to be last night, under a full moon . . . and I got held up in Christchurch. But never mind . . . that moon will rise over the Inlet again tonight!'

It did. First Monique and Edouard walked down to the little Post Office near the wharf. Monique posted a letter to Aunt Amabel. In it she had said, 'You wrote that your bequest was to bring me joy. It has, a cup full and brimming over, as my great-grandfather once wrote to my great-grandmother.' That letter would go on the first leg of its journey to Canada, by the first mail-launch to Lyttelton tomorrow morning. They talked of many things. Monique teased Edouard that the first

morning after he got back from Australia he'd just
prevented himself saying he wished she'd never come
here. He thought back, shook his head. 'Not so,
sweetheart. Even then, when I was still wary, I found
myself wishing I wasn't going to introduce Emilie into
the household. I didn't want to be distracted. But I was
nursing resentment because I thought you'd brushed me
off. Any more doubts?'

'No, I was terribly jealous of Emilie, even when I
couldn't help loving her for herself alone.'

He looked startled. 'Oh, you idiot! As if she could
compare with you? But I'm glad you could feel that
way. Well . . . if that's all, the moon is rising.'

They walked among the Bourbon roses, saw the
Normandy poplars tall against that moonlit sky, knew
the fragrance of the gilly-flowers whose ancestors had
been brought from France in little seed-packets, by
Louise. They looked down to see the lights of the little
port ringing the beach at the foot of the cliffs where
Philippe had first beached his whaleboat with all their
earthly possessions . . . they knew their destiny and the
destiny of their children lay here . . . knew that all old
sins were forgiven, all wounds healed.

They paused under the big tree grown from a walnut
that had fallen from a tree in France long, long ago.
'Today was for the ancestors,' said Edouard softly. 'But
tonight only the present matters . . . and the two of us.'
He reached her lips and thereafter was silence.

# Harlequin Romance

## Coming Next Month

**#2767   SECRET LOVER  Kathryn Cranmer**
Bitter memories flood back to an Englishwoman when the man
she'd once loved turns up at her country cottage needing help
for his daughter. She can't refuse—even knowing he'll discover
their son!

**#2768   THE MATCHMAKERS  Debbie Macomber**
Her son's advertisement for a father in a Seattle newspaper
shocks his widowed mother and infuriates a noted sportscaster
who has a low opinion of marriage-minded women!

**#2769   WILDFIRE  Alexandra Scott**
Relief! That's the first thing Leone feels when her fiancé's
accident postpones their wedding plans. Then she wonders
why. Doesn't she love him? His yachtsman friend's persistent
pursuit of her doesn't clarify the situation....

**#2770   SONG WITHOUT WORDS  Betsy Warren**
Having a composer set her poem to music disturbs its writer;
his intention to record it with a new sexy meaning distresses
her. What if the composer should suspect its passionate
message was for him?

**#2771   COMEBACK  Nicola West**
Six years and marriage stand between their last meeting and
now—but the old feeling is still there. A woman faces an
agonizing decision—to continue her marriage or wreck it for
an old love....

**#2772   THAT MAN FROM TEXAS  Quinn Wilder**
A young Alberta woman is fascinated by a Texas drifter's tales
of his rodeo exploits. But she's even more interested in the
mysterious past he doesn't talk about, and whether their
attraction has any future.

Availabe in June wherever paperback books are sold, or
through Harlequin Reader Service.

In the U.S.
901 Fuhrmann Blvd.
P.O. Box 1397
Buffalo, N.Y. 14240-1397

In Canada
P.O. Box 2800, Postal Station
5170 Yonge Street
Willowdale, Ontario M2N 6J3

# Can you keep a secret?

## You can keep this one plus 4 free novels

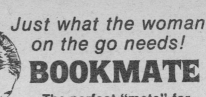
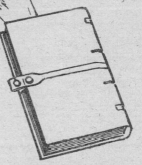

# WORLDWIDE LIBRARY IS YOUR TICKET TO ROMANCE, ADVENTURE AND EXCITEMENT

## Experience it all in these big, bold Bestsellers— Yours exclusively from WORLDWIDE LIBRARY WHILE QUANTITIES LAST

To receive these Bestsellers, complete the order form, detach and send together with your check or money order (include 75¢ postage and handling), payable to WORLDWIDE LIBRARY, to:

**In the U.S.**
WORLDWIDE LIBRARY
901 Fuhrmann Blvd.
Buffalo, N.Y. 14269

**In Canada**
WORLDWIDE LIBRARY
P.O. Box 2800, 5170 Yonge Street
Postal Station A, Willowdale, Ontario
M2N 6J3

| Quant. | Title | Price |
|---|---|---|
| _____ | **WILD CONCERTO,** Anne Mather | $2.95 |
| _____ | **A VIOLATION,** Charlotte Lamb | $3.50 |
| _____ | **SECRETS,** Sheila Holland | $3.50 |
| _____ | **SWEET MEMORIES,** LaVyrle Spencer | $3.50 |
| _____ | **FLORA,** Anne Weale | $3.50 |
| _____ | **SUMMER'S AWAKENING,** Anne Weale | $3.50 |
| _____ | **FINGER PRINTS,** Barbara Delinsky | $3.50 |
| _____ | **DREAMWEAVER,** Felicia Gallant/Rebecca Flanders | $3.50 |
| _____ | **EYE OF THE STORM,** Maura Seger | $3.50 |
| _____ | **HIDDEN IN THE FLAME,** Anne Mather | $3.50 |
| _____ | **ECHO OF THUNDER,** Maura Seger | $3.95 |
| _____ | **DREAM OF DARKNESS,** Jocelyn Haley | $3.95 |

|  | YOUR ORDER TOTAL | $_____ |
|---|---|---|
|  | New York and Arizona residents add appropriate sales tax | $_____ |
|  | Postage and Handling | $ .75 |
|  | I enclose | $_____ |

NAME _____

ADDRESS _____ APT.# _____

CITY _____

STATE/PROV. _____ ZIP/POSTAL CODE _____

WW-1-3

One of America's best-selling romance authors writes
her most thrilling novel!

# TWIST OF FATE

## JAYNE ANN KRENTZ

**Hannah inherited the anthropological papers that could
bring her instant fame. But will she risk her life and give
up the man she loves to follow the family tradition?**

 **WORLDWIDE LIBRARY**

# HARLEQUIN BRINGS YOU

## *Janet Dailey*

★ ★ **AMERICANA** ★ ★

**A romantic tour of America with Janet Dailey!**

★

**Beginning in June, enjoy this collection of your favorite previously published Janet Dailey titles, presented state by state.**

JDA-A-1